Jenny McCartney grew up in Northern Ireland and lives in London, where she works as a journalist. *The Ghost Factory* is her first novel.

THE GHOST FACTORY

The Troubles turned Northern Ireland into a ghost factory: as manufacturing industries withered, the death business boomed. Belfast, 1990s: In trying to come to terms with his father's sudden death, and the paramilitary violence meted out to his friend Titch, Jacky is drawn to confront the bullies who still menace a city scarred by conflict. However, after he himself is attacked, he flees to London to build a new life. But even in the midst of a burgeoning love affair, he hears the ghosts of his past echoing, pulling him back to Belfast, crying out for retribution and justice. Their voices are very much alive, and so Jacky reluctantly returns, in an attempt to reconcile the young man he used to be with the new path he has tried to forge for himself.

JENNY McCARTNEY

THE GHOST FACTORY

Complete and Unabridged

CHARNWOOD
Leicester

First published in Great Britain in 2019 by
4th Estate
An imprint of HarperCollins*Publishers*
London

First Charnwood Edition
published 2020
by arrangement with
HarperCollins*Publishers*
London

The moral right of the author has been asserted

A catalogue record for this book is available from the British Library.

ISBN 978–1–4448–4391–0

Published by
F. A. Thorpe (Publishing)
Anstey, Leicestershire

Set by Words & Graphics Ltd.
Anstey, Leicestershire
Printed and bound in Great Britain by
T. J. International Ltd., Padstow, Cornwall

This book is printed on acid-free paper

'634–5789' (recorded by Otis Redding), by
Steve Cropper and Eddie Floyd (1967)

W. H. Auden: 'Musée des Beaux Arts' (1938), in
Collected Shorter Poems 1927–1957 (Faber and
Faber, London, 1966).

'Walkin after Midnight' (sung by Patsy Cline),
by Alan Block and Don Hecht (1954).

For my parents

One need not be a Chamber —
to be Haunted —
One need not be a House —
The Brain has Corridors — surpassing
Material Place —

Emily Dickinson

Part One

1

Belfast, 1995

I grew up in a rainy city, walled in by dark hills, where people were divided by size. We came in one of two sizes: big or wee, with no real words for those who fitted somewhere in between.

Mostly the reason for a fella's nickname — Big Paul, say, or Wee Sammy — was staring you in the face, or the chest. But sometimes strangers were puzzled when they heard some great lump, with arms on him like two concrete bollards, being spoken of as Wee Jimmy.

The explanation was simple: he was obviously the son of a Big Jimmy, and had contracted the term 'wee' early, from the pressing need to distinguish the child from the father. Although he had long burst out of his wee name it clung to him as he surged through life, a stubborn barnacle on the side of the *Titanic*.

I was once Wee Jacky. But when Big Jacky, my father, collapsed on the street one day, his hand flapping towards the astonishing pain in his heart, the need for my title ebbed away on the pavement. I became just Jacky, because I was now the only Jacky.

Then there was my friend Titch. His name belonged to the third and rarest category: he was so enormous, but so unthreatening, that his bulk

3

could safely be referred to in ironic terms. So he was dubbed Titch, a miniature word synonymous with a small perspective on life.

The clash between Titch's name and his appearance made strangers laugh. From the moment of introduction, he was a walking contradiction, an ambulatory joke. But he turned out to be no joke for me. That big soft eejit, and what he stumbled into, was the trigger for the whole nasty business that swallowed me up like a wet bog.

★　★　★

I grew up in Belfast: my beloved city, baptised in tea and drizzle, sprinkled with vinegar-sodden chips and cigarette butts. You turned off the Lisburn Road, with its smattering of boutiques and cosy coffee shops, and just kept walking over the metal footbridge until at last you made it to our battered grid of streets with its two-up, two-down terraced houses crammed together in different shades of brick, paint or pebbledash. Every so often there was a derelict one with boarded-up windows, dismal as an eyeless face. And there I was, walking down Lucan Street towards the house where Titch lived with his mother.

It was the best time of the day for me: the fading hour when a long summer evening tips into the night, and mothers come to their doors to reel their grumbling children back in from patchy football games on scrubby grass. One of them was sitting on the brick wall near the waste

4

ground as I walked past, scuffing his heels on the graffiti. He yelled after me in his reedy voice: 'Mister, lend us a quid would you?' I would have walked on, but there was something about the pally delicacy of his *lend* that made me laugh, the wily pretence that I had a hope in hell of ever getting it back.

I turned round to look at him. He was slouched up there, about eleven years old, puffing on a cigarette and screwing up his eyes like a bad imitation of James Dean. He wouldn't have known who James Dean was, of course: he thought he had made up the squint himself. He had a ratty skinhead and one of those childish old man's faces, the fine skin stretched over the sharp bones a bit too tightly for someone so young.

'What would you do with a quid,' I asked him. 'Go and buy yourself some more fags?'

'Sure a quid wouldn't buy me a whole packet anyway,' he answered, quick as a ferret.

'At the corner shop, they sell them as singles,' I said. A second's pause. The wee dervish knew I had him on the hop.

'I was gonna get a bag of chips,' he countered, sliding his eyes away in expectation of defeat. I handed him the coin: 'Don't be spending it all in the one shop.'

He grinned, a sudden flash of pure joy, and faked falling off the wall in amazement as payment. I watched him saunter down the road to the chippy, trying to flick his fag-end into the gutter like a practised smoker. In about a month's time, he'd have it just right.

The moment sticks in my mind: his dwindling, cocky figure in the grey light. It was the last time that things in my life seemed clean, the smiling photograph snapped minutes before the car crashes. Seconds after I walked into Titch's house I could smell the first cracklings of trouble, like something softly burning in another room.

⋆ ⋆ ⋆

The years had dealt Titch's mother a few thumping blows, and you could see their impact in the depressed sag of her shoulders. She was like a sofa that too many people had sat on, and the heaviest arse was Titch's dad, a salesman and raconteur who drank up the housekeeping money, and then the rent money, and then buggered off to leave her precarious and alone with Titch, her hulking, simple-natured son with a penchant for stealing things from shops. Titch's dad had since shacked up with a hairdresser from Omagh, by whom he had two more children in quick succession. He sent Titch occasional birthday cards with a fiver or tenner tucked inside, and the scrawled words 'From Your Dad' beneath the glaringly false inscription To The World's Greatest Son.

When Titch was younger he hoarded all his dad's cards from year to year and used to pore over them sentimentally. Then one year the dad's card arrived ten days late, bearing the gold-piped legend Happy Birthday Son, and in his furious disappointment Titch threw the entire carefully

6

saved stack on the fire. Now he filleted the money wearing a bored, sulky expression, plump fingers rustling speedily inside the envelope, and threw the card into the bin without even reading the message. At least, that's what I had seen him do, but it might have been for effect. I bet he fished it back out and had a proper look at it later.

There was a kind of sweetness running through Titch's mum: she wasn't a whinger. She never hinted that God had dealt her a bad hand. She had dealt it to herself, she said, the day she first saw Titch's dad relating a joke in a smoke-filled city centre bar, with his gleeful face shining as he approached the punchline, and the men crowding round him already in stitches at the way he was telling it. She should have seen he was a bad egg from the word go, she said, but then again that might have been why she had liked him. Maybe the whiff of sulphur had attracted her.

I knocked twice: the front door opened, more slowly than usual.

'Ah hello, Jacky,' she said. The day's worries had seeped into her voice.

'What's up?' I asked, hanging my jacket in the narrow hall. She ushered me into the front room and nodded towards Titch's bedroom.

'He got into bother at McGee's shop. The old man caught him taking a packet of biscuits he hadn't paid for and there was a bit of a row, I think.'

She watched me warily, the hazel eyes waiting for a definitive reply.

'Oh dear,' I said. It was worse than she knew. I

had heard that the McGees were hardmen, heavily involved. The older McGee was a nasty piece of work: rancid with an unnamed resentment, quick to anger and loath to forget any slight. He hung about in a couple of local drinking clubs with a guy called McMullen, who had a pot belly and weaselly eyes, and who was said to have killed at least three people himself. I didn't know if he had or not, but bad rumours clung to him.

There was no missus on the scene. People whispered that oul McGee's wife had abandoned the family and Northern Ireland years ago, when her two boys were young, never to return. This was a maternal crime alluded to only in hushed voices, although I heard Titch's mum say once — as though uttering a small heresy — that she was a good-looking woman and the only one in that family with a civil tongue in her head. For most people, though, the wife's flight had given her husband a reason for the drop of arsenic in his soul.

From what I remembered, McGee's grown son now called round after work twice a week to take him to a drinking club where he stayed until the small hours, diligently feeding the next day's irritable mood with copious amounts of spirits. The son lived a few streets away from me. He had an Alsatian dog tied up in his back yard that growled if it heard anyone walking past.

As a shopkeeper, the da maintained a testy politeness with his regular customers, but he wouldn't take kindly to some fat chancer just wandering in for a free packet of chocolate bourbons.

8

'What exactly happened?' I asked.

'I don't know. You go and speak to him. I can't get any more out of him.'

I started walking up the stairs towards Titch's room. Titch was lying on his long-suffering bed, ostentatiously scrutinising one of his mother's very old *Hello!* magazines. He had heard me come into the house long ago, which is why any moment now he would affect a sudden surprise at my appearance.

Titch. *Physique*: overweight, shambolic, implicitly threatening the trembling frame of his single bed. *Eyes*: pale blue, currently glued with manufactured attention to a picture of Ivana Trump. *Mood today*: laconic, with a strong undercurrent of surly defiance. His left hand dangled speculatively above a half-open packet of Jacob's Custard Creams, like one of those mechanical claws you try to pick up prizes with at fairgrounds.

'Hello,' he said, without looking up.

'Is that a tacit acknowledgement of my presence, or are you just rehearsing aloud the title of your reading matter?' I said. I liked talking this way to Titch.

'What?' he said. You had to hand it to Titch, he was a genius of repartee. He was a lord of language, drunk on the endless permutations of the spoken word.

'You're a lord of language,' I said.

'Bugger off, Jacky,' he said, mildly. He shifted slightly: the bed frame winced and shivered. I could see he was working up to some tremendous pronouncement. 'How do you think that Trumpy woman gets her hair to stay like that?'

9

That did it. I went over and pulled his head round to face mine. The pale blue eyes carried a look of resentful surprise.

'Listen, you big eejit,' I hissed. 'Never mind Ivana fucking Trump's hairdo. What did you do today in McGee's shop?'

The eyes widened slightly in recognition, and then floated lazily away from mine. 'The old man caught me taking a packet of Jaffa Cakes.'

'Why didn't you take them from Hackett's? At least your ma settles up with them at the end of the week.'

'Hackett's was closed.'

There you have it: Titch's immortal logic. Hackett's shop, his usual stomping ground, was closed. So what did he do? He took himself over to McGee's, and straight into a row with a muscular wee psycho.

'So what did he say when he caught you with the biscuits?'

Titch sighed. He wanted me to go away now, but he could see there was no dodging the question.

'Oul McGee saw me putting them inside my coat, and he came over. He said 'What do you think you're doing you thieving bastard?' I s-said I was going to pay for them. He was squeezing my arm till it hurt, Jacky, and he said 'You were not, you big fat bastard.' And he kept on squeezing.'

'So what did you do?'

'He was hurting my arm, Jacky, so I told him to f-f-fuck off and gave him a push. He skidded and went flying into his tins of tomato soup.'

10

In the midst of his self-righteous distress, Titch's shoulders began to heave with laughter at the memory.

'Did he fall down? Did anyone see?'

'Aye, he fell down with all the tins rattling round him. There was no one else in the shop but them two oul Maguire sisters. They were letting on they were shocked, but I saw one of them laughing into her coat collar.'

I sat on the chair beside his bed and stared at him, hard. He looked back at me, guiltily, but still with that little smile twitching somewhere beneath his smooth, pasty skin. I knew he was secretly freeze-framing the image of old McGee toppling backwards in furious disbelief, his arms and legs waggling comically as the soup tins clattered around him. Titch was savouring that moment like a mouthful of stolen Jaffa Cakes.

'It's not as funny as you think. You know your aunt in Newry,' I said. 'If I were you, I'd go and stay with her for a while.'

His mind slowly wheeled round to face this new and unwelcome proposition. The mouth made a brief 'O' of apprehension.

'I don't like that aunt. She's always nagging me and she never gives me enough to eat. Why?' he said.

'Because you knocked down old McGee and made him look stupid,' I shouted. 'And McGee's son is apparently well connected. So the next time you go dandering down the street, looking for new biscuits to stuff into your fat face, you're liable to get a severe hammering. You think that it hurt when McGee squeezed your arm. It'll be

11

nothing compared to this: you won't be able to walk right for a year.'

'Aw Jacky, they would never do anything about that. I only gave him a wee push.' He picked up his *Hello!* magazine again, stubbornly. 'And I gave him his Jaffa Cakes back.'

There was no talking to him. Sometimes Titch reminded me of a vast, impenetrable animal: a whale maybe, drifting through yesterday and today, in some unreachable element of his own. Warnings bounced off him. He swam around in the blue water of his mother's love, and the harsher currents of my affection. He couldn't understand that something entirely different, something much darker and nastier, might be waiting out there for him.

I could warn him about getting a hammering, all right. I could also warn him about the grave possibility of a Martian invasion in ten years' time. It was all part of the meaningless, potential Future: all one and the same to Titch. Defeated, I took one of his custard creams. He looked up: 'Hey Jacky don't be eating all my biscuits. I've only got twelve left.' He was trying, clumsily, to charm me out of my mysterious bad mood. I got up to leave: 'Don't be looking for women in those gossip mags: you'll end up with an ex-wife who takes you to the cleaners for your Hobnobs.'

His mother was waiting at the bottom of the stairs, an unravelling parcel of nerves. I told her: 'He knocked old McGee over. I'd get him up to your sister's in Newry if I were you.'

She was on the verge of tears: 'There's no way he'll agree to go.'

In the days that followed, I pushed the business about Titch to the back of my mind like a stack of unpaid bills. Titch wouldn't go to Newry, and I was in no position to kidnap twenty stone of struggling biscuit-snatcher and take him up there by myself. And it wasn't just Titch, there was something else, too. No one ever really believes in something bad until it happens. Not even the one who predicts it.

2

At the time Titch nicked the Jaffa Cakes the armed gangs in Northern Ireland had been fighting for over twenty-five years, and they had only recently grown weary of it. They had differing aspirations for our little state of six counties and one and a half million people. The IRA wanted a united Ireland, while the Loyalist UVF and the UDA preferred us to stay part of the United Kingdom. They had formerly reached consensus on one thing, though, which was that the best way to persuade ordinary folk on the other side of the sincerity of your argument was to build a large stack of their corpses and promise more of the same until your demands were secured.

We called our situation the Troubles, and the longer it had dragged on the more fitting that genteel euphemism became. The murdering was sporadic but fully expected, like some recurrent, rumbling agony in your unmentionables. The populace soldiered on through it, mainly keeping their heads down and quietly hoping that splashes of terror didn't land on or near them. In between shootings and bombs there were businesses to be run and children to be raised. Things didn't fall apart, quite. They kept on, but more painfully.

At long last the killing had grown stale, even for past enthusiasts. The whole thing had lost its mojo. No one knew where it was headed any more. All armed groups had recently agreed to stop the violence — the headline stuff, at least — while they reconsidered their options.

* * *

Given what had gone before, this period of relative calm was much appreciated, but energies need somewhere to strut their stuff. Muscles require flexing. Now that the loyalists were no longer officially engaged in killing Catholics, they had begun to consider more closely the question of discipline nearer home. Certain young Prods were stepping out of line, giving cheek, failing now to understand the long-established principle of who was in charge. They needed to be dealt with.

I had concerns that Titch, who had never before been considered an example to anyone, might finally become one now.

In our house, we had never been big fans of the local paramilitaries. Big Jacky didn't sound off about it beyond the front door, because in our neighbourhood you never got anything but grief by gabbing. But he used to tell me how in the days before this bother got started he would dander freely up the Falls, and Catholics came over here without any problem. Now we were walled off from each other in raging wee cantons.

Like his father before him, Big Jacky stood up in grave reverence for 'God Save the Queen' and scrupulously arranged the poppy in his lapel on

Remembrance Day. He had a notion of Britain that I couldn't quite boil down, but that stood for something larger and more historic than the territorial daubs of red, white and blue that marked the kerbstones near our house. A photograph of his grandfather who died at the Somme stared out at us, handsome and doomed, from a frame on the bookshelf. Big Jacky said to me from when I was small that all this killing ever did was slather on misery.

So when the young fellas came to the door collecting money for 'the prisoners' he would say gently, 'Och boys, sure I have my own charities, and it's hard enough now just to pay the rates,' steering them on their way as though he had already forgiven them their presumption in asking.

They mostly seemed to take it okay, although once I saw a younger guy give him glowering looks, muttering about freeloaders being made to pay the price or get the fuck out, before the older guy with him quickly whispered something to shut him up.

Big Jacky had lived around there for a long time, I suppose, and he knew some of the players from school to nod to, but I understood that wasn't the only reason why he got more leeway than most.

It was this: once or twice a week, Big Jacky helped out at a club down the road for disabled kids, and he had got especially close to one wee boy there called Tommy.

Tommy's legs were heavily unreliable, which meant he needed a wheelchair, but every so often he could flash you a smile of heart-liquefying sweetness which he used to his advantage. His speech was slow and woolly, and you had to bend right down next to his mouth to make out what he was saying, but his mind was sharp. With his snappy observations and his pale, fragile body, he was a Venus fly trap masquerading as an orchid.

The club was run by a bosomy, middle-aged woman called Barbara, an energetic matriarch who made up in practicality what she lacked in imagination. What creative flair she did have went into her hair, dramatic stabs at glamour which varied wildly in their success rates. Hairdressers rubbed their hands at her approach like pushers welcoming a star junkie.

Given his difficulty in speaking, Tommy was tight with his words, but he had great timing. One afternoon I walked in to look for Big Jacky and Tommy immediately started agitating for me with his arms. I got up close to hear him say in his distinctive voice, as if transmitting from several leagues under the sea, 'Barbara's had her hair done.'

The next second big Barbara steamed into view, dead serious beneath a majestically awful new custard-coloured bouffant, and the pair of us cracked up.

Tommy's dad was a very senior Loyalist, above even the likes of McMullen in the hierarchy, and — despite his readiness to okay the shattering of other families — he dearly loved Tommy, who held a place in the one small compartment of his heart that had not yet ossified. He had a slack

17

face and hard-working eyes, and he observed how much Tommy liked Big Jacky, who was endlessly patient with him, taking him back and forth to the toilet without complaint and listening carefully to whatever he said.

Big Jacky didn't like Tommy's dad, though. I could see that in the tension of his jaw in the man's presence, the way his natural reticence retreated even further into the guarded handover of monosyllables. But he gave him the minimal courtesy due to any father of Tommy's. And perhaps because of this chance connection down at the club, Big Jacky never had too much trouble from anyone. You couldn't rely on that, though. You couldn't rely on anything.

⋆ ⋆ ⋆

Mrs Hackett in the corner shop sometimes filled me in on stuff that was going on locally, so long as no one else was in earshot. I had learned that good timing and a modest outlay on a tin of Buitoni ravioli and a packet of Punjana teabags could purchase some thought-provoking snippets. She had long ago developed the habit of confiding in Big Jacky — something perhaps to do with the natural fraternity of shopkeepers in a volatile city — and now it had transferred to me. What Mrs Hackett wasn't told, she overheard. She was an assiduous wee gatherer of information. I couldn't be entirely sure of its direction of flow, even though I trusted to her good intentions, and so I never told her anything I didn't want others to know. Given my caginess, that limited the scope of our chat, but I kept the ball in the air with pleasantries. Thank God for the weather in all its variations.

'Another oul rainy day,' I observed.

'Och, will it ever stop?'

As she handed me my change she took a quick squint down the central aisle of the wee shop, then right and left. A signal to linger. She leaned over the counter and whispered: 'Say nothing but there was another beating last week.'

'Who was it?'

'A wee boy from Arnold Street. Only sixteen. I know his mother. She was in this morning in an awful state, a bag of nerves.'

'What happened to him?'

'Four of them jumped on him on his way home and battered him with iron bars. He's up there in the Royal now. Head injuries, broken leg.'

'What was it over?'

'Some row over a girl, his mother said. Him and another lad argued over a girl but it got out of hand and the other boy's uncle is, *you* know.'

A meaningful glance from behind the thick glasses. She would never say the actual word.

The door suddenly swung open and a stout, middle-aged man I had never seen before walked in. Mrs Hackett's voice grew abruptly louder —

'Well enjoy the ravioli, now. I hope you have an umbrella.'

'Don't worry, sure I've got my waterproof jacket.'

★　★　★

19

The thing I had liked about living with Big Jacky was his capacity for silence. It wasn't a brooding silence, with argumentative storm clouds waiting to burst overhead. You could relax in the expanses of Big Jacky's silence. It was the mental equivalent of an endless highway stretching out of sight, carrying within it peace and possibility.

These were the sounds that punctuated an evening with Big Jacky: the soft rustling of the newspaper, the hiss of the kettle, his belly-chortle at some fresh piece of idiocy issuing from the gabbling television, a courteous observation about the rain, the spit of sausages frying in a pan. He didn't ask me too many questions. I suppose that's why I told him almost everything.

I wondered sometimes how I, with my spiky edges and tangled imaginings, could have sprung from the quiet bulk of Big Jacky. He did, too. As a child, I would sometimes catch him looking at me strangely, as I gyrated wildly in my Indian chief's headdress or danced with frustration over a difficult puzzle. I heard him once saying in a low voice: 'You're like *her*.' I knew who he meant: my dark-haired snapshot mother, the fine-boned, smiling face that lay in his bedside drawer with his most precious things. She was frozen there, next to an earlier model of him grinning broadly beneath a modest dirty-blond pompadour. I don't remember her. She died of meningitis when I was two.

In deference, perhaps, for me being *like her*, he fed me with books: shyly, at first. He brought home the daily newspapers and historical pamphlets from his newsagent's shop. He bought dusty, dog-eared volumes from church fêtes and charity shops: everything from *Oliver Twist* to paperback Westerns by authors with names like Buck Tyrone and Cliff Ryder. He filled in little forms from the back of the Reader's Digest in his sloping, careful hand, and sent off for handsome, maroon-bound tomes with titles like *Strange Stories and Amazing Facts*. They came thumping on to the doorstep, bursting with the lurid, illustrated mysteries of Spring-Heeled Jack, the fiery devil that terrorised the good citizens of Victorian London, and of the wailing faces which had appeared on floor tiles in Spain, mouthing inaudible agonies because the house had been built on the site of a medieval graveyard. There was even a photograph of the wailing faces: they were all smeary and open-mouthed, as though shocked at the cheek of the energetic Spanish housewives who had tried to wipe them off the tiles with a damp cloth.

He brought home the gleaming satin memoirs of Hollywood movie stars; and the autobiographies of long-dead sportsmen; and assorted poetry anthologies, trickling out lines of Larkin and Betjeman, Hughes and Heaney. Big Jacky didn't say much, but every week floods of new words spilled from the pockets of his brown overcoat, and I danced around with expectation. The books piled up: Aunt Mary and Aunt Phyllis, my mother's sisters, observed developments from a distance, darkly, twitching to take over. He must have sensed the conversations bristling self-righteously over their Carrickfergus

21

kitchen table (*Something should really be done. There's just him and the wee boy in there now, and the place is coming down with all these books he buys, and the child looks as peaky as bedamned*) and stubbornly ignored them.

If Spring-Heeled Jack and his clawing cohorts sprang into my dreams, and I woke up dry-mouthed with terror, I made my way to the room where Big Jacky slept. When he felt the nervous phut-phut of my breath on his sleeping cheek, he would stir and lift a corner of the quilt. 'Get in,' he said and I would lie awake, comforted, next to my big, flannel-wrapped bulwark against the dark.

★   ★   ★

Every so often the aunts would pay us a visit, motoring sedately into Belfast under the patchy pretext of a birthday (mine or his) or a spurious shopping trip (for one of those fine wool cardigans, a Christmas present for Anne next door, *you* know, can't get them for love nor money in Carrickfergus, not even at McGill's, just thought we'd call in and see how you two were getting on.)

Aunt Mary, her husband Sam, and Aunt Phyllis all lived together. Phyllis had never married. 'Phyllis was too much of a lady to get married,' said Aunt Mary, meaningfully. It was as though the goatish attentions of a man, all beard and raw lust, might have catapulted Phyllis on to a precipice of mental distress from which she would never claw her way back.

When Sam and Mary went on holiday, Phyllis

22

came along with them. 'Three's company, four's a crowd,' Aunt Mary would carol gamely, although sometimes — when Phyllis was off peeling potatoes, drooping over the sink in her long brown cardigan — Mary would whisper: 'Of course, sometimes Sam and I would like a wee fortnight on our own. But it wouldn't really be fair on Phyllis, to leave her behind in charge of the house, away from all the fun.'

Mary's whispers had a tendency to carry. Now and again I wondered if Phyllis could hear.

Sam enjoyed his bowls and his television. He was retired from his job as a bank clerk. We saw him about once a year, when we visited them in Carrickfergus, and then he would say: 'Long time no see, Jackies Senior and Junior,' and excavate himself from his armchair to fetch Big Jacky a whiskey.

He was a tame man, really. Any rebellious sinews in him had long ago been replaced with a convenient machine-washable stuffing. Mary had him kitted out in pale lambswool pullovers, like Rupert Bear. His clothing was organised to match the house, an overheated cave of squashy velveteen sofas, pastel Chinese rugs, and polished tabletops sprinkled with lace doilies. You could sink back into those soft furnishings and not be seen again for a week. It was a miracle Sam was still alive. One day scientists would discover him dead there, the suburban equivalent of the leathery men they found preserved for centuries in those Danish peat bogs. He would have his eyes still wide open and his hand stiffened around the remote control. They'd dub him the Bungalow

Man, and scientists would marvel at the contents of his stomach (a diet of oven chips and chicken nuggets, specifically designed by Mary to generate no kitchen mess).

China figurines of dancers sprang from the sideboards, suspended in eternal pirouettes. Brass lamps gleamed from shining coffee tables. The furnishings of the house demanded a vigorous cleaning regime. They got it with blasts of spray and polish, worked in deep with triple applications of elbow grease.

Our front room in Belfast clamoured for no such attention. It had a brown 1950s sofa with wooden legs, and a fraying green armchair. A low, rectangular coffee table provided a stationing point for mugs of tea. Big Jacky accommodated himself in the armchair while I extended myself on the sofa, where years of pressure had made convenient buttock-shaped dents. When the aunts came to our house, I could see that the sparseness of Big Jacky's taste dismayed and unsettled them. They fluttered around, hunting for a corner on which to perch. They besieged my father with pointless knick-knacks: fringed, furiously patterned cushions, knowing china squirrels with nut-packed cheeks, Belleek pottery sweet-dishes and embroidered tablecloths, to take the edge (although they never actually said this) off his spartan, miserable life with his peaky, odd son. He thanked them politely and pressed them to take some more tea. When they had gone, he put the things away carefully in a cupboard, and brought a small selection back out only before their next visit.

One day when we had waved off Aunt Mary,

amidst a rapid hail of queries and promises, Big Jacky sat down in his armchair and took out his pipe. Pressing the springy tobacco into the bowl, he sighed and said: 'Normal service resumes.' He lit up, and took a puff. Then he said: 'They drove your mother mad too.' That was it. The pipe smoke drifted my way. I drank it down with the brandy-glow of conspiracy.

After Big Jacky died, normal service never resumed again.

3

A few days after I heard what Titch had done in McGee's shop, I was walking past his house down to the chippy. I looked in the window: Titch was beached on the floor of the front room with a pint glass of orange squash beside him, and his mum was lying on the sofa with her shoes off. They didn't see me, because both of them were in hysterics at some crappy film on the television.

Why didn't I go in? Normally I would have. But it's a bore, when you're in the middle of watching something, to have to start explaining the whole plot to the enquiring, only half interested visitor (*He's the blonde one's husband, but he's doing a line with the brunette who's married to the police inspector. No, not him, the other one, with the moustache*). And I suppose I didn't want to take my claw-hammer to the fragile shell of happiness that surrounded them. I carried Titch's trouble around with me now. The pair of them had unburdened themselves of it, and burdened me. I'd walk in there as gloomy, responsible Jacky, with a miserable long face on him like a Lurgan spade, and the talk would suddenly be all about McGee, and Titch going to Newry, and Titch refusing to go to Newry, and his mother trembling again on the edge of weeping. The funny film would be forgotten and the laughter stowed away, and who knew

26

if anything would ever happen to the big eejit anyway?

I walked on. The midget James Dean with the skinhead was hanging around outside the chippy, with a can of Sprite in one hand and a burning cigarette in the other. He acknowledged my proximity with a curt wee hardman nod.

'Hello,' I said.

He proffered his crumpled packet of Embassy, eyes narrowed: 'Smoke?'

'No thanks,' I said, 'I'm frightened it might stunt my growth.'

'Very fucking funny,' he said, mortally offended. The swear word was thrown in as proof of his maturity. He hauled all four foot seven of his dignity up on the wall and sat there, puffing away and ploughing all his energies into ignoring me.

I bought my chips, soaked them in vinegar and salt, and came back out. I had poked a hole in the warm paper to eat them while I was walking and keep them hot. He was still there, working hard not to look at me.

'Chip?' I asked him.

I was sorry I had made that crack earlier, after he had offered his ciggies with such ill-concealed pride. He turned his head slowly, still offended, but he couldn't be bothered to keep it up. The hand came down and rummaged around for a chip: it salvaged two. I sat up on the wall beside him.

'What's your name?' he said.

'Jacky. What's yours?'

'Marty.'

A pause, bulging with contemplation.

'I seen you walking around with that big fat fella from up the road,' he said eventually.

'Is that so.'

'He's not right in the head, that fella.'

'Maybe not. His name's Titch,' I said. 'Are *you* right in the head?'

He laughed, showing his pointed, irregular teeth: 'My ma says I'm a headcase.'

'Good, then you and Titch would get on fine. Two prime headcases together. Joint gold medallists at the Headcase Olympics.'

'My ma says he takes things from shops.'

'Your ma keeps her eyes peeled. Do you ever take anything from shops?'

'Took a couple of Crunchie bars once from Hackett's, when Mrs Hackett was away in the back getting newspapers. And a Walnut Whip, a few times.'

I thought of poor old Mrs Hackett, carefully exploring the familiar confines of her shop like some ponderous old turtle in a crumbling tank. It was almost impossible to imagine her young. She looked as if she had been born with a granny perm. I pictured the doctor saying to Mrs Hackett's mother, 'Congratulations. You have a lovely baby girl,' and both of them looking down fondly at Mrs Hackett's tiny wizened face, framed with the hollow sausages of grey-beige hair.

God help her, anyway, when even eleven-year-olds saw her for a soft touch. And God help Titch, when even an eleven-year-old knew to take things from Hackett's, and not McGee's.

'You shouldn't steal from Mrs Hackett,' I said. 'She has trouble with her arthritis, and she's always nice to the customers, even wee headcases like you.'

'Aye she is,' he conceded. 'She gave me an ice lolly once when I told her it was my birthday.'

'See?' Something struck me: 'Was it your birthday?'

'No.'

He dug his paw in for some more chips.

A pause.

'The thing about telling lies to people,' I said, slowly, 'Is that one day they find out you've been lying. And when they do, they don't like you as much as they did before.'

'Mrs Hackett never liked me that much anyway,' he said. 'Think she knew about the Walnut Whips.'

There wasn't really much I could say to that: it had the probable advantage of being true. I got down off the wall, and passed the rest of my chips over to him: 'You finish them. I don't want any more.' He sat watching me as I walked back up the street. As I turned the corner I saw him squinting into the greasy paper, diligently hunting out the best bits, the crunchy pieces of fried potato that lurk around the sodden corners of the bag.

★   ★   ★

When Big Jacky died, Aunt Mary and Aunt Phyllis made a pilgrimage to Belfast to sort out the funeral. They took charge of all the phone

29

calls to friends and family, such as there were. I could hear every word they said as I lay in my room, looking at the shadows the lamp cast on the ceiling. (*Yes. An awful shock. Quite sudden. Just passed away right there on the street. Still, at least he didn't suffer for too long. Thank you. You know how much we appreciate it. Him? Oh, taking it very hard, you know, can't get too much out of him as usual.*)

They put the death notice in the *Belfast Telegraph*. Aunt Mary wanted a poem, but Aunt Phyllis thought not. I thought not, too. God knows what doggerel the pair of them would have come up with.

They held lengthy, respectful consultations on coffins and services with Mr Gascoigne, the undertaker. They mulled over flowers. Fine choices were sifted and weighed. The Porchester (handsome oak, satin-lined) or the Wellington (slightly more accommodating, less costly wood)? They could have mummified him in newspaper, tied him up with brown string and lowered him into the Lagan, for all I cared. All I knew was that he was gone for good. I didn't say that, of course. I dug up an empty opinion. On balance, the Porchester, I said.

The aunts annexed the kitchen with the speed of two peacetime generals suddenly placed in charge of a military campaign. Odd, I thought, that it took a death to bring them fully to life. They churned out doilied plates of tray-bakes and delicate, pan-loaf ham sandwiches carved into tiny triangles. They went shopping for teabags, milk, sherry, whiskey, beer: the full equipment for the perfect funeral. I should have been grateful. God knows I couldn't have done it by myself. And yet I wasn't, particularly. I thought I could smell a faint triumph buried somewhere in their help, the way a dog can sniff out a bone deep in a dustbin.

Sam dug himself out of his sofa, prised his hand off the remote, came up for the day to commiserate, and motored sedately back to Carrickfergus that night. The aunts stayed over. It was like a terrible dream played out in slow motion, and this time there was no waking up. I didn't want to stand there after the burial in my Sunday suit as the kind, creased faces came up one by one and said: 'I'm sorry for your trouble, Jacky. He was a great man.' I wanted to haul myself off into waste ground and howl like a wolf, dash my head against the wall until my forehead poured with blood. Anything to distract me from the pain coming from the void deep in my chest, the small hollow the size of the universe where Big Jacky had been.

Titch and his mother came to the house: he was in his Sunday suit, too, but it fitted even worse than mine. The too-short sleeves exposed his bluey-white, plump wrists. His mum was running around helping, but Titch stood in the corner at a loss for what to do and ate nearly two plates of sandwiches. I saw jowly Aunt Mary shooting him a glance of distilled venom as he started in on the tray-bakes: it was the only thing that made me smile all day. Before he left, he came up and said to me in a rush, 'I'm very sorry, Jacky. I liked Big Jacky an awful lot.' I knew he meant 'loved'. His anxious face was pale and clammy with sweat.

I told him: 'He really liked you too.'

★ ★ ★

The ambush came the day after the funeral. I was sitting in the kitchen on a hard wooden chair, drinking lukewarm tea and watching a shaft of sunlight falling through the window. I was counting the minutes, waiting for the aunts to go home. They would say: 'Will you be all right?' and I'd say graciously, 'Yes. I'll be fine. Thanks for everything. I'll give you a call tomorrow.' And then I'd wave them off and go upstairs and lie on Big Jacky's bed and stare at the ceiling and think about him quietly as the light faded and darkness slowly filled the room like black ink pouring into water.

I might go and get one of his shirts out of the cupboard, with the pipe-smoke smell of him still on it, and put it on the pillow beside my head and just lie there a while thinking about the things we did together over the years. I wanted to remember him taking me to the Botanic Gardens when I was younger, and both of us standing silently in the hothouse watching the big, leathery water lilies floating in the pond.

But it didn't happen like that. Suddenly the two aunts padded into the kitchen with manifest intent, a pair of soft-soled missionaries circling a recalcitrant native. Aunt Mary had her coat on, I noted. Aunt Phyllis, ominously, didn't.

Mary broached the subject first: 'We were

thinking it might be better if Phyllis stayed here for a little while, and helped you get back on your feet. She could help out at the newsagent's too, until you sorted something else out.'

The *newsagent's*: I hadn't even thought of that. It had been closed since Big Jacky died.

Aunt Phyllis was looking at me, expectantly. I stared back at her, wild-eyed. I was appalled. Every fibre of me was screaming *no, no, no, this mustn't happen*. I made a flailing effort to push their fait accompli away: 'Oh you don't need to do that, Aunt Phyllis. I'll be fine here, sorting things out on my own. Please don't put yourself to that trouble, honestly the two of you have done enough already. More than enough.'

Mary struck a firmer tone, her cheeks puffing out with confident authority: 'No, really, Jacky. We are certain it would be best.'

You big bloodhound, I thought, fuck off and sniff round someone else. It was a dirty trick, to mob someone the day after their own father's funeral. My heart was pounding with the injustice of it.

'I'll be fine, honestly,' I said.

I looked again at Phyllis, at the worn, expectant face, the tightly permed hair, the fussy wee cardigan with the careful bow tied at the front. It was a miserable enough life she had up there in Carrickfergus with Mary and her husband, and Mary queening it over her. I was her bid for independence, the last raft drifting past on an isolated river. She was clambering aboard me with a horrible tenacity: didn't she realise she would sink us both? *No, no.* I struggled to fight off the pity. Pity makes weaklings of us all.

Phyllis said: 'It would only be till you got yourself set up again, Jacky.' *No, no.* Mary chipped in quickly with: 'You can't be expected to manage here on your own like this. Phyllis can sort things out around the house.'

A brief stab of utter hatred, followed by a little flood of guilt. They had me now. I was sliding underwater.

I looked at Phyllis, and said: 'Just till I get myself sorted then. That would be kind of you.'

Phyllis smiled. Mary remembered there were some more of Phyllis's things in the car, and bustled out to fetch them.

★   ★   ★

Tick-tock. Tick-tock. That night Phyllis moved herself into Big Jacky's room, so I couldn't very well go in there and lie down, as I had planned, unless I wanted to give her a heart attack as well. I lay in my own bed, seething.

Tick-tock. Tick-tock. The bathroom had quickly filled up with Phyllis's bits and pieces, her aspirin and cuticle scrapers. Towelettes and hairnets, Q-tips and denture grip. Like the Dana song: all kinds of everything remind me of you.

Tick-tock. How about if I plastered my face in Phyllis's Pond's cream, backcombed my hair to stand up like a fright wig, wrapped my sheet around me like a toga, and walked into Big Jacky's room saying, 'Phyllis, get up. It's exactly this time every night that we slaughter the cat'?

She'd leg it all the way back to Carrickfergus in her long nightie, squealing like a stuck pig.

Tick-tock. Or, still with the face cream on, but in a voluminous nightdress to look like my mother, whispering, 'It's Grace, your dead sister. Leave wee Jacky alone, he's mine, after all, not yours.' But that would be a wicked thing to do. Big Jacky would be ashamed. I pictured him up there, looking down at me and smoking the pipe, slowly shaking his head in grave disappointment. 'Don't torment Phyllis,' he would say. 'She's not a bad soul.'

Tick-tock. I could just about hear her snoring. Does that mean, if she woke up, she could just about hear me crying?

Tick-tock. The starlings singing, puffed up with the importance of the morning, balancing on the telegraph wire with their gnarled little feet. The grey dawn creeping through the fine curtain. The piglet oink and whistle of Phyllis snoring. Me wide awake.

And all of that was just one night.

4

'Your big mate got a beating last night.' There was a mixture of fear and excitement in Marty's voice as he ran up next to me: fear at the darkness of what had happened, excitement at the size of his news.

It was a lead weight casually pitched into the bowl of bad soup already swaying in my stomach.

'Which mate?' I said. I didn't need to ask.

'Your big dopey mate, Titch you said his name was.'

'What happened to him?'

'I heard the shouting in the night. Four fellas with balaclavas on pulled him out of his house, I seen them out my window. They yanked him out over towards the waste ground, and I couldn't see, but I seen the one left behind pushing his ma back into the house. She was screaming too. The ambulance came later.'

How much later? I thought. They had got organised and cocky about the beatings now. I had heard that they dialled the ambulance themselves before they gave someone a doing. I wondered what they'd hit him with. I hoped to God it wasn't the planks of wood with rusty nails in it. The last boy that got that had infections and was in the Royal for weeks.

I could picture him there, flailing around, a clumsy bear prodded with hot pokers. It made me wince even to imagine it.

'Thanks for telling me,' I told Marty. He nodded abruptly and sauntered off down the street.

* * *

Round the corner, the birds throatily singing, the children squabbling over the football like seagulls with a piece of bread. Everything was just the same and everything was different.

Titch's house had brown cardboard tacked over the frame of the living-room window, where the glass had been. The red paint was coiling back from the dents in the front door, where boots had kicked it in. This was now the bad-luck house, singled out from all the houses in the street. The plague house.

I knocked. The door stayed shut. I knocked again. Nothing. I looked towards the window. As I stared at it, I saw the bottom edge of the cardboard peeling inwards: an eye was staring at me through the small triangle of space. Titch's mum's eye. My two eyes looked back into her single eye.

'Let me in,' I whispered.

A few seconds later the front door opened. I went into the hall and looked at her face. My God, she had aged twenty years in a night. Her swollen eyelids looked as though they had been scrubbed with the pan scourer. I went into the living room and sat down. 'What happened?'

'They came at about three in the morning. I ran downstairs when I heard them kicking in the door and they said where was Titch? I said he was at his aunt's in Newry and one of them said 'You're effing lying you oul bitch' and two of them pushed me to one side and went upstairs to find him.'

She was crying now, pulling in the air with big, hungry gulps, her hands dipping and soaring. The words choked her as they came out.

'And then they dragged him out of bed and down the stairs. He didn't know what was happening and he kept shouting for me. Pulled him out the door and I tried to follow but one of them pushed me back and said 'You stay out of it.' The same fella cut the phone and threw it out the front window, and then he said, 'You effing stay in here. I'll be in the hall and if you try to get out I'll sort you out too and make sure he gets a worse one.''

'Where's Titch now?'

'Upstairs, lying in his room. He wouldn't stay in hospital so eventually they let him home. When I brought him back from the hospital the only thing he said was 'Don't let anyone in.' He's got a broken arm, a fracture in his leg and his face is all swollen up. The doctor said it was with baseball bats. He's pushed his desk against the door of his room.'

'I'll leave him alone today then,' I said. 'Maybe call in on him tomorrow.' I bent to give her an awkward kiss on the cheek. She wasn't expecting it. It wasn't our usual parting gesture. Her head was bowed and hot, the cheek damp and stiff, crusted with a layer of dried tears. I walked out on to the street.

I took a few steps. Then something made me look back up to Titch's bedroom window. I hadn't expected to see anything, I don't even know what made me turn round. But what I did see nearly stopped my heart: a swollen, malevolent thing looking back at me, standing in the space made by a tugged-aside curtain. It took me a second to realise that it was Titch. His head seemed monstrous, the eyes shrunk to sunken currants, the face a blackened, purple mass of bruises.

Those watching eyes, I knew, had soaked up all the horror on my face. I stopped and raised a hand to him from the street. After what seemed a long time, one bandaged hand rose slowly in reply. I turned back then and kept on walking.

As I walked, I was trying to think what he had reminded me of. Something from childhood. The lonely monster, shut up in a tower. That, but something else too. Then I got it. When I was younger, we used to play with a kit called 'Mr Potato Head'. You took an old potato, and stuck plastic eyes and a nose and stringy hair on it, and turned it into a bit of a character. For a couple of hours you'd prop him up in fruit bowls and push him around in empty egg cartons. But then you would go on to something else and forget about it, and two weeks later you'd find oul Mr Potato Head lying somewhere behind the bin, with his head turning all purple and yellow, and accidental eyes sprouting out of him.

So that's what they'd done to Titch. Except he had felt and heard it all: every kick, every spike, every burning word. And he wouldn't have understood why this evil had fallen upon him. For a packet of biscuits? Dumped by the bins to bloat and rot, my best mate, Mr Potato Head.

⋆　⋆　⋆

I couldn't go back home. There would be too much chat out of Phyllis. By the time I usually came in Phyllis was always hungry for my presence, even though it was invariably unsatisfactory. She yearned for gossip and confidences. I found myself unable to provide these things. She could have wolfed down a six-course banquet of discussion, and I was only capable of passing her the occasional bruised windfall.

Sometimes I would struggle to do my best, courteously assembling snippets from here and there, but I couldn't tonight. How could I hand over the happenings of the day? 'Four men in balaclavas came round to Titch's house last night, dragged him on to waste ground and gave him a terrible beating. Could you change over to BBC 2, I think the snooker's on?'

But it wouldn't be left at that. The story would make too big an impact. You can't drop a boulder into the centre of a still lake and not expect to create some ripples. There would be a silence — not a dead silence, but a busy one, building to a gush of who, what, why, where, when, and now what will happen? And I knew the answer to most of these things, and yet had no heart to begin explaining any of it to Phyllis or even to myself. None whatsoever. An immense weariness came over me: it would have been very good to curl up in a dark corner away from it all, and sleep for a thousand years.

I started the walk into town, moving through the fine rain, the shining, shifting curtain of small falling needles. Nowhere does drizzle like Belfast. It's our speciality. We should parcel it up and export it to the Saudis. They're gasping for it, by all accounts.

5

Drink. The clatter of laughter, and raw shouts, and mists of smoke rising from wood-panelled cabins. Light filtered through stained glass. I was in the Crown Bar, Belfast, ornamented Victorian gin palace and liquor saloon: a doughty old coquette who had her fancy windows shattered every time the IRA attempted to blow up the Europa International Hotel opposite, which it did with a zeal undimmed by repetition.

Just a couple of years earlier one of the IRA's 1,000-pound car bombs had hit the jackpot, and not only blasted a large, jagged hole in the side of the Europa, but instantly reduced the wedding-cake pomp of the nearby Grand Opera House to rubble as well. The Europa's head concierge said afterwards that if he stood at his desk in the lobby he could now see straight through to the Opera House stage. Anything really nice we had, it got wrecked. After a while you got used to it.

For over a century, in and out of disturbances, the Crown had flung open her doors and spilled men out at night into the path of horse-drawn traps, trams, trolleybuses and finally motor cars. They were her roaring, weeping, brawling, laughing men, their walnut brains pickled and petrified in alcohol, pushed out to confront the cold, stony pavements and their icy wives. Or maybe their women were there with them too, arm-in-arm as they both swayed home in a side-long pavement dance, bloodstreams running warm with beer and port.

Sometimes in the afternoons wee boys of the urchin class still swaggered in, so edgy you could cut yourself on their banter, and made deadpan offers to sell you three jokes for a pound.

I ordered a whiskey.

'Jacky!' I turned around, and there was Sammy who I went to school with, his face shining with the pleasant sweat of four pints, and a russet-haired girlfriend beaming by his arm. He was a couple of years older than me. It was a long time since I had last seen him.

'Jacky, how *are* you?' He placed an authoritative, amicable hand on my shoulder. He was heavier than I remembered him, kitted out in corduroys and a navy fisherman's sweater: he looked oddly well-to-do. 'How's things? How's your dad?'

Years ago, he used to come over to my house after school sometimes, to watch TV or play football. Big Jacky always called him the Sergeant Major, because of his blond brush-cut and his precocious capacity for organisation. He said that on his way home from work he could hear Sammy from halfway down the street, bawling us all into position for some pitched battle.

'My dad died, Sam. Heart attack,' I said, and gave a small smile to show that I was aware of the social awkwardness of my answer. He looked genuinely grieved: his girlfriend had the decency to look grieved too, even though she didn't know me.

43

'Och Jacky, that's terrible. When did it happen?'

'A few months ago. It was bad, I miss him.' I hustled him past the expected condolences: 'Anyway, what about you, what are you up to?'

'Well, I'm getting married in the autumn, to Shauna' — he indicated the girl beside him, with a proud flourish of introduction — 'and I'm running a car valeting business now, employing about ten people. It's going pretty well, we're getting a lot of corporate accounts. But listen, how are all the rest of them — do you still see Titch?'

In truth, Sammy had always been a bit impatient with Titch, who was a human liability in Sammy's embryonic money-making schemes. When we were twelve, Sammy had set us up with buckets and sponges to wash all the cars on our street, at a cost that undercut the nearest carwash (Sammy took his cut, naturally, for supplying the materials and sweet-talking the neighbours). We were all raring to go: Sammy had sketched for us a tantalising picture of entrepreneurial rewards, with bouncy new footballs and cinema tickets ripening as the fruits of our labours.

It all began smoothly on day one, with the Sergeant Major strenuously demonstrating the correct procedure on his own father's gleaming red Ford. It was to be Titch's job to fill the water-buckets, and mine to rinse and clean the different cloths. Then we set to work, but by midday I could see Titch's mouth drooping sullenly, and a lead-limbed, lackadaisical quality sneaking into his polishing. Titch never really understood the concept of delayed gratification. At one point he went off down an alleyway on his own, and was sitting there gratefully peeling a chocolate bar when I found him and dragged him back.

The next day, at the appointed hour for beginning the car-washing, I was there all by myself. There was no sign of Titch, or the water-buckets which he had carted home the day before, grumbling. Sammy and I went round to Titch's house: nobody there, and no explanatory note — nothing. Sammy was livid. He had to go begging for water-buckets and help me do it himself, abandoning his superb supervisory role as our manager, or risk angering his new customers. He damned Titch — the lazy big fathead — to high heaven. When Titch and his mother arrived back the next day, from a visit to his grandmother in Larne, the Sergeant Major wouldn't speak a word to him for a fortnight.

'Titch isn't too good,' I said. 'Four paramilitaries dragged him out into waste ground last night and gave him a terrible hammering.'

Sammy's expression took on a curious mixture of surprise and intimate understanding. He leaned close, and asked in a lowered voice, 'Was he dealing drugs?'

I stared back at him. 'Sammy, catch a grip. Titch can hardly get around to dealing you a hand of cards, there's no way he'd be up to drugs.'

'Well why did they do him, then?'

'He got into a row with old McGee, who runs

that corner shop. Titch nicked a packet of Jaffa Cakes. McGee's son is involved.'

'Jaffa Cakes.' He gave a bark of laughter. 'And they did him for that?'

'They did him for that.'

'Poor bastard.'

Sammy started chewing over this information, soaking up its future implications for himself. He shook his head, slowly and sorrowfully: 'They're really getting out of control now. Everything you want to do, or think of doing, they're on your back. They came round the other month asking for a slice from the car valeting business.'

'And what did you tell them?'

'I cut them down. What they were asking for at the beginning was a joke: there wouldn't have been any business left in a year to take anything out of. But you've got to give them something, or — ' he broke off, raised his eyebrows, and mimed striking a match ' — and I don't want to collect any insurance money on my place just yet. I like it where I am.'

There was a seam of absolute pragmatism running through Sammy. He just did whatever he had to do to keep going. It wasn't a question of right and wrong. That stuff didn't keep him awake at night. There were simply certain people that had to be dealt with and paid off. Whether it was the government taxman that came banging on his door or the local hoods demanding their protection money, it was really all one and the same to Sammy. Yes, it would be better if the system was straight, but was it Sammy's fault if it wasn't? It did pain his businessman's heart, though, to have to pay out over the odds.

Sammy wasn't a bad guy, at all. He was even kind, at bottom. There are businessmen like him all over America, gently rolling their eyes as they slide their monthly envelope over to the local Mafia. I could have seen Sammy keeping shop in small-town Nazi Germany, mournfully complaining about the boisterous antics of the young Brownshirts, maybe even occasionally passing his dwindling band of Jewish customers a wee something they were officially forbidden — but making sure he always kept the framed picture of Herr Hitler on the wall and a little nip of schnapps for the visiting SS man.

In that moment's pause, he must have caught a flicker of what I was thinking. Whatever else, Sammy was never slow. He looked me in the eye: 'Jacky, I'm not Charles Bronson. And if I was, I'd have a nice big pile of rubble and ten more people on the dole to show for it.'

I smiled at him and shrugged: 'I know.'

He finished up his pint in one expansive gesture. 'Listen, tell Titch I was asking for him, will you? If there's anything he or the ma needs . . .' A protective arm moved around his fiancée, who was already making a 'we're leaving, but it was nice to meet you' face.

For a departing second, Sammy's astute eyes rested on me, taking in the stubble on my chin, and the loose hang of Big Jacky's oddly cut overcoat. Casually, as though it was an afterthought, his hand rummaged in his back pocket and produced a business card: *Cleen-Sheen Cars.*

'I know you've probably got a lot else going

on, but if you ever fancy a few hours on the side, we always need people with a bit of sense. It's very flexible. Or give me a ring anyway, if you just want a pint.'

I took his card, and shook his hand. I had to give it to Sammy, the offer had been made with a certain panache. I watched the two of them go out the door, huddling together against the rain while his girlfriend struggled to put up her umbrella. As I said before, he wasn't a bad guy.

* * *

When I finally got home, the house was dark. Phyllis had gone to bed. I was relieved at this, and sad too. I could see the *Belfast Telegraph* lying open at the television page, where she had marked out her evening's viewing in pencil, alone.

Everything suddenly had a drunken clarity. The thought of her specially picking out which programmes to watch made me want to weep. I should have rung and told her where I was. I hadn't. She wouldn't mention anything about it the next day: that made it worse. I failed her as a companion, I knew. Would she be happier back with bloodhound Mary and remote-control-man Sam? Probably not.

She loved working in the newsagent's: she hoarded little bits of information about everyone. She helped people out, sending them cards and chocolates when they were sick, and they never stopped being grateful. At least Phyllis was busy making herself part of something real. She was a spider at the centre of the sticky human web of fussing and affection. Not like me. I just hung around on the edges of things, ineffectually watching. Phyllis was trying to mean something to people. I didn't mean anything to anybody.

I could have saved Titch, with more effort and conviction, and I hadn't. I had guessed this would happen to him, I had even warned him, and yet there he was trussed up in bandages anyway. My superior knowledge had made not the least impression on events. The terrible, predictable misery had unfolded just as though I had never spoken, never even existed. Why had I let him learn it for himself? Had I wanted, somehow, to be proved right?

I remembered a story from a long time ago, told by a friend of Big Jacky's who called in to see us one night. His son had been given a pet rabbit, not one of the little dwarf rabbits that are as limp as an old fur glove, but the real article: a big buck number with restless ears and a prominent will of its own. This rabbit was a source of great pride to the son. The father had watched the son building a run for the rabbit in the back garden, where the boy had made plans to observe it frolicking and chomping grass to its heart's content.

The boy was assembling the run from loose bricks, card-board boxes and bits of wire all shambled together, and the father saw that the rabbit could easily escape from it. So he warned the son: 'Your rabbit will break out that run, and you'll not see it again.' And the son ignored him, and went on fixing up the flimsy pen.

49

The preparations continued, and the father saw that the moment was approaching when the rabbit would be released into the run. He said again: 'I'm telling you now, the rabbit will be able to escape from that run,' and then off he went to work.

When he came back that night, the house was soaked in tears. The sobbing son told him what had happened. The rabbit had duly spent a few minutes enjoying its new run, amiably grazing, and then it had suddenly bolted over a cardboard box and disappeared. He had searched everywhere for it, in neighbours' gardens and out on the road, but it was gone. And the father, although pained by his son's misery, couldn't help himself from saying: 'Son, I told you the rabbit could break out of that run.'

But the son didn't say meekly 'I know you did, Dad,' or simply let the unwelcome reminder wash over him. He turned on his father with something approaching rage, and said: 'Well, if you knew it would happen, why didn't you *stop me*?'

The father laughed guiltily, telling it: the boy was right, in a way. The father could have stopped him, but he hadn't. The boy had never owned a rabbit before, or seen one escape, so how could he be expected to believe how easily this predicted disaster would happen? Yet if the father had actually stopped him, the rabbit would never have got away; his warning would never have been proved right, and the resentful boy would have despised his father's bullying caution. And so, the price of knowledge: one lost rabbit.

But Titch — what good had it done him, to see his judgement proved wrong? In his way, he had even been right to laugh at the thought that he might end up in pieces after a row with old McGee over a packet of biscuits. For wouldn't it have been laughable anywhere else but here? He was the sane one, really: the rest of us were the headcases, to expect such an event and plan for it, cravenly. He had thought the world a funny, benign place. He was wrong. His uncomplicated vision had now been blackened, like burned glass. Mine had been tested and proved clear. But none of that explained why a voice inside my head, coming from a patch of waste ground, kept repeating with sorrowful insistence: 'If you knew it would happen, why didn't you *stop it*?'

* * *

Every morning, I opened my eyes to the rhythm of the creaking floorboards as Phyllis padded towards the bathroom. She had a habit of clearing her throat loudly en route to the basin. I had long ago concluded that this was partly from necessity and partly a vocal tribute to the new day. When this emanation reached my ears, I shut my eyes once again.

Phyllis's preparations for her daily appearance at the newsagent's were as follows: the procedures of washing and dressing, the teasing of her fine mouse-brown hair into a respectable cloud, the careful application of powder and a rose-tinted lipstick, and the ingestion of two pieces of toast washed down with a cup of tea.

The execution and conclusion of these matters took approximately forty-five minutes. Then, for fifteen minutes after Phyllis shut the front door, I would lie in a fitful haze, wallowing in solitude.

After that, I got up. To be honest, I had sort of lost my way since Big Jacky's death. I had few bearings left. I'd studied English at Queen's University after school, but dropped out before finishing the degree. I somehow couldn't dissect the books in the style I thought my tutors wanted. My approach seemed in some obscure manner to be frustrating them, or so it felt to me. I began to lose heart — and anyway, by the time you had prodded and tugged everything out of a book it had often quietly died on you, like a patient left open for too long on an operating table.

Before Big Jacky died, I had spent much of my time helping him in the newsagent's shop. People used to ask me questions about the university course and whether I was returning to it, but their curiosity had receded now. They had come to accept my apparent lack of ambition as a fact of life, something which relieved and depressed me. Now day ran into day in a kind of purposeless fog. My usefulness had fallen away since Phyllis took over the shop, although I still helped her shift heavy deliveries when she asked. There were a couple of other people who helped us out sometimes, and when she saw I wasn't handling things too well in there without Big Jacky, Phyllis had quietly upped their hours.

Phyllis had changed since she first came to live with me; she was no longer the bowed plant she had seemed in Carrickfergus. The submissive droopiness, assumed as a protective mantle under the domineering shadow of Mary, had been cast off. She was swelling into a larger, more exuberant presence, in the house and in the shop.

Well, good for Phyllis. She was waxing. I was waning. I had anorexia of the soul. I got a bit of money from the dole: that did for my food, some of the bills, and the occasional drinks I spun out across my evenings in town. My books sustained me, but erratically. I would read the same one, again and again, for hours, and yet it seemed to lead me nowhere but in a large, loose circle, like some clapped-out oul donkey on a beach.

Anorexia of the soul. Would I ever even have thought of exactly those self-pitying words, if I hadn't drunk in so much daytime television? I watched it a lot of the time now, especially the chat shows. They drifted before me, an endless string of enormously fat people, bulimics with bad perms, shameless adulterers, weeping adulterees, feckless spend-thrifts, part-time prostitutes, busted drunks and heartbroken gamblers. I applauded them all, every one, the whole limping chorus line of flawed humanity.

The American shows were the best by far. There, at least, they were all going to hell in flamboyant style, spurting out fierce jets of accusation. They were pouring the energy that built the American dream into wreaking the American nightmare. I admired that. Here at home, I was just fading into the soft Irish mud as the rain fell on me.

Take Kimberley, for example, a blowsy,

bleached blonde with a mouth that raced in several directions at once, most of them ill-advised. She was fighting for the affections of Charlie, her philandering boyfriend with a long, rodenty face. But Charlie was in love with the misnamed Chastity, a sixteen-year-old minx.

Then Kimberley explained that she intended to stick by Charlie 'because of stuff that happened in our childhoods that we're both having a tough time getting over'. But the audience were hollering and chanting with their prissy, pleased little mouths. And then one of them stood up, a smug woman in an appliquéd top, and said triumphantly, 'I just wonder what trailer park y'all came out of!'

Everyone laughed and yahooed. For a split second, Kimberley's face collapsed in genuine dismay. I fell back on the sofa and started to weep, the tears soaking my face and neck.

It was then that I realised I really had to get out of the house.

6

Mr Murdie was a short man, with sharp eyes that had totted up a million bar bills and a stainless steel brain that never failed — ping! — to calculate exactly the right change. If a cannibal had killed and eaten Mr Murdie, he would probably have detected an unusual flavour permeating the leathery meat, for as Mr Murdie had spent his entire working life steeped in the nicotine fug of Belfast bars, his flesh had almost certainly been deeply and satisfactorily smoked, like a mackerel hung above a wood fire.

Mr Murdie had observed enough alcoholic bonhomie to grow mistrustful of bonhomie altogether. It was, as he knew, a slippery and deceitful customer. He had watched it sway into gross sentimentality and lurch into frightening belligerence. That is why when Mr Murdie's regulars sometimes slumped over the counter at the end of the evening and told him — amid slurred, urgent confidences — that they actually loved him, loved him as a best, best friend, Mr Murdie answered with an economical wee smile, and the words, 'Aye well if you really love me, boys, you'll clear off to your beds now and let me wipe the counter.'

Mr Murdie knew that Mrs Murdie really loved him. She wasn't much of a drinker, though, and so she hardly ever said it.

When I walked into the Whistle Bar, where

Murdie was the manager, and enquired of him whether they needed any barmen, I had reason to believe that he would help me out. Big Jacky and he had played together in a showband called the Janglemen when they were in their late teens. Mr Murdie had played the guitar and Big Jacky had been on the drums. I had seen a picture of them in their stage suits, with both of them managing somehow to look eighteen and forty-five at the same time. But there was an expression of subtle pride on Murdie's saturnine face beneath a glossy Brylcreemed quiff, suggesting that a secret craving for flamboyance had been momentarily satisfied.

Murdie remained a friend of Big Jacky's, and he would call round to our house on some nights to play cards and eat bacon sandwiches. When I was small he had a habit of greeting me with the words: 'What happened — did your school burn down?' This threw me into a pleasurable confusion. I hadn't the least idea what Mr Murdie meant. Why on earth would my school burn down? And yet the thought that it might burn down some day was unsettling but exciting. If I woke up one morning, and Big Jacky just said, 'No school today, son. It's burned down, I'm afraid,' would that be the business of school over for good, would I ever have to go again?

When I got a bit older, I used to reverse the charges and ask Murdie: 'What happened — did your bar burn down?' This was less of a joke than it seemed. Two of the bars that Murdie had worked in really had burned down. One was razed at a time when sectarian furies were running conveniently high in Belfast, and the owner torched it himself for the insurance money. The other was intended to act as a city-wide warning to those who chose to ignore the final reminders on their protection money. Murdie kept silent as a Sphinx throughout, observed all that happened, found himself fresh employment and carried on pouring customers' whiskey.

He was polishing the beer glasses when I walked into the Whistle, and he seemed pleased to see me. It was a quiet enough afternoon. There were two drinkers slouched over the bar, but they were too engrossed in the horse racing on television to slide me more than a desultory glance. Murdie had been at Big Jacky's funeral along with Mrs Murdie. I hadn't talked to him since.

'Well, well,' he said. 'Here's the man himself.'

He poured me a pint of lager, and then — with a quick look towards the pub door — lit up a cigarette. 'So, wee Jacky, what are you up to?'

'You won't believe it,' I said. 'My school burned down.'

Murdie's face cracked into a broken smile: 'Who did it?'

'I did. I decided I was getting too old for detention.'

He laughed, and then waited, smoking. There is an amateur and a professional style of smoking. The amateur style is floatily indulgent, expansive in the movement of the smoking arm, casually squandering the cigarette's little life. The professional style extracts the maximum value from every puff, the smoking arm moving quickly and in a straight line, in the knowledge that the pleasure of the cigarette might soon be cut short by some external demand. Murdie smoked in the professional style.

'Aunt Phyllis is living with me now. She's sort of taken over the running of the newsagent's.'

'Is the business going well?'

'Aye, I think it's going all right. It seems to have plenty of customers. Most of them come in to talk to Phyllis. She's certainly got the gift of the gab.'

Enough said. Murdie nodded, and looked at me with the unspoken understanding that there are times when you would like to put the people with the gift of the gab in a large room along with everyone who has kissed the Blarney Stone, lock the door and let them all jaw each other to death.

'The thing is, though, there's not really enough for me to do there. Phyllis has it pretty much all under control. I was wondering if you might need a barman here, or know anyone else who does.'

Consideration. He stubbed out the cigarette as punctuation to his thoughts. His mental machinery was doing some speedy calculations: I could almost hear it clicking and revolving.

'Davy's leaving next week, to go and work on a cruise liner,' he said. 'You could fill in for him for a while. But you'd need to come on a few afternoons, when there's just me here, to get the hang of the place. Come in on Tuesday.'

I was delighted. I finished up my pint. Murdie walked me to the door, and, as I left, he hit me a stern, playful whack with the rolled-up copy of the *Belfast News Letter* he had been using earlier on to kill flies.

★ ★ ★

I went to see Titch to tell him about the job. Ever since the beating, it had been a gala performance to get him to come downstairs at all. In the past he used to get a bit of spare cash for helping out at the chippy but there was no prospect of that now. His mother was at her wits' end. There was mostly silence from him in the daytime, when he often slept, and then a rumpus during the night. His mother said that she could hear him getting up at two and three in the morning and struggling to shift the furniture around in his bedroom with his one good arm.

He had said to me, one afternoon, 'I'm going to get them back for what they done, I swear it.' It made me sad even to hear him say this. It wasn't going to happen. The sentence started out with defiance in it, but it tailed off halfway through from a lack of conviction.

'Och Titch,' I said, 'Leave it now. Don't make things worse for yourself. Soon they'll all land themselves in jail anyway.'

Titch had a counsellor. The Victim Support people had got in touch after the beating, and now a woman in a paisley-patterned duvet jacket came round regularly to ask him, in a professionally hushed voice, how he was feeling. Titch confirmed regularly, in monosyllabic form, that he was feeling bad. As the awkward silences lengthened, the counsellor was forced to stare with false, fixed interest at the family photographs displayed on the mantelpiece. Titch's hand moved with increasing frequency towards the open packet of Viennese Whirls by his side. He wouldn't even look at a Jaffa Cake now.

Titch's mother said that once she had read, upside down in the counsellor's notes, the single phrase: 'uses food, mainly sweet things, as a comfort blanket'. Titch's mother remarked to the counsellor that she had obviously never had the chance to observe Titch at work among savouries, in the Kentucky Fried Chicken restaurant in Shaftesbury Square. The counsellor stared blankly at her for a moment, with her biro quivering above Titch's case notes, and then said without smiling, 'Ah. Joke.'

The whole aim, said the counsellor, was to allow Titch to 'achieve full closure' with his experience at the hands of the paramilitaries. It would be useful if Titch could first learn to forgive himself for behaving as a victim, and then somehow — and she recognised this might take a while — forgive his attackers for perpetrating the assault. Titch's mother said that she had a First World War bayonet, a family heirloom, and that she would first like to 'achieve full closure' with the backsides of his assailants. The counsellor looked at her oddly again, she said, and then made some quite extensive notes which she casually shielded from view with her arm.

When I called round Titch was up in his room. He was lying on his bed, reading his mother's *Bella* magazine. He had it pulled open at the recipe section. When he saw me come in, he let it slide to the ground: a full-colour picture of Thai fishcakes with a tiger prawn garnish winked garishly up at us both.

I skated over the pervasive air of hopelessness. 'I've got a job, Titch. I'm going to start as a barman at the Whistle on Tuesday. If you come into town to see me, I'll treat you to a pint of lager, cider or orange squash for free, as an introductory offer. We need new customers.'

I knew there was no way he would come into town yet, but I wanted to ruffle him out of this awful torpor. I wanted to goad him into being cheeky to me again.

'I'm not going out of the house,' said Titch, sulkily. 'I don't want them fellas to get hold of me and do what they done last time.'

'Titch, they're not going to do you all over again just for the heck of it. They've already done you once.'

'They're not in jail, are they? There's nothing to stop them, if they want to.'

I couldn't argue with that. He had the relentless, correct logic of a child sometimes. The hopelessness came back to fill the small room, washing over me, touching the useless frills on the beige nylon curtains and the pointless, grinning Toby jug on the windowsill that his uncle had brought him back from Yorkshire. In my desire to shove it away, to jolt Titch out of his own grim reasoning, I threw in something even worse.

'But Titch, it makes no difference anyway whether you go out or stay in. In fact, you'd be

61

better off going out. They came up and got you here, didn't they? They pulled you right out of this room, didn't they?'

As soon as the words were out of my mouth, I knew I should never have said them. He stared at me for a second as though I had just smacked him full in the face. And then his expression began to disintegrate, falling apart into shapes that would have been almost comic if they hadn't been so terrible. He was moving violently from side to side, putting his elbows up to shield his head, and all the time making the high-pitched wailing sound of some trapped animal in distress.

I waited until the worst of it had passed and then I went over and put my hands on his heaving shoulders. I told him gently: 'Sshh. They won't come for you again.' The shoulders moved gradually to a shaking halt. And then he started to whisper something all jumbled together, like a child's babble, and so softly that I had to lean in very close to hear. It was the same sentence, over again: 'I don't have anywhere to go. I don't have anywhere to go.'

7

The Whistle was a great place to work. It was an old, established bar on the way in to the city centre: a bit dilapidated, but it had charm. We got a lot of students and gentle wastrels in the daytime, and a more eclectic, fired-up clientele by night.

It was never too busy in the afternoons, and in between serving customers Murdie demonstrated to me some of the little tricks of the barman's trade: how to polish glasses to a high sheen without smearing them again when you set them down; the correct way to serve a whiskey and water; how to pull the perfect pint of Guinness; and the proper proportions of the constituent elements in a port and lemon.

When we had the basics of the bar sorted out, said Murdie, we'd move on to learning cocktails.

At a certain point in the day, if things were quiet, he would pour a single whiskey for each of us, to be drunk slowly and without ice. We would savour the peaty burning at the back of our throats while Murdie's favourite song, Van Morrison's 'Tupelo Honey', spun lazily out of the CD player. It was a surprisingly lush choice for such a self-contained man. The golden afternoon light would float in through the frosted pub windows, spilling in widening patches on the polished wood of the tables, and for that moment all the worries that clodded to me would flake away.

One day I was staring at the fat, corrugated worm lying at the bottom of a bottle of mescal. One of the regulars had brought it back from a trip to Mexico, as a present for Murdie. He had displayed it behind the bar, unopened, and the function of the worm had begun to nag at me.

'What's that thing for?' I asked Murdie.

'That's the mescal worm,' he said. 'It soaks up all the lunacy in the bottle. If you eat that worm, you'll start hallucinating. You'll see demons.'

He could be quite poetic, Murdie, when you got him going. We both stood contemplating it floating there wickedly like a baby's thumb.

'If you ate that worm, Murdie,' I said, 'could you remember, in the moment of insanity, why you and my dad called your band a name like the Janglemen?'

'It wasn't us that thought of it, Jacky,' he said: 'it was your mother. She thought it would be funny, and it was. We got lots of bookings just because of that name.'

'What was she like, Murdie?'

'She was a laugh,' he said gently, 'a really good laugh. But kind, too, and a great dancer. And she was crazy about you.'

Then he started to empty all the ashtrays, to rinse them out before the evening crowd started coming in after work.

★ ★ ★

In the evenings, when things hotted up, the door at the Whistle was manned by Joe and Jimmy. They both wore tuxedos, the traditional doorman's costume, and they were both built like brick shithouses, the historic doorman's physique. Joe was dark-haired with a bristly, neat moustache. Jimmy was blond. Joe did weights at the gym to keep himself in peak condition. Jimmy probably kept fit by twirling his little brothers around like drumsticks on the Twelfth of July. I wouldn't have liked to mess with either of them.

The year before had been a particularly bad year for Belfast doormen, security guards and taxi drivers. Doormen, whether Catholic or Protestant, were used as exclamation marks to punctuate the long-running argument between the IRA and the Loyalist paramilitaries.

The argument had long followed certain clear, established lines. The IRA would, for example, let off a bomb. The Loyalists, to emphasise how enormously they disapproved of this violence, would kill a Catholic doorman who was standing outside his workplace, musing on what to buy his son for his birthday. The IRA, to show how furious they were at this outrage, would gun down a Protestant security guard who was thinking about where to go with his girlfriend on his next night off. The Loyalists, to demonstrate their anger at this atrocity, would phone a taxi driver from a Catholic firm and shoot him point-blank in the back of the head as he politely asked them for directions. And so their discussions on morality continued.

This year, however, had been better for doormen and taxi drivers specifically, and worse generally for young Catholics who annoyed the

IRA and young Prods who irritated the Loyalists. Nonetheless, Joe and Jimmy were mindful of the pitfalls in their chosen occupation.

Joe could be funny when he had time, and he had a lot of that on the door. He told me one night, stroking his lapels, 'If they start shooting doormen again, at least I'm going to go dressed in a tuxedo. When I get up there they'll stick me straight on the pearly gate with Saint Peter, to keep the troublemakers like you out.'

I told him: 'You've been watching too many Mafia films. Knowing your luck, they'd get you when you were dandering back from the gym, in your big floppy shorts. The best you'd get then is a part-time job as a personal trainer to Matthew, Mark, Luke and John.'

He wouldn't hear of it.

'I'm going on the gate,' he said, puffing out his chest. 'And when I see you coming, I'll tell you: 'I'm sorry, you're underage. You'll have to go to hell.''

'Nobody's underage for heaven,' I said.

'No, but you'll still need ID before they'll serve you a drink,' he said. His shoulders shook with pleasure at getting the last word, and then he wheeled round and grimaced at three girls who were teetering in high heels and an atomic cloud of perfumed body spray at the door, all of them plastered in make-up and none a day over fifteen.

'Date of Birth,' Joe demanded flatly, with his stern official's face on. He stared with meaning at the smallest one, a sharp-faced wee blonde who looked all of fourteen. She glared back, pursing her glossily enamelled lips as though deeply, personally affronted by the question, and then reeled off a fake date of birth that would have made her eighteen exactly two months before. Joe mimed exaggerated disbelief. They carried on this little war of nerves every couple of weeks. It was splendid to watch.

He turned towards each of the others, as though by now deeply bored and suspicious, repeating the mantra: 'Date of birth'. They were all pretty good at it, really, apart from a plump gormless brunette who had obviously had a bit to drink already. She stumbled over the year, and then stood blinking under her heavy purple eyeshadow, trying to work out which date she needed in order to get in.

'Sorry, you're not getting in,' Joe told her.

At this, the others began to squawk and flap in protest.

'Mister, she is eighteen,' chirruped the blonde, 'but she's just had her birthday. You just confused her there, the way you asked her that.'

The brunette had worked it out by now, and even caught up with the necessary, offended tone of voice. She repeated the entire date of birth again, slowly and deliberately, as though Joe had failed to understand her the first time because of his own bestial stupidity. The others fell silent in anticipation, knowing not to push things too far.

'Happy Birthday. And congratulations. You're the only eighteen-year-old I've ever met that still gets a bedtime story from her mammy,' said Joe sarcastically.

The three of them started to snicker and

preen, sensing that he was softening.

'Get in . . . and next time bring your ID,' he called after them, in pretend irritation. He turned and winked broadly at me as they stampeded towards the bar, tittering in glee and triumph, waving their crumpled fivers and asking for vodka and orange.

★ ★ ★

It's strange at first, working behind a bar. You feel like you've been pushed on to a stage without knowing your lines, with the lights shining on you and a host of querulous faces looking on. And then after a while you get used to it, and the bar becomes your little square arena, your illuminated patch.

The important thing, Murdie told me, is that you're never seen to be standing idle. If you're not serving customers, then you should be polishing glasses, or stacking beer mats, or wiping up real and imaginary spillages with a damp cloth. But you are never performing these tasks to the exclusion of the customer's most vital interests. All the while, you are watching out for the thirsty, expectant face in the crowd, the frantic signalling that someone is dying for a drink.

When things get busy, said Murdie, you must learn to keep in your head the chronological order in which these thirsty faces appear, and serve them accordingly. If you mix them up you must quickly apologise. You must not disregard the short man (for Murdie was short himself) or the plain woman in favour of those individuals who naturally catch the eye and thus seem to be blessed with Bar Presence. The tall, burly man and the beautiful woman have already queue-jumped in life, said Murdie, but they should not be permitted to do so at the bar. To the truly professional barman, Bar Presence should be irrelevant. Order of appearance is everything.

I was hardly ever bored behind the bar, apart from very early in the evening or late at night when you got stuck with the tedious pub raconteur in the Aran sweater who had bolted his corduroyed arse to the bar stool. I liked it best at the height of the evening, when the place was packed with people and noise, and everyone was laughing and shouting for more drink, and you started to work with a feverish rhythm that drove everything else out of your head. I liked having a bit of money, too. Murdie paid me a decent chunk of cash in hand at the end of every week.

It was Phyllis's birthday halfway through the month and I asked Murdie for the night off. I'd been feeling guilty lately about how grumpy I'd been with her since she moved in. She had been dropping wee hints about her birthday, and how Mary and Sam would be away on holiday together and sorry to miss it but she had thought this time she would just stay in Belfast for it. 'Is that so,' I had said, distantly, as though my radio wasn't even picking up on her faltering signal.

I knew she thought I'd forgotten all about it. On the morning of her birthday, I got up half an hour early — well before her throat-clearing operation — and put a bunch of pink roses outside her bedroom door. I'd bought them the day before, and kept them in a jug of water in my wardrobe so she wouldn't see.

I got back into bed. Half an hour later, I heard the floorboards creak. Then a crash, a stumble, and a yelp of surprise. Phyllis had kicked over the roses by accident and they were all strewn about the floor, but I could see she was pleased. She kept saying 'Oh my goodness' as she collected them up in her nightie.

I took her out for dinner later on, to a French restaurant in town. She put on her best blouse, with a fussy wee frill at the neck, and her pearl earrings, and a daub of blue eyeshadow to set off the rose-tinted lipstick. When I saw her appear like that at the bottom of the stairs, all done up to go out, I felt an awkward pang of love for her.

In the restaurant, she had a couple of glasses of white wine with her dinner, and got a bit tipsy. The conversation got on to Mary and Sam's holiday: they had gone to Tenerife.

'It's good for them to go somewhere on their own without me,' she said. 'I sometimes felt as though I was a bit of a spare part.'

I said nothing, sawing away at my steak. I could sense the faint electricity of something meaningful approaching.

'I mean, I wouldn't have wanted Mary along all the time when I was going out with my boyfriend,' she said. There was a second's hesitation before the word 'boyfriend', as though she had doubts about whether to mention it, but had ploughed ahead anyway.

I had never heard Phyllis talk about a

boyfriend before. I couldn't imagine Phyllis with a boyfriend. Mary had always said that Phyllis was too delicate to get married. I carried on cutting my steak without showing surprise, so as not to scare the revelation away.

'When were you going out with him, Phyllis?' I asked.

'When I was nineteen,' she said, 'He was a medical student. We used to go out to dances together. Mary didn't like him. She said he was sly but he wasn't, he was just shy of her because she tried to bully him with too many questions.'

She smiled suddenly. 'He used to call her the Iron Lung, because she was always hunting after me, shouting my name.'

'How long did you go out together?'

'Two years. Your mother liked him. The pair of us used to give Mary the slip sometimes and go out to the dances together.'

I couldn't leave it now. I had to get to the bottom of it before the wine wore off and Phyllis clammed up about the only really important thing that had ever happened to her, and went straight back to talking ceaselessly about hairstyles and pork chops.

'So why did you stop going out?'

'He was killed in an accident,' she said matter-of-factly. 'I wasn't with him because I wasn't feeling well that night. He went out to a dance with his brother, and his brother was driving him home along a country road late that night when a van hit their car. The van's driver was drunk.'

'Did the brother survive?'

71

'Yes,' she said. 'He only had a broken arm. He got married the year after. But after my boyfriend I never felt like going with anyone else.'

'I'm so sorry, Phyllis,' I said. Then we both started looking, quickly, at the list of puddings. After some deliberation over the pavlova and its possible disappointments in texture, Phyllis played it safe and plumped for the chocolate mousse.

8

The next day, I was back in the Whistle. It was a soft night, and the city was quiet. Blond Jimmy was on the door. Murdie was behind the bar with me, complaining about Mrs Murdie's younger English cousin Gavin, who had come to stay with them for a few days and was still there three weeks later, sleeping in the spare room and expecting a full Ulster fry on weekends when he roused himself from his bed at midday. He was between jobs, which is a dangerous place for a house guest to be.

The cousin had elected to go on an extended 'Troubles Tour' of Belfast in a black taxi, in which the taxi driver took him round a miniature history of the Troubles, complete with a running commentary. They had gone up along the Peace Wall, that separates the Protestant Shankill Road and the Catholic Falls Road, and up to the shop on the Shankill where an IRA bomb killed nine Protestants queueing to buy fish, and all around the murals that use the gable walls like storybooks to tell the highly coloured version of events from each side.

The worst of it was that the cousin was very interested in the roots and origins of it all now, and when Murdie got home exhausted at night the cousin was waiting for him there at the kitchen table, with a drink already poured out for Murdie from Murdie's own whiskey bottle, and a million questions about the Troubles along with his own answers to the problems.

Things had finally come to a head the night before, said Murdie, when he came back in at midnight and there was the cousin, sitting up with a glass of Murdie's whiskey and a copy of the *Belfast Telegraph*, raring to go. Why, asked the cousin, did the Protestants who lived in a county with a majority of Catholics not move house to live in a county with a majority of Protestants, and the Catholics do vice versa, and then the counties that were then a hundred per cent Catholic could go over to the South if they wanted, and there could be a much smaller Northern Ireland just for all the Protestants who wanted to stay British?

Could we talk about it tomorrow, said Murdie, because I haven't really much energy left after a day in the bar.

Of course, said the cousin, but did Murdie not see that if things were sorted out that way, then it would be much easier for everyone who wished to remain in the new, smaller version of Northern Ireland, and the state that was left would demand far fewer resources from the ordinary British taxpayer? Would Murdie not agree on that?

And then Murdie snapped and said I'm sick of effing politics, you've done nothing but talk politics since the day you got here and I wish you'd give my head peace. People don't move house because they don't want to move and that's it. I've come home tired from a long day at work and the last thing I want to talk about is your effing blueprint for the redesigning of Northern Ireland, because I've had blueprints for a new Northern Ireland every single day of my life for the last effing twenty-five years.

There was an awful silence. And then the cousin finally got his breath back and said, with deep affront, Well I can see exactly why you've had the Troubles for so long if you've got an attitude like that. If you lot are not even prepared to discuss your problems rationally round a table with other people, it's no wonder your whole place is in such a mess. And the worst of it is, you all expect English taxpayers like me to foot the bill for it.

That did it. Foot the bill? said Murdie, maddened with anger, Foot the bill? This city was blasted to smithereens in the Blitz for standing up to Hitler alongside England, would you like the fucking bill for that? And in any case you haven't stuck your hand in your pocket for so much as a pound of sausages since you arrived.

There was no recovery from that, Murdie said, because it was the truth. And now there was a poisonous atmosphere in the house, and Mrs Murdie was livid, and the cousin had got up ostentatiously early this morning and appeared grim-faced at breakfast with his hair all combed over to one side, and would only accept a cup of tea with a lightly buttered piece of toast before going out for the day.

I told Murdie he shouldn't worry: 'Maybe he'll take his leave altogether now, and you'll get a bit of quiet.'

Murdie was racked with guilt: 'No, it's not right, son. I shouldn't have spoken like that to him, he was a guest in my house. And now he'll go back to England and tell everybody there that Mrs Murdie is married to a madman.'

Then he said, 'The joke of it is Mrs Murdie can't stick him for long either. But she says I shouldn't have insulted him: it's the principle of the thing.'

He started laughing: 'But it was true what I said about the sausages. That fella's tighter than a fly's arse.'

Consoled, he went back to checking the beer barrels, whistling a tricky little twirling melody.

★   ★   ★

Murdie told me about his wife's cousin in the afternoon. It was the last afternoon I spent working in the Whistle.

I had set up everything ready for the evening rush, but it was a Wednesday night and we had no band booked to perform, so the customers were just trickling in. I was playing a few tapes of Big Jacky's, soul music from the sixties, and was half listening to them and half thinking about other things.

And then, at about half past nine, a dark-haired girl came in who I remembered from school. She was good-looking enough, in tight jeans with teased hair and all the jewellery on, but there was something I never liked about her face, something almost birdy. She had a hard, thin mouth, and I remembered her always hanging around the corridors with three or four girls in her gang, shouting out raucous stuff to torment the quiet ones or embarrass the plain ones. But I couldn't remember her name.

She remembered mine, though. It was all hair-tossing, and 'Hiya Jacky, I haven't seen you in ages', and she perched herself up at the bar with her boyfriend on a bar stool beside her. He wasn't best pleased by the whole scenario. He looked vaguely familiar, too, although I knew he hadn't been at school with me: he was wiry, muscled but not overly tall, with a tattoo of a rose with a face in the middle of it bulging on his left arm. It didn't look much like her face, but then maybe the tattoo artist's hand was shaking when he did it.

The boyfriend was edgy drunk and she was over-the-top drunk, an explosive combination, and anyone who came near them was likely to get whipped up by the corner of their personal typhoon.

She wanted a double vodka and tonic. He wanted a pint. I was civil enough to her, but I was keeping my distance. There was a hum of trouble off the pair of them. I served them both their drinks, and kept myself busy with the other customers. There was plenty going on elsewhere to keep me well away from them without it looking deliberate, or so I thought.

A few vodkas later, she started up again. Her eyes had locked on to me with the peculiar, fixated stare of the slightly belligerent drunk.

'You're not very friendly, Jacky,' she said, mushing the words a little. 'I bet you can't even remember my name.'

I couldn't, as it happened. I had been racking my brains for it all night. I'd gone out with one of her lesser friends briefly at school, and I had the dim memory of it ending in some kind of minor dispute with the potential for wider hysteria from which I had quickly retreated. But the worst thing would be to take a stab in the dark at the name and get it wrong. That could reasonably, or very unreasonably, be interpreted as an insult.

'Of course I can,' I lied.

'What is it then?' she said.

'If you don't know it yourself, I'm not going to tell you,' I said. 'It's a state secret. Do you think I'd go giving out your name to just anyone?'

My lame little joke enjoyed far too spectacular a success. She went off into stagey peals of laughter. I bet by the time she had finished she had forgotten what I had said in the first place. I winced inside, and then I looked over at him. He had obviously interpreted my remark as an unwelcome attempt at flirtation. His face was a thundercloud waiting to burst. I didn't want to be standing there when the rain came.

I busied myself up at the other end of the bar. When I came back, to pour two pints of Guinness, the pair of them were having a spat. I caught the tail end of his words, 'that wee smart-arse'. I concluded from the direction of his stare, and without wishing to be immodest, that I was the wee smart-arse in question.

When I came back, five minutes later, they had obviously made it up again. They were all over each other now: he was kissing her, aggressively, with her head bent back at an awkward angle like a rag doll's. She looked as if she was going to fall off her seat any moment, and her hand was flailing around for some steady port of call. On the way down, the blind fingers struck a vodka glass. It fell and shattered on the floor, the malign shards skittering across the tiles. They both surfaced from the beery whirlpool of their kiss, blinking.

'We've had a spillage,' he yelled. He raised his fingers above his head, snapping them and pointing to the floor. 'There's broken glass down here. Somebody clear it up.' He was looking straight at me, his eyes glittering with hard, pissed malevolence.

I wasn't in too big a hurry to race over there like an eager scullery maid with my pan and brush, kneel down next to him, and then have my face ground into the debris. It sounded like a recipe in the French restaurant where I'd gone with Phyllis: tonight we have mashed face on a bed of broken glass, with a blood coulis, the house speciality of our resident thug. I felt a thin jet of hysteria squirt through me. It always did when I got nervous. I almost wanted to laugh out loud.

Murdie glanced over, and absorbed the situation in a second. He had antennae for trouble. Years of working in bars had given Murdie a talent for instant invisibility, beyond price in moments such as these. He simply withdrew his personality as a snail draws in its horns. He became his pure function and nothing more. I had watched him do it before. He didn't make eye contact, he remained scrupulously civil, but he didn't utter a spare word. There was no dangling hook left out for a drunk to hang an argument on.

While the fella was still staring at me, Murdie nipped out from behind the bar with the pan and brush, and swept up all the glass. It was over in an instant: as far as anyone else was concerned, the brush and pan had simply danced up and done it by themselves.

When Murdie came back, and we were both turned towards the cash register, he whispered to me out of the side of his mouth: *don't stand effing rubbernecking around here, get you up to the other end of the bar.*

I did. Soon, I thought, they would just leave, stumble off acrimoniously into some boozy argument at home, and fall into their pit of a bed taking oafish swipes at each other and missing. And I would have a whiskey with Murdie and then walk home alone, letting the cool night air wash the alcohol, and the stale smoke, and all the fury off my back. I still wish it had happened that way.

It didn't. An Otis Redding song came on, the one where he keeps telling some girl that his telephone number is six-three-four-five-seven-eight-nine. I always used to wonder what happened to the people who actually had that telephone number, whether they were driven mad by hordes of drunken Otis Redding fans ringing them up in the middle of the night, or whether nobody bothered them at all.

'*If you need some good loving, just call on*

me . . . ' sang Otis, 'And if you wa-a-a-nt some good kissing, call on me . . . Lord have mercy.'

I had started listening to the song, letting the words drift around me as a cocoon against the pair sitting up at the bar. But the guy at the bar had started listening to the song too, and now he was bawling out his own parodic version of the lyrics: 'If you wa-a-a-ant, a good kicking, call on me.'

I began watching him. He was horrible all right, but he wasn't stupid. It took a certain amount of ingenuity to fit those new words tightly into the song, especially when you were as drunk as he was. And he was singing them in exactly the same rhythm as Otis.

He had a flicker of charm in his face, too, something in the curve of that cheekbone that suggested good humour, sitting right next to his viciousness. But that flicker would always be enough to attract certain women to him, enough to assure him the place of popular class clown who beats up other pupils at break-time.

I hated him. I hate people who ruin a good song, plastering stupidity all over something great. And I hated his chanting face, pumping out its thick stream of cunning idiocy.

On and on it went. When it came to the chorus, he had another little twist up his sleeve: he began bellowing, at the top of his voice: 'Six-three-four-five-NINE-NINE-NINE,' the ambulance number, and banging his fist on the counter so that the pint glasses danced a rickety jig. People were moving away from him now, edgily, and Jimmy was looking over from the door to see

81

what was going on, but the girlfriend was still screeching with laughter. I could see her distended, open mouth, the dirty pint glasses, Jimmy's anxious face. It was like riding round and round, strapped to a fairground horse on some nightmare carousel. My head was beginning to spin.

The song ended. I tried to steady myself. And then I heard him turn to his girlfriend and assert, with slurred deliberation, 'Nobody fucking messes around with you or my fucking family.'

She looked back at him hazily, with smudged eyes, trying to pacify him now, repeating, 'Yes, yes . . . och sure I know that.'

He kept on: 'You should have seen the last fella we done. He was a big fat slabber, but he couldn't even make a fist when it came down to it. When we pulled him out of his house, he just kept squealing for his ma-a-a-mmy.' He rolled his eyes stagily like Al Jolson as he delivered the punchline.

I felt a terrible coldness coming over me, as if I was being dipped in a bath of ice. It was a single realisation, pumping into my brain in waves, each wave bigger than the last, sickening my stomach, filling the empty space behind my eyes with a red, pounding mist. I realised exactly who he was. He was McGee's son.

He kept on: 'He had insulted my da.' His voice rose to a screaming falsetto, a drunken pastiche of a terrified woman's voice: 'Mammy! Mammy! Ma — '

I leaned over and hit him on the jaw as hard as I could. He tumbled off the bar stool with a crash. I heard girls screaming, and Murdie saying 'Jacky, what the fu — ' I climbed over the bar and slammed him again twice, when he was moving back up off the floor.

I don't remember much about what happened next, except that Murdie pulled me off, and Jimmy and Joe moved in to surround him and bundled him outside, befuddled and jabbering with rage, before he could take a swing at me. His girlfriend was left behind, yelping and hissing at me like a vicious, scalded cat, 'Why did you do that, you bastard?' before someone propelled her outside as well.

I could hear roars coming from outside the bar, and Jimmy's voice saying firmly, 'I'm sorry sir, you're not getting back in. If you keep trying to get back in, I'll have to call the police. We're closed now.' Then more shouts, and threats: 'I'll be back for you too, you fat bastard.' And, finally, a calm that was somehow worse than the noise.

In the centre of the silence I thought: why did you do that? But I knew why I had done it. The phrase drifted into my mind, 'to get him back for what he did.' And then I thought: no, Jacky, you haven't got anybody back. They've got *you* now.

*   *   *

That night, Murdie told me not to come back to the Whistle. It was for my own good, he told me, and he was right. It was also for his good, I told him, and I was right too.

He poured me a large whiskey, and one for himself, and then looked at me with shrewd, troubled eyes.

'Why did you do that, Jacky?'

83

'He gave my friend Titch a beating, along with three of his mates. You remember Titch, you met him at our house one night. He's a bit simple. He hasn't been out of the house again since.'

'But how did you know it was that fella?'

'I didn't have a clue until I heard him boasting about it at the bar.'

Murdie took a cigarette out of his crumpled pack, tapped it and lit it contemplatively.

'He's a guy called Ronald McGee,' he said, 'Nickname 'Rocky'. To be honest, Jacky, of all the people you could have had a dig at tonight, he wasn't the best one to choose.'

'I know,' I said.

'He's well in with the Loyalist paramilitaries.'

'You don't say,' I said.

Murdie poured us both another whiskey.

'If you keep working here, Jacky, they'll come in and get you here.'

'I know.'

'And if you go home, they'll find you there.'

'Home Sweet Home,' I said. I was almost getting the hysteria again.

'You can stay at my house until you get yourself sorted out. I don't think anyone would think to look for you there. I've a sofa bed in the front room, and I'll lend you a bit of cash to tide you over.'

He was a good man, Murdie.

* * *

When we got back to Murdie's house that night, Gavin the cousin had gone to bed. 'That's a

84

first,' said Murdie. Then he picked up his whiskey bottle: there was only a miserly tea-coloured dribble in the base of it. 'That's not,' he said.

Mrs Murdie had gone to bed too, leaving a note that said simply, 'Stew on the cooker'. The premeditated brevity of the stew note, said Murdie, was a sign that she was still livid. It was actually worse than no note at all, because by continuing to consider his dietary requirements, even while furious, Mrs Murdie was taking care to retain occupation of the moral high ground. That could only mean she was gearing herself up for a long and painful campaign: 'The Deep Freeze,' he muttered, 'Mrs Murdie's Stalingrad.'

Murdie clattered about, pulling out the bed in the front room and getting me clean sheets. The place was very tidy. He handed me a clean towel and a glass of water. Then he dug around some more and added a toothbrush he said he kept for spare and a disposable razor for the morning.

He said: 'I'll warn Mrs Murdie you're about the place, so she doesn't get up in the night and beat you over the head with the frying pan in mistake for me.'

Then he leaned closer and whispered: 'But if Gavin should come in here, I give you permission to hit him with any implement that should come to hand. You haven't seen him before, after all, and from his demeanour you might assume that he is a violent intruder.'

He laughed, enigmatically. I wondered had all the whiskeys gone to his head, or maybe his nerves had just been scrambled by the evening.

I told him: 'You seem like a good host,

Murdie, and I've only been here ten minutes.'

He gave a regretful little smile. Hospitality was still a sensitive point, after the incident with the cousin. 'Sleep tight,' he said, and went up the stairs on leather-shod tiptoe so as not to wake Mrs Murdie with the groaning floorboards.

The yellow light of a street lamp came through the window, falling across my brown blankets. Out on the street a solitary drunk was stumbling home. I heard him singing a mournful song in a voice wet with alcohol and stirred with sadness. I could have lain awake all night, turning over the implications of what had just happened in the Whistle. But I didn't. I just fell back on the clean pillows like a dead man, into the soft arms of a deep, black sleep.

9

I came round early and lay very still, trying not to wake my dread up. But it was already lying in me like stagnant water, and it began to stir when I heard the sound of Gavin clanking around in the kitchen.

There is a poem I have always liked, by W. H. Auden, that I first came across years ago in one of the books Big Jacky bought. It is about how perfectly the Old Masters understood suffering: how, in their paintings, when one person was enduring torments, everyone else was simply carrying on as usual, 'eating or opening a window or just walking dully along'.

While Titch sat terrified in his airless bedroom, and I was thinking about being exiled from my own house, Mrs Murdie's cousin Gavin had remounted the summit of his own good spirits and was digging noisily in the fridge for bacon and potato bread.

Gavin was a tall and robust fella in his early thirties: ruddy-cheeked, with a busy, loose-lipped mouth. There was an air of greedy carelessness to him, something almost unfinished, as there is with some hectic, sizeable people. The blueprint for Gavin had been sketched with a thick charcoal pencil and in great haste.

This cousin was always half in a hurry, although he never had anything really important to do. If there was a vase set next to Gavin's elbow, you knew that it was destined to crash to the floor, the casualty of some sweeping gesture. If he loaded his clothes into the washing machine, you knew that he would shove them all in with reckless speed, and then twist the dial just hard enough to break it and leave you ankle deep in churning, foamy water not long after. He never did break the washing machine, to be absolutely fair, but you always felt that he was right on the verge of it. And in one way that was worse.

He liked his food, although he was large rather than obese. In a few years, though, he would almost certainly slide into a corpulence that would be lent dignity only by his height. For now, a vast amount of fuel was needed to keep his bandwagon on the road. The Murdies' fridge door swung back and forth like a hurricane lamp in a high gale. Much of its contents eventually poured into the same deep pit: Gavin's perpetually masticating, chattering, questioning, exclaiming, capacious gob.

After a few minutes, I wouldn't have cared if I had never seen Gavin again for the rest of my life. After a few hours, I would have been actively and powerfully grateful not to. I observed politely to Murdie that Gavin certainly seemed to have more energy than the rest of us.

'That's because he does eff all but lollop about Belfast like an effing Labrador dog,' said Murdie sourly. It was uncharitable, but I took Murdie's point. A generous heart was a luxury he could no longer afford. It was costing him enough just to keep Gavin in sausages and soda bread.

★ ★ ★

On the first day at Murdie's, after Mrs Murdie
departed for her secretarial job and Murdie went
off to the Whistle, I was left alone with Gavin
and a large pot of tea. Gavin had his map of
Belfast out and a couple of paperback books
about the Troubles, and leaflets about forthcom-
ing events all spread across the table.

'So,' he said, 'what brings you to the Murdie
Family Hotel?'

A revealing choice of pleasantry, I thought.
But I didn't really fancy telling Gavin all my
business, especially with him rattling around
Belfast on Troubles Tours in black taxis, gabbing
on heedlessly about things he shouldn't.

'I'm having a few family troubles,' I said. 'Mr
Murdie kindly offered to put me up for a few
days. He's an old family friend.'

He slathered crunchy peanut butter on a hunk
of bread and looked back at me with undisguised
curiosity. 'What sort of family troubles?'

'I'd rather not talk about them, if you don't
mind,' I said tightly.

What a secretive little prig I must sound, I
thought. Still, as I didn't like Gavin, I didn't
suppose it mattered much whether he liked me
back. We could have a conversation without any
concern for the future.

'That's okay,' said Gavin mildly, chawing away
on his bread. But he continued looking at me
with an odd directness, like a screwball scientist
who has seen something interesting suddenly
develop on his agar plate.

'Are you Protestant or Catholic?' he asked abruptly.

So that was it. I did a mock double-take: 'Didn't your mother ever tell you that it was rude to bring up a man's religion at breakfast?'

'No, but which are you?' he kept on, doggedly.

I was damned if I was going to tell Gavin what I was, and be slotted into some pre-prepared slot he had gleaned from the introduction to his Welcome to the Northern Ireland Troubles book.

'I'm not telling you,' I said.

'Why won't you tell me? Are you ashamed of what you are?'

All right. I took a deep breath, and got stuck in.

'Because that's what's at the root of all my family problems. I desperately want to incorporate some elements of Islam into my private spiritual wardrobe, but my family are dead set against it.'

'Are they Protestant or Catholic?'

He didn't give up easily.

'Neither, I'm afraid, Gavin. That's the real difficulty. They are deeply militant atheists. They even started up a paramilitary group of their own once, in the late seventies, the Atheist Liberation Army. One of its core demands was that all citizens in Northern Ireland must publicly deny the existence of God. But unfortunately my parents were the only members of the ALA.'

'What happened to their paramilitary group?'

'It came under very serious, sustained attack by Republican and Loyalist paramilitaries, both of whom thought it was immoral. I remember that once my parents made themselves the target for Loyalist gunfire while attempting to hoist an atheist flag over a Free Presbyterian church.'

'What was the flag like?' asked Gavin. His interest, worryingly, was far outstripping my initial expectation.

'It carried a picture of a scowling man with a long beard — the traditionalist's representation of God — but crossed out in red, as in a no-smoking sign. Mother and Father were frankly lucky to escape with their lives on any number of occasions. The problem was, they never knew who to thank for their miraculous survival. All the other paramilitary groups had God for that, you see.'

I kept on talking, staring bleakly into my tea as though I could barely stutter out the painful memories. Gavin was soaking it all up.

'The lack of focus confused and divided my parents. My mother broke away and formed a more radical, violent splinter group: the Atheists' Defence Force. The ADF and the ALA began feuding over conflicting views of the struggle. The house turned into a battle zone, both physical and ideological. I was stuck in the middle, the only neutral ground. I started to pray.'

This had all gone far enough. I was enjoying myself, but I was also beginning to feel ashamed. No matter how credulous Gavin was, it wasn't right to deceive him. And, however playfully I talked about these joke parents, I was really insulting the memory of my own mother and Big Jacky.

He started looking them up in the index of his

book, excitedly. 'I've never heard of this. What was it called again, this group?'

The fizz had gone out of me.

'To be honest, Gavin, all that stuff there was just a bit of a joke,' I said sadly.

Gavin looked at me mistrustfully, as though I had just confessed in a wee squeaky voice: 'I'm a Munchkin, actually.' He seemed angry. Well, he had every right to be.

He slowly collected up his books and leaflets and moved towards the door with a certain amount of self-possession.

'I hope you have an enjoyable day,' he said stiffly.

'You too,' I said.

The door banged shut. I slumped over my tepid mug of sweet tea. It had all been pure nonsense. I felt horrible.

★　★　★

The fierce jollity I had felt in teasing Gavin evaporated, leaving behind a nasty, bitter taste. Here I was, camping in a kind friend's already overcrowded house, jobless and homeless, cheaply taunting some gullible English cousin. What had I got to be a smart-arse about?

I hadn't hit the McGee fellow out of bravery, either; I couldn't even comfort myself with that. I had no desire for dangerous thrills: the mere thought of pursuing a sport like white-water rafting or bungee jumping had always filled me with horror. Why would someone pay money to be dangled by their heels from a long piece of elastic until their retinas detached? Round here that was the sort of thing that happened to you if you were caught in bed with an IRA man's wife.

The only time I ever had any physical courage at all was when I was in a blind rage, and then I temporarily forgot about being afraid. More fool me. Big Jacky had always warned me: 'That temper of yours will get you into trouble one day, son.' Well, he had been right. But I wasn't in a rage now, far from it. I was miserable and worried. Why hadn't I left McGee alone last night, banked the information, and worked out some clever, subterranean way to punish him properly? As it was, I probably hadn't even hurt him. He had fallen to the floor, unhorsed by pure surprise, but I hadn't seen any blood on him when they were hustling him away. There would be a few bruises, maybe, but it was a poor revenge for what had happened to Titch.

I went outside to a phone box — I didn't want to call from Murdie's home phone — and rang Phyllis at the newsagent's shop. She sounded distant and reedy, as if testing out this new-fangled speaking device for the first time from somewhere in the nineteenth century: 'Hel-lo?'

'Hello Phyllis, it's Jacky.'

'Where are you?'

'I'm staying at a friend's house. I'll be here for a while, Phyllis. I've had a row with a Loyalist guy, a nasty piece of work, and I'm staying away from home for a bit. I'll not be at the bar either.'

'Oh my goodness.' Phyllis's voice had gone all quavery.

'If anyone comes round looking for me, no

matter who, you tell them that I haven't been home since Wednesday morning. Pack up some of my clothes and stuff and put it in the attic. If they start asking you questions, tell them that I phoned you late on Wednesday night and said I wasn't coming home, and that I was going to Scotland on money I borrowed from a friend, and not to worry about me. Tell them I wouldn't tell you where I was but that I've promised to write.' That sounded convincing.

The deluge of instruction was too much for Phyllis. I could hear her struggling to breathe.

'Listen, Phyllis. Calm down. Don't worry, seriously. You don't need to tell the Iron Lung about this yet. She'll only go berserk. I'll ring her myself in a week or two.'

A bemused silence. I had been trying to make her laugh, but she had probably forgotten about telling me that her boyfriend used to call Aunt Mary the Iron Lung.

'But what if they come round here?' she said, uncomprehending. She hadn't even worked out who 'they' were yet. That would all happen later, in some messy tangle of reflection.

While talking, I had become doubly conscious of the ammoniac reek of urine in the trapped air. Since phone boxes now doubled as pissoirs, a long conversation had become an exercise in endurance on several levels. I couldn't wait to get out.

'Just like I said. Tell them I phoned to say I'm going to Scotland. You don't know exactly where, but I said I'd write.'

'Are you going to Scotland?'

'I don't know yet, Phyllis. But if anyone comes

94

round, just tell them I have.'

'Where are you now? Are you in Scotland?'

It was turning into one of those Bud Abbott and Lou Costello sketches, where the pair of them play around at frustrating confusions for a full hour, until even the audience wishes they would pack it in. I had never found those sketches very funny to watch. It was even less funny to be starring in one with Aunt Phyllis.

'I'm at a friend's house.'

'Which friend?'

'I'm not telling you, Phyllis, because I don't want you to be frightened into telling anybody.'

'Who would frighten me into that?'

The more I tried to reassure Phyllis, the worse I made it.

'Phyllis, I have to go now. Don't worry about me. I love you, and I'll be in touch as soon as I can.'

A plaintive, panicky voice: '*Will* you write from Scotland?'

Firmly: 'Goodbye for now, Phyllis.'

I went back to Murdie's house and made a cup of tea. Then I spread myself flat out on Murdie's sofa, and repeatedly bounced the back of my head off the firm cushions, all the while emitting a low moan of pain from deep within my chest. I had to do this for a very long time before I began to feel even a little bit better.

★   ★   ★

There wasn't much else to do, so I spent the afternoon in the Botanic Gardens. It was a sunny day, and there was a hint of August heaviness in the air, the delinquent, late summer laziness that seeps into your bones and turns them to warm rubber.

It is a calming place, the Botanic Gardens, a green park set behind a pair of heavy Victorian wrought-iron gates. I sat down there on a wooden bench and looked at the organised pinks and reds of the flower beds, and thought of the gardeners plotting precisely this spread of colours, and ordering in all the bulbs, and carefully planting them, and then watching the flowers straggle up and grow to their full, brazen moment before they begin their gradual drooping towards death. I thought of how a gardener might take pride in that, and of how — as the hectic world outside the gates chased stupidities and bred its failures — the flower beds in the Botanic Gardens might be counted a rare thing, a modest and complete success. If you died and were forced to justify your existence before God, and you told him, 'I made the flowers bloom every year in the Botanic Gardens in Belfast,' it would not sound a shabby way to have spent your whole life.

The gardens were full of schoolchildren in their uniforms, temporarily released for lunch-time, waving their dripping ice lollies and bawling amiable insults. Young women, who had worked all the morning in nearby offices, unpacked first their sandwiches and then their lard-white legs beneath the sun. On the grass, university students kissed and alcoholic tramps hunted casually for cigarette ends on the path.

I used to come here with Big Jacky. First, we would go into the Ulster Museum itself and straight up to see the main attraction, the Egyptian mummy in her glass case. The mummy was a fine-boned, shrunken thing, short of stature, and her head and one hand were left unwrapped for the benefit of onlookers. The leathery little face was all cheekbones, and you could still see some of her teeth, like small, stained squares of brown pottery. There was even hair, too, a patchy custard fuzz.

Back then, I just used to look and look at the mummy, without even thinking. But today, up close again beside her transparent tomb, I thought how very strange it was that this desiccated thing was once actually a young woman who ran around and laughed in the sun, and was quiet or talkative, and who maybe fell in love and sang songs and stroked cats. If anyone had told her where her body would end up, how unbelievable it would have seemed.

Now, everything that remained of her was lying in a glass case for generations of Belfast schoolchildren to gawp at. Big Jacky had told me once about a school friend of his, a real head-the-ball, who screwdrivered open her case one time they were all knocking about up there, reached in and shook her frail dark hand. The others were excited and half scared by the act of sacrilege. But that was back in the old days, when you could do nearly any mad thing.

After the spectacular dryness of the mummy, Big Jacky and I always used to walk back to the gardens, and into the splendid damp of the hothouse, billed on a brass plaque outside as The Tropical Ravine. It was a Victorian glass dome that, once you stepped inside, was suddenly bursting with humid jungle. You could have sliced the air with a knife inside the hothouse, and it would have poured out water. Plants with fleshy stalks as thick as a child's arm juddered near the little waterfall, and bulbous fruits drooped from thick, unidentifiable vines.

I opened the door and went in again, for the first time in years. The humidity was just the same, a tender slap on the face with a wet flannel. But the glasshouse seemed darker and smaller than I remembered. Inside, a man was taking his daughter round on the wooden pathway, holding on to her hand tightly in case her chubby, unsteady legs gave way. She must have been about three or four, an outspoken child in a short red coat. They stopped briefly to stare into the water beneath them.

'Is there frogs in that?' she said. She had one of those sweetly rasping childish voices like a scouring pad on silk.

He didn't pay attention to her question: he was kneeling down to point out a giant water lily.

'Is there frogs in that?' she said again, louder this time.

The piercing question made me smile. For a second I yearned for all the brackish impurities in my life to be boiled away, and myself distilled back to some clear childhood moment when the most important thing, the only really important thing, was whether there might be frogs in that.

10

Back in Murdie's house, the local news was on the radio. '*The Chancellor of the Exchequer pledged to keep inflation rates down . . . there has been a train crash in the Midlands, two people have been injured . . . speaking today, the Northern Ireland Secretary confirmed that the IRA and the Loyalist ceasefires in Northern Ireland are still in place . . . police confirm that a 77-year-old Catholic man last night became the oldest victim of a paramilitary attack, thought to be linked to Republicans: four masked men broke into his flat in North Belfast, and beat the old age pensioner with iron bars in his legs and ankles. The victim is said to be in a serious but stable condition in hospital. And now over to Martin Rawlins for an hour of country music from Nashville, Tennessee . . .* '

★　★　★

It has always interested me, how the truly momentous happenings in life, the great solid chunks of luck or misery, must swim in the grey soupy water of something trivial.

A lonely man is walking home from work, wondering what to have for dinner: bacon, he thinks, and then he thinks no, fish. At the fish counter he gets talking to the smiling woman beside him in the queue, they fall in love, and he stays with her for the rest of his life.

A woman is walking towards the bus after shopping in the city centre, when she suddenly remembers that her niece has just given birth to a baby boy. Should she get a present for the baby tomorrow? Och no, sure she might as well get it today. She nips into a department store, and in that very instant a bomb explodes just inside the shop door and the woman is lucky, they tell her later, because the people right beside her die but she only loses her legs.

People marvel at it, how the thin tug of an impulse can yank a whole life into a fixed shape. The man thinks: 'What if I had gone to the meat counter instead?' and the woman thinks: 'What if I had just carried on walking to the bus stop?'

But sometimes we know, or think we know, what the terrible result of an action might be, and yet we go ahead and do it anyway. We trust to luck. We overtake on a blind bend and hope that there is nothing hurtling in the opposite direction. We realise, on the way to an appointment, that we have left the front door unlocked but we carry on, telling ourselves that today no one will test it. What makes us do it? The desire to escape from something, I suppose, and the desperate hurry to get to somewhere else. And the fact that ninety-nine times out of a hundred, we come out of it still laughing.

★   ★   ★

Murdie came back on Thursday night to tell me that someone had been in the bar looking for me — not McGee, but a hard-looking young fella with a thick neck and short fair hair.

'He came in and said 'is Jacky working tonight?' I told him that you had given in your notice. He said 'Why was that?' I said 'Haven't a clue. Maybe he got sick of being stuck behind a bar.' He said 'I heard he got into bother last night.' I said 'Aye, there was a bit.' He said 'If you see him, tell him Mr McGee would like a word with him.' I said 'I doubt he'll be back, but if I happen to bump into him, I'll certainly pass on your message.' So I'm passing on Mr McGee's message,' said Murdie, falling into his armchair.

'That's very kind of you, Mr Murdie. Did Mr McGee's friend mention what sort of a word Mr McGee wants with me? Perhaps he wants to invite me to a cocktail party, or some other variety of social event.'

Murdie gave a short laugh, a bronchial seal's bark. 'Probably some other variety of social event, son.'

Mrs Murdie carried on diplomatically with her knitting. Gavin glowered from above his paperback book. He knew there was something alluringly fishy going on in our conversation, but he couldn't quite work out what. He had been a bit shirty with me ever since that morning's conversation. I felt guilty, naturally, but then a dose of standoffishness from Gavin was a drink of ice-water on a desert march.

The trouble was, I couldn't go to bed until he went to bed. My bed was the sofa in the front room, which was where Gavin liked to park himself of an evening, with his Troubles books

101

and the How-To Guide to Playing the Tin Whistle, or whatever else he had concealed in his backpack.

As the night wore on, I could sense his coolness to me wearing off, at exactly the time when I would have liked it to be building up. He was snouting me out as a potential companion for a long, late-night conversation, moving inexorably back towards me like flickering toothache heightening to a reliable stretch of solid pain.

After draining his cup of tea, Mr Murdie stood up with a histrionic stretching motion, and then said, a shade too emphatically, 'Well, I think I'll turn in. It's been a long day.' Mrs Murdie did the same. Mrs Murdie's Stalingrad appeared to have fallen.

Was there anything either of us needed? she asked. She was assured that there was not. Well, in that case they would both see us in the morning. Gavin made no move to get up. As Murdie turned towards the door, he caught my eye in a fleeting, sardonic glance. I was too weary even to want to laugh.

The silence hung in the air for a little while. Then Gavin said, magnanimously, 'I see what you were trying to say this morning. You've had enough of religion, eh?'

'Well, maybe just not enough of the right sort,' I conceded. I wasn't going to be so pompous as to claim any great philosophical intent behind baiting Gavin, even to Gavin.

'So, has Belfast changed for the better since the cease-fires?' he said, with a fresh heartiness.

Oh no, now we were back into the whole

shebang all over again. I began to see what had driven Murdie to lose his self-control.

'There aren't any big bombs going off, and that's a nice change. But the IRA and the Loyalists are dragging even more people out of their houses to beat them up. The press calls them 'punishment attacks'.'

I really didn't want to get into this.

'So you're saying that now the IRA are attacking Catholics, and the Loyalists are attacking Protestants,' he said, showily figuring it out.

'Yes.'

'But surely much of it is just stopping their own people from stepping out of line? Wrong, of course, but I've heard that a lot of it is about cracking down on drug dealers and car thieves, and it's actually pretty popular with the local community. My car was stolen from outside my house in England last year, and I can tell you, if I had got my two hands on the little bastard that did it I would have — '

'Got together with five friends to beat him with a nail-studded plank of wood, shattering his shin bones so that he could never walk right again? Is that what you would have done?' I said. My voice was rising.

'Well, I wouldn't have gone quite that far, no,' Gavin said.

'How far would you go, then?' I said, in a strange, strained voice that came from somewhere in the pit of my stomach. 'How far?'

He just looked at me.

I stood up. I was really beginning to feel quite unwell. I was cold and the palms of my hands were sweating. There was too much of this stuff crowding in on me now. My eyes began to focus on a piece of white bread that was clinging to the side of Gavin's face, hanging on to the dark bristles that sprouted vigorously, indeed with almost obscene strength, from his cheek. That was like me, I thought. Just hanging on temporarily, about to be swept away by someone else's gesture.

'Are you all right?' said Gavin. He was staring at me oddly again.

'I don't feel very well, Gavin. Excuse me, I'm just going to the bathroom.'

I went upstairs, locked the bathroom door, and was quickly sick into the toilet bowl. Then I rinsed my mouth and splashed my face with cold water, again and again, letting it run in and out of my eyes and down my face. I did this for a long time. I dried my face slowly, patting it with a towel, and sat down on the floor until things became bearable again.

When I walked back down into the front room, Gavin had gone to bed.

* * *

Two days later. The lunchtime radio news: '*House prices are soaring again for the first time in five years . . . schoolteachers are warning of possible strike action after their annual pay rise failed to keep pace with inflation . . . a gang of six masked men, thought to be linked to loyalists, entered a house in Ballymena in the early hours of this morning and beat a 24-year-old man in a paramilitary-style attack . . . the 77-year-old man assaulted in*

North Belfast on Wednesday has spoken in hospital about his ordeal. He said that he had pleaded with his attackers to leave him alone, but they continued. It is now believed that the paramilitary-style beating was a case of mistaken identity, and that the gang, thought to be linked to Republicans, was looking for another man in the same block of flats.'

★ ★ ★

I woke up on the fourth day and decided I couldn't stay at the Murdies' any longer. It was partly because I slept in their front room. No matter how early I got up, or how late I went to bed, I was condemned to be a bulky presence camping in the heart of their home, hammering my tent pegs into their domestic peace.

Murdie was getting edgy, smoking more cigarettes and speaking in staccato sentences when he came back at night. The main source of his irritability was Gavin, whose mere presence now played a frantic cantata on Murdie's nerves. An extra guest couldn't help matters. I tried to repay them by filling up their fridge. Then it drove me twice as mad to see most of the food disappearing straight into Gavin before Murdie even made it through the door. It was a race against time. Chomp chomp. It couldn't be long, surely, before they would just order him to leave. Or maybe he would stay there for ever — a gigantic cuckoo, squawking at the small, busy Murdies — compulsively fattening and jabbering as they grew thinner and more worn out.

I had decided to get out of Belfast. The simplicity of that decision exhilarated me. I didn't really want to go to Scotland, in spite of what I had told Phyllis. It would be too much like here, with all the canny-eyed folk in the close wee kirk wanting to know exactly who you were, and why you left and, 'Belfast, did you say? Which part? Och, maybe you knew the McClenahans who used to come here for their summer holidays.' I wanted to go to some big, callous place where nobody had the inclination to squander too much inquisitive energy on a stranger. I could only breathe easily in a great fog of indifference.

I walked into the city centre, and booked a one-way flight to London for the following day. The travel agent said, 'Are you sure you won't be coming back in the next three months?' and I answered, in a confident voice which pleased me, 'No. Definitely not.' There was something clean and precise about a one-way flight. It was a straight arrow flying into the future, the big maze of the metropolis.

I would go round to my house late that night, in a minicab, say my goodbyes to Phyllis and write a letter for her to give to Titch. Then I would pack my two suitcases and retrieve the bit of money I had stashed away for an emergency. Very early in the morning I would leave my house, once again using a minicab which would take me to the airport. I would worry about what happened in London only once I was en route. The minicab company I'd use would be from the other side of town.

The cumulative effect of these decisions was to make my heart beat faster and my head lighten, as though I was in love. And I was. I was in love with the idea of getting away.

Mrs Murdie gave me a kiss and a slightly tearful hug goodbye. Gavin gave me a handshake which managed to be both clammy and a real bonecrusher, and said 'Bon Voyage'. I bet he was pleased I was going. Murdie said gruffly, 'Goodbye, son, don't forget to write,' and then shoved two hundred pounds in twenty-pound notes into my back pocket. I tried to give him some back, but he danced away neatly, frowning and making angry gestures of refusal.

He wanted me to pick up my stuff while the minicab waited, and come straight to his house before leaving for London, but I wouldn't. It was late enough anyway.

'Let's not get it out of proportion, Murdie, McGee isn't bloody Don Corleone,' I said.

Murdie shook his head in despair at me. Then he said, 'Right again, boy genius. Don Corleone is probably more forgiving.'

The truth was, I wanted to calm Phyllis down before I went, and I didn't want to have a taxi driver tapping his fingers on the dashboard outside while I mulled over which things to take with me. It would have made me nervous.

11

It was just off midnight, and dark, when the cab pulled up outside my house. There was a light on in our front room. I paid the driver and got out.

The night was still and dry, and our street was quiet. But I had the feeling that someone was watching me. I looked around. There was a figure sitting on the wall opposite the house, wearing a jacket with a hood. The face was half turned away.

What or who was it? It could have been anyone, anything, even a slumped scarecrow or a stuffed Lundy of the kind they burn on bonfires on the Twelfth. But a single orange point was moving up and down in the shadows: whatever it was, it was smoking a cigarette. The figure looked as though it was watching our house. I started to walk quickly towards it, my blood beginning to cool. It was better to find out now.

The face snapped towards me, into focus: a familiar, sharp little triangle, lit by the street lamp, and I almost laughed with relief. It was Marty.

'What the hell are you doing here, Marty, you gave me the creeps,' I said.

'Nothing, sure. Just sitting here.'

There was something slightly strange about his manner, something I couldn't place. He seemed almost sullen, his narrow eyes not quite meeting mine.

'Why are you out at this time of night? Is your ma not looking for you?'

'She's sitting up with Vicky and Jeanette, watching a film. The back door's open, so I can go in whenever I want,' he said.

'All the same, you don't want to be hanging around out here half the night.'

'Where've you been?' he said.

'Just staying with a friend.'

'There was some fellas round here looking for you,' he said.

I could feel my heart starting to sprint.

'Is that so. What were they saying?'

'They were just saying where were you and had I seen you because they wanted a word.'

'When was this?'

'Last Thursday and Friday.'

That wasn't so bad. Maybe they thought I'd left Belfast by now.

'Were they giving Phyllis any bother?'

'I don't think so. They just asked me had I seen you.'

I started to think.

'Marty, if anybody asks you again, you didn't see me tonight, all right? Remember that.'

He just stared back at me, with that strange look on his face.

'I've got to go inside now. You should be off to your bed.'

I took a few quid out of my pocket, and slipped it into his chilled hand. 'Here. Buy yourself some chips tomorrow. And an ice lolly, for your dessert.'

He didn't say anything. He wouldn't lift his

hand to take the money.

I moved to unlock my front door. He was standing on the grass verge now, not moving.

'Goodnight, Marty,' I said. He was beginning to infuriate me. God knows I didn't want to be hanging around outside the house for too long. I might as well do a tap dance there on the pavement with a 'Here I Am, Boys' sign round my neck.

But he seemed reluctant to leave, dragging his shoes along the grass in circles.

'Are you going away?' he said. He had lost all his cockiness: he seemed like a very young child again.

'Yes, sunshine. Pretty well as soon as you'll let me get into my house,' I said.

'Go soon, you shouldn't stay in there long,' he said animatedly, almost desperately. 'Please.'

I couldn't quite understand his urgency. I definitely understood mine, though.

'I promise. You look after yourself,' I said. I opened the door, and he turned suddenly and bolted up the street as though Spring-Heeled Jack was after him, without once looking back.

★　★　★

Phyllis was still up. She jumped a mile when I came in. She had the television turned up so loud that she hadn't heard me outside. Her face looked subtly appalled, as though I had casually walked back in with half my head missing and said, 'Now how about a nice cup of tea?'

I told her that I was going to London, and

110

then I told her roughly why. She couldn't take it all in. At one point she said, 'Why don't you call the police?'

I said, 'Come off it, Phyllis. Do you think they're going to give me a round-the-clock police guard and a medal because I performed a public service and hit some Loyalist in a bar?'

She looked down at her slippers silently, a chastened child.

'You'll be able to run the newsagent's,' I said. 'And then if things calm down maybe I'll be able to come back. I'll phone to let you know how I'm doing, and write you letters.'

Her powdered parchment face crumpled slightly. Tears were welling in the downturned corners of her eyes.

I said again, uselessly, 'I'll phone you all the time, to see how you're doing.'

I had the minicab booked to pick me up at six in the morning. I didn't plan to go to bed. Phyllis wouldn't go to bed either, although I sort of wished she would. She said she'd keep me company while I was packing.

She got some of my things down from the wee loft cupboard, where she had put them. I didn't have that many clothes: I bundled them all into one suitcase. Phyllis took them out again and folded them up into rectangles, meticulously laying them flat.

Then I started hauling out my books, choosing which ones to leave, which to take. I had to leave *Strange Stories and Amazing Facts* behind, on the grounds of its weight. Pity. I didn't feel unhappy during the packing. I felt as though all the messy foliage of my life was being pruned into a clear, clean shape, the tidy form of two medium-sized suitcases.

At three in the morning, Phyllis went off to bed. She set her alarm and said she'd get up in two and a half hours, to make me tea before I went off.

At four in the morning there was the sound of our front door being kicked in, and I realised I wouldn't be going to London on the early morning flight after all.

First fear paralyses you, and then it makes you move twice as fast. I went into Phyllis's room and shook her awake. I said: 'They're here to take me. Put your dressing gown on and get back into bed. Don't worry, they'll leave you alone.' She was mumbling something, waking up, but I couldn't make out the words.

Then I opened the window in her room: it was a long drop from there into the backyard. If I pushed myself out and dangled down off the windowsill I would be all right. I could hear one of them shouting, 'Where are you, you wee bastard?' as the thump of boots came up the stairs. There was no time. I was leaning out the window, getting ready to climb, when I looked down below me and saw two other men with black balaclavas waiting in our yard. I wanted to be sick.

They were looking back up at me and encouraging me to jump. One of them had a baseball bat, and was standing tapping it off his leg. The other one shouted out, crooning, 'Go on, Jacky boy, come into our arms.' His balaclava was more of a hood, a black bag with eye-holes in it, like some medieval executioner's. I was flooded then with the feeling of despair. If there had been a way to kill myself, I would have taken it. If I jumped, I jumped to them. If I ran back, I ran back to them. I could see Phyllis on the bed, her mouth slack and her face turned the grey of cold ashes and dead people's skin.

I left the windowsill and picked up a lamp. Two more men, both wearing masks, came in the bedroom door, and with all my strength I threw the lamp at the one nearest me. It glanced off his shoulder and shattered on the floor into jagged china clumps. He kept on coming towards me, even angrier. The lamp had been the last thing between me and them. Now I had nothing.

My arms and legs liquefied with fear. It is an awful thing to feel yourself utterly powerless. It takes you into a place where very few people ever get to go, and it is difficult ever to come back fully from there. It is a place where nothing you can say, nothing you think, nothing you can do matters any more. Something terrible is going to happen to you, you know it is, and there is nothing you can do to change it.

Every nightmare you ever had where evil people were chasing you, and your feet were dragging heavily as though made of lead, was a thin echo of this. And you know it is. For this isn't a dream. This is real, and they can do to you whatever they like. And they will like to do the very worst things, because they hate you.

They took hold of my arms and started to pull me down the stairs. The banisters were shuddering as I banged against them. I heard Phyllis's tremulous voice saying 'Don't hurt him' sounding very far away now, a muffled, twittering plea from a distant universe. And one of them answered matter-of-factly, as though this reply had become as routine as the acts they were about to commit, 'Shut your face you stupid oul bitch.'

★   ★   ★

At the bottom of the stairs, one of them held my arms down while the other made me open my mouth and then tied a gag round it. It was a thick bit of white cotton, and it smelled faintly of paint. We went out the front door, and the other two were waiting. Three of them picked up their baseball bats from where they had set them beside the door. One of the bats, I saw, had nails in it. They were silent and business-like, intent on their common purpose, like men setting out together on some fine morning for a fishing trip.

You don't really think when four people are walking you towards waste ground. But there are almost-thoughts, embryo thoughts that are conceived and just as quickly miscarry. How had they known that I was in there? Had they been watching the front door all the time? What were they going to do: would I get just the baseball bats? Did they have guns?

There was a big moon out that night, sailing lazily across the sky. As we moved down the street, we passed Titch's house. All the lights were off. There I had been, warning Titch. I

114

thought he had been stupid not to get out. He wasn't half as bloody stupid as me.

I turned my head to look over at the house where Marty lived. I hadn't expected it, but there he was, watching from his bedroom window. For a second, I saw his face pressed up against the glass looking straight back at me, the gagged hostage walking in the centre of the four hoods. His pale, triangular face seared itself on my memory, a red-hot iron on a thin cloth. It bore a strange expression, one I had never seen on him before: fearful, transfixed, but with something else in it, too. Something like complicity. And it struck me then like a hammer blow straight to the back of the head: *He had known. He had known they were coming for me.*

★   ★   ★

We got to the patch of waste ground. It was dark. They walked me deeper into the darkness, further and further away from the street lights. Then one of them said to me flatly, 'Lie down, you wee fucker. If you try to move about it'll be worse.'

I lay down quietly on the ground. 'Prisoners Out' was scrawled on the wall in front of me, just visible in white paint. The ground was cold and hard, with tiny bits of gravel on it that scourged my cheek. But the beating didn't come. I lay there, waiting.

I still waited. Then somebody, I think it must have been McGee, said, 'What do you think, Jacky? Do you think we should stiff you?'

I turned my head on the ground and looked up towards the black hood where the voice was coming from. The hard glint of something metal caught what little light there was. Christ, he meant it. He was holding a gun.

I said nothing. The voice said again, 'Should we shoot you?'

'Please don't,' I said, through the gag. It came out as a strangulated gargle.

'Why not? Say pretty please, and then I might do it anyway.'

'Pretty please.'

Oh fuck, why were they forcing me through these hoops?

I felt the cold metal pressed against my cheek. At the same time, a warm patch of urine started to spread across my trousers. I hoped they wouldn't notice.

'He's pissed himself,' said one of the voices. They all laughed.

'Bang bang. You're not the hard man now,' said McGee. 'Not like the other night in the Whistle.'

He was kneeling down close to my head now: I could smell the tang of stale beer.

'That was a mistake,' I said absurdly.

'You hit me by mistake?'

'Thought you were someone else.'

'No you didn't, you lying wee fuck. You were pissed off because we did your big fat friend, the one who was squealing for his mammy. Well now you're going to be squealing for yours.'

'Mine's dead.'

Why did I tell them about her? Did I think I

116

could invoke her protection, like a hovering saint?

'I'm not surprised, when she saw what a toe-rag she had for a son.'

He jumped up. The others sniggered again.

'Give him the treatment,' he said.

The crack of a baseball bat came down on my arm and everything spasmed in the white heat of pain. And another, and another. I heard the blows whistle through the air as they came towards me. I was yelping like a dog now and snivelling for them to stop. I tried to curl up, but the blows kept on coming. A fist hit my jaw, with a sickening smack. The copper taste of blood filled my mouth, and — oh look, there was a loose tooth swimming in it. My stomach started to heave. I fought for air through the blood-soaked gag.

I don't know how long it went on for. I can't remember. Maybe I passed out, and then came round again. One of the last things I remember is another kick in the side and the hissed words, 'You'd better get the fuck out now. I wouldn't waste a bullet on you.' Hands untied my gag. Then the sound of feet moving away, and someone whistling.

I lay there. I couldn't move. Blood was still leaking from my open mouth. Blood was clogging my nose, but the smell of my own urine and the garbage from the bins was filtering through it. An empty Tayto crisp packet fluttered near my eyes. I thought pointlessly 'Here's me.' That's what wee kids say, happily announcing themselves to a room full of smiling adults. But here's me, a broken thing now, choking on loose bits of myself, trapped face-down in the gritty dirt. If I tried to stand up, I didn't know which pieces would come with me, and which would stay behind. I didn't even want to find out. Here's me.

12

At first, I was mildly elated just to have survived. Elated and heavily sedated. I had lost quite a bit of blood, they told me, before the ambulance came. I still don't know who called it. They gave me a lot of painkillers in the hospital, and I spent much of the time only half asleep, and the rest only half awake. The nurses brought me cups of tea, and I could listen to the radio. I jumbled up the voices on the radio with ones in my sleep. Together they made a soothing babble, a flowing river of sound.

They were going to keep me in for a while, they said. Stitches and a brain scan and a few broken ribs and a dislocated jaw, they said. Black eyes. Antibiotics to fight infection. Tetanus shots. All fine, I nodded, load me up with everything you've got, test me to destruction. They said I'd got off lightly, all told, compared to many other cases they'd seen. Maybe out there on the waste ground I'd inherited a slim line of credit from Big Jacky after all.

Phyllis came to see me. She said her nerves had gone to pieces since what happened, and the doctor had given her sleeping pills. I said not to worry, it would all be fine. I wasn't worried about anything much now. The worst thing was over.

Murdie came to see me too. He looked sad, and said that he had told me not to stay at home that night. I know you did, I said. It was a bit like a dream, with all the faces from the past appearing one by one at the side of the bed, looking mournful and wagging their heads and waving.

In the bed next to me there was a boy called Gerard. He had short hair that he had bleached blond, with the mousy roots sprouting through, and a silver ring through his left eyebrow. He was sixteen. They were keeping him in for some operations because his IRA punishment beating had gone wrong.

His right leg was held together with steel pins, and the doctors were pleased they had been able to save it, he said. His ordeal was more formal than mine: he had been required by the IRA to turn up for his beating by appointment, under threat of suffering something unimaginably worse if he didn't. I thought about what it must have been like for him, watching the hands on the clock creep towards the agreed hour.

A year or so earlier he would certainly have been shot in the legs, he said, but out of respect for the fact that there was a ceasefire on it had been decided to do him over with baseball bats instead.

'It was the Provies,' he said. 'They told me to keep very still and take it. But I moved when they were doing it and it shattered the bone. Then they said it was my own fault.'

'Why did they do it?' I asked him. The sludgy words came dropping out carefully. It hurt to talk.

'Joyriding,' he said. 'People were complaining

120

about me. Me and my mates gave some cheek to the Provies. Sick of them fellas standing on the corners and bossing us about.'

Gerard played techno music on his Sony Walkman all day. I could hear its tinny pounding leaking from his head-phones, as his skinny torso twitched to the music. It kept him distracted. He was probably escaping into some endless fantasy about scooting round his housing estate at full pelt in a stolen car.

'I've got to stay in here for weeks,' he said. 'I'm bored out of my nut.'

His mother came sometimes and pleaded with him to keep out of trouble when he left hospital. When she went home, Gerard would look over at me and sag his upper half in dramatic mock relief at the end of the lecture. Sometimes his girlfriend Roisin came, tottering in her high heels and caked in black eye make-up. She looked about fifteen.

Gerard looked forward keenly to her visits, counting the hours, and then was slightly offhand with her when she finally arrived. He would deign now and then to let her pull the plastic curtain round his bed and kiss him, though.

Roisin was kind-hearted. She always brought chocolate for me as well as Gerard, because she felt sorry for me. I just posted the milky squares into the slot of my mouth and let them melt on my tongue, leaking out sweetness. Anything else involved too much unpleasant working of the facial muscles. I appeared more badly beaten than Gerard, although he was actually far worse off than me. I had needed rows of stitches in my head and cheek and some more on my arms and legs. My face looked like an old piece of fruit, dappled with rot, the kind you might make jam out of if you were feeling very thrifty. Otherwise you would chuck it away.

Gerard's bother was all in the legs department, and his baby face was unmarked. He said: 'There's a bad apple in every barrel, my ma used to say, and in this ward it's you.' We got on well, him and I. He was refreshingly short on self-pity.

My tongue kept probing the empty space in the back of the top row of teeth. I doubted if you would be able to see the gap when I smiled, but it hurt too much now to find out. I was vain enough to care about how I looked at the end of all this. I was no pin-up, but there was something about my face that women liked — some suggestion of romantic complication — and I didn't want to lose that small advantage. God knows, I didn't have many others.

When I got bored I would mumble a comment at Gerard, just to get him going.

'What do you want to be when you grow up, Gerard?' I said to him one day.

He answered exactly as I knew he would, 'I am fucking grown up,' furiously moving the top half of his body to some imaginary techno beat, apropos of nothing.

Then he gave it a second's more consideration: 'Make loads of money.'

'They don't put you on a big salary for joyriding, do they?'

'They do for racing driving,' he said. 'Look at

Eddie Irvine. Loads of money, gorgeous women hanging off his arm, international rally-races. I do exactly the same thing in Belfast and I get my leg wrecked by the Provies.'

'That's because you're driving someone else's car,' I said.

'So's Eddy fucking Irvine.'

He was quick enough, was Gerard.

'Such an innocent wee face, and such a foul mouth,' I baited him.

'You should swear more, then, it might make your big fat mug look better,' he said.

Then he stuck his earphones back on. I settled my painful pumpkin head gently back into the piecrust of pillows.

★   ★   ★

I sort of liked it in hospital. It was like resting in the centre of a soft cloud. I felt that no one could get at me there. I was taken care of, and the nurses were kind to me in a brisk way. I didn't have to run around explaining things and trying to make ends meet. One night when neither Gerard nor I could get to sleep we made a pact to tell each other the name of the person who had directed the attack on us, names that each of us would keep close and remember on behalf of the other.

It wouldn't make any difference to anything, we both knew that, but there was some satisfaction just in banking the cold truth with another young human being. We had this idea that if anything worse happened to either of us, at least someone outside our family would know who was responsible. McGee's name meant nothing to Gerard, and I had never heard the name he told me before, but I promised to remember it, and I did: Frankie Dunne. One other thing stuck with me. Gerard said that Dunne had suddenly pulled out a gun before the beating got started in earnest, and whispered softly in his ear: 'I could just flip my wrist and plant one in your brain.'

There was an old man up at the end of the ward who kept calling for his wife in the night. I don't know if he was asleep or awake, but he would say, 'Mary, are you in there?' in a sorrowful voice, again and again. Gerard said that when he got out he was going to turn the phrase into a techno record, and make a fortune playing it in the dance clubs for all the Belfast ravers: 'M-m-m-mary, are you in there? Are you in there, Mary?'

The old man didn't get many visitors, although his middle-aged daughter came sometimes, and sat there with an air of permanently distracted affection. The nurse told me that his wife had died last year, that was why he kept calling for her. He had a gentle old patched face, full of seams and lines, and fine white hair sprouting in clouds from either side of his head like some absent-minded professor. One day when he was having his afternoon cup of tea, I sent the nurse over with a bar of the chocolate Roisin had brought for me. I watched the nurse telling him who it was from. He looked over, and then his wandering, bleary eyes found the bed she had indicated, and me in the middle of it. He slowly raised one gnarled hand in a majestic gesture of acknowledgement. Thereafter, on his way to the bathroom in his striped dressing gown, he made a sort of little joking half-bow at the foot of my bed. A delicate gent.

★　★　★

Hospitals are peculiar places, and the dressing gown is a great equaliser. They ought to make it a compulsory uniform on the outside. Mostly everyone's nice to each other, exchanging shy comradely smiles, a bit abashed that fate has knocked them off their feet and into their bedclothes. You become a benign connoisseur of other people's troubles, musing to yourself as the new arrivals stumble in, 'I wonder what happened to him?' and 'What's she got?' It's not a bad idea to be put in hospital along with other sick people; it keeps misfortune in perspective. It's when you get back out among the well that your vision really starts to blur.

I was dozing at visiting time one day when the nurse said, 'There's someone to see you.' I opened my eyes and there were Titch and his mother, carrying grapes and newspapers. 'It's the first time he's been out,' his mother whispered to me as they sat down.

Titch was staring at me, with his mouth half-open. There was still a vulnerable, exposed quality to his bulk, a sense that he had recently emerged, blinking, into an over-bright and hostile world. I suppose I must have looked terrible to him.

'Don't worry, Titch,' I said. 'They say I'll have my old face back in a few weeks, but with a couple of extra lines on it.' He had to work hard to decipher what I was saying.

'What happened to you?' he said.

'The same guys that did you over, took me on a trip to the waste ground,' I said. 'You can probably imagine the rest of it.'

'Phyllis told us about it,' his mother said.

Titch kept on staring, as though his eyeballs had stuck to my stitches.

'When are you coming home?' he said finally.

'I don't think I will be coming home,' I said. 'When they let me out of here, I'm going away for a while.'

'I came home.'

'I know you did, but it's different with you. I don't think they'll give you any more trouble. Anyway, how are things?'

'He isn't getting the counsellor any more,' said his mother.

'What happened?'

'He spilled his orange squash on her case notes when she was in the bathroom, and accidentally ruined them,' she said.

I saw a prim little smirk on Titch's face, of the sort that Queen Victoria must have worn when she first glimpsed John Brown in the nude.

'Attaboy,' I said, 'I hope you bought the poor woman a new jotter.'

'She wrote down about me liking biscuits,' he said, with a passable stab at indignation. 'And then she wrote that I was unhelpful. But she was supposed to help me, not the other way round.'

He was obviously perking up.

'Send her over to me. I'll give her something to write in her notebook,' I said.

I would have, too. They had offered me a counsellor as well, but I had said no thanks, I'd have to get over this in my own way.

Two days later, Phyllis visited in an even worse state. Her lipstick was put on all awry, as if it had made an escape bid for the safe territory of her right ear. The Loyalists had issued a death threat against me if I came back into the area. Posted through our front door, it was signed with the military-sounding pseudonym of Captain Grey. Phyllis had called the police, who had been very pleasant about it, she said. They had sat down and taken a cup of tea with her. Their sympathetic advice was that, since they hadn't the means to guarantee my future safety round the clock, it might be better if I left the area for a while. 'A cooling-off period,' was how they described it.

The Loyalists and the IRA were ordering people out of Northern Ireland all the time now, as if they owned the place. We were supposed to go and skulk about in other countries, dreaming about a moment when they would finally turn round and suck their teeth in lofty contemplation and maybe let us slink back in.

Because they were all on ceasefire no one in authority would really challenge them, in case they got annoyed and started swinging the big wrecking-ball again. The government thinking was that in the meantime you had to allow them their wee patches of control. Gerard and I, unfortunately, had our postcodes in those wee patches.

I was leaving anyway, I told Phyllis, so it didn't make things any different.

'At least I have it in writing,' I said. 'If I come back and they don't shoot me, I'll be able to sue Captain Grey for breach of contract. Hope he has money.'

Phyllis just looked at me.

But I wasn't feeling half as witty as I made out. I didn't want to leave the hospital ward. My bed was next to the window. At night I could lie motionless between the clean sheets and watch the clouds moving across the sky. There was the faint smell of detergent in the air, keeping our poisoned exhalations clean. I could hear the music still trickling out from Gerard's earphones, although he had fallen asleep. Even the old man calling softly for Mary was a kind of comfort, although he did so less often now. I feared being left absolutely alone. I feared travelling into the heartless expanse of a city I didn't know, and that didn't know me.

On the day that they said I could go, Gerard was quieter than usual. His eyes were red-rimmed and he wasn't playing his techno music. The doctors had told him that morning that he would walk with a limp for the foreseeable future, which Gerard took to mean for ever.

I had a bath, and slowly got back into the clean clothes that Phyllis had brought. It felt like a different me inside them now, warier and more fragile. If I breathed too deeply or bent over, my ribs shot out a suffocating strand of pain. I began to understand why Titch had refused to leave the house for all those weeks. It was as if the memory of the beating had sunk into my bones. I moved around like a much older man, as though even the breeze was hiding a knife.

I looked different, too. The scars set me apart, although the nurses had given me cream to put on them and told me they would fade with time. People see your damage and aren't sure how you got it, whether for being a bully or a victim. Either way, it makes them a little uneasy. Their eyes climb aboard the scars and travel down the tram lines.

Gerard was lying in bed, staring into the plastic curtain. I went over to him and said, 'Forget that racing driver crap, Gerard, they all burn out eventually. Get into the DJ-ing. You'll make a packet at it, and all the women will go mad for you.'

He smiled and shook my hand. I waved to the old man down the ward: he raised his hand in reply. I said goodbye and thank-you to the nurses, backing away like a retreating vaudeville entertainer. Then I got into the big, clanking lift, specially designed for wheelchairs and trolleys, and pressed the button to descend into the rest of my life.

Phyllis and Murdie were waiting to pick me up. They had got a bit more money together for me and bought me a new plane ticket. Phyllis had packed my cases all over again. Murdie gave me a lift to the airport straight from the hospital. He even had an address for me to go to in London, a cousin who he said would put me up for as long as I needed ('A decent fella. My side of the family,' he stressed. Gavin, he said, had finally departed after Mrs Murdie told him bluntly that a sick friend was moving in and required the room in two days' time.)

The fields looked very green as we drove up to Aldergrove airport, a deep bright green. It seemed calm here outside Belfast. I wondered if one day I could maybe just live somewhere round here, in a secluded house away from the road.

The rain clouds were pewter, but the sunlight was coming down between them, falling on to the quiet fields. The light was oddly intense, like a pale yellow stone set in dark granite. I used to think that this kind of light could be found everywhere. It was only when I went away that I realised it can't.

Part Two

13

London

I moved from a place where I mattered, but in the wrong style, to a place where I didn't matter at all. Whether this was better I found hard to say at first. But I knew then that people don't come to an unfamiliar city just to get away from their old homes, but also to escape their old selves.

Everything about London was strange: the hustling crowds that seethed out from the mouths of Tube stations; the double-decker buses that reeled drunkenly around the crammed streets; the truncated way that people spoke, their words chopped in mid-air by some invisible knife that cut 'a's down to a sliver, and whittled off their 'r's and 't's altogether.

I was rich in nothing but vowel sounds, and even they were a bloody hindrance. Hardly anyone here seemed able to understand me. I could see their faces ruffling with confusion when I spoke, like the sea beneath an angry wind.

⋆   ⋆   ⋆

Murdie's cousin, Mr Norman Wharton, owned a tall house in Hackney. This he shared with his wife, Mrs Nellie Wharton. Their two sons had long since gone: one to join the navy, and the other to run an import-export business in Southampton. The Whartons had bought a boxer dog to fill the space in their affections left by their departed children. It was a wheezing, slobbering, bow-legged lump called Rollo, now advanced in years.

Whatever core of independent character Rollo once possessed had long decayed beneath the weight of the Whartons' indulgence. He slavered by the dinner table, where he lingered in hope of falling bits of meat, growling if his greasy manna was too slow in descending.

In the evenings he staggered in and prostrated himself before the electric fire, sometimes letting loose a rogue fart or a dreaming squeak. Rollo had hated me from the very beginning. The day I arrived, dragging my suitcases through the front door, he stood snarling at the bottom of the stairs, his jowly little mask contorted with rage.

Ever since, he had conducted himself with cussed obedience when the Whartons were there, but the moment he and I were alone in the house his behaviour changed. When he was awake he stationed himself at doors, nipping at my trouser leg when I tried to pass by.

I had, in revenge, invented a game called 'Baiting Rollo' which I played on the rare occasions when the Whartons went out and left me to have dinner alone. The kitchen, where the Whartons usually ate, was separated from the hall by a glass-panelled door. Sometimes I was able to make it into the kitchen before Rollo noticed.

Once the dog and I were safely on separate

sides of the door, I would unpack the meat which I had bought to cook for dinner — a pork chop, perhaps, or a piece of calf's liver — and wave it back and forth while the hungry Rollo watched me through the glass door, yapping with frustration. When I finally cooked and then ate it, sitting behind the glass, the bad-tempered beads of Rollo's eyes followed each movement of my fork. Then I would dole a tin of Matey dog food into his dish, as I had promised the Whartons. When the door opened he would rush in, wheezing and growling, uncertain whether to bite me or bury his muzzle in the Matey first — but the lure of the Matey always won, and the monotony of chewing gradually sedated him.

The top of the house, where I lodged, was a Rollo-free zone: he was too fat and idle to mount the stairs. Mine was a high-ceilinged room, vacated by the naval officer son and left with few adornments: a model ship, now permanently docked on the surface of the dresser, and a small, framed oil painting of a storm at sea.

I liked this painting: it showed furious waves rearing up towards a swirl of dark grey skies, lit by a single streak of lightning. That was all. The fact that man was entirely absent from this struggle lent the picture a rare modesty. The artist had not felt minded to include any kernel of human interest in the form of some tiny, plucky vessel battling against the high seas. It made me think with relief of how nature ticked on without us in all the places that we can't see. I asked Mrs Wharton who had painted it, but she just muttered something about a relative of Mr

Wharton's and carried on with her dusting.

On windy nights my windowpane rattled in its frame, and I would lie in the dark listening to the hum of traffic from the street and thinking about home. Rollo lay in the dark too, two storeys down, snorting and dreaming of a falling rain of pork-gristle.

★   ★   ★

Mr Wharton was a tallish, stout man, with a face the colour of a rare steak and iron-grey hair that ascended from his head in a hopeful Marcel wave towards heaven. Mrs Wharton was a birdy little cockney woman, with a pair of permanently startled eyebrows, a topiary frizz of poodle-cut blonde hair and a furious energy. In life, Mr Wharton liked a steak-and-kidney pie, a couple of pints of Guinness, Mrs Wharton and Rollo. He was well disposed towards me — not so much as an individual, it often seemed, but as a benign ambassador from his own, distant Belfast past.

For the first month I just got accustomed to the place, and some evenings I would join the Whartons in their living room. They sat in velour-upholstered armchairs on either side of the giant, wide-screen television. They liked the television to operate at a reassuringly loud volume, spouting out jingles and soap operas like some oblong, idiotic god. If discussion became necessary, they never turned the television down: they turned their conversation up. There were times when between the jabbering of the television, the

136

heckling of the Whartons, the wheezing of Rollo and the thrum of the cars outside their door, I thought my head would split.

If an advertisement came on which featured an egg sizzling in a pan, or a couple of bacon rashers spitting under a grill, Mr Wharton would dash me a stagily conspiratorial look and shout across a roguish reference to Belfast delicacies, unavailable in London: 'I bet you could handle that between a couple of bits of soda bread, eh? And a big bit of plum duff on the side?'

I would push my face into an expression of pleasurably tortured yearning, and sigh: 'Oh aye I would, Mr Wharton. I really would.'

★   ★   ★

A visitor's voice rang out in the Wharton's kitchen — 'So when I came back from a month away in Spain, I found that my flat had been burned down, along with everything in it. Video, TV, curtains, carpets, all destroyed. And six-hundred quid's worth of clobber, that I bought before I went — all off the back of a lorry, like — jackets, shirts, trousers, you name it. All burnt to a facking crisp. All I had left was the clothes in my suitcase, and what I was standing up in.'

Harry Smiley — balding native of London town, minicab driver and friend of Mr Wharton's — took a contemplative slug of beer from a can and screwed up his knowing eyes in squinting recognition of the caprice of fate. Mrs Wharton leaned forward in her chair, drawing heavily on her John Player Special, and asked urgently, 'Did you get it back off the insurance?'

'No. My insurance had expired two weeks before, and I hadn't even realised to renew it. It cost me fifteen grand.' He paused, aware of the dramatic power of his bad luck.

Mrs Wharton gaped for a moment. 'How did the fire start?' she said.

Harry took another swig before answering: 'It was the old geezer that lived upstairs. He came back pissed from the pub one night, got into bed, lit up a cigarette and fell asleep. Next thing the whole place was burned to a bleeding cinder, his flat and mine.

'He'd only moved in a couple of weeks before, and I'd helped him carry in his stuff. Then he goes and burns my flat down. My first thought when I heard was 'Where is the old git? I'll kill him,' and then I heard he'd died in the fire and I felt bad, like.'

'Poor old bloke,' said Mrs Wharton.

'Yeah,' said Harry.

He lit a cigarette, inhaled deeply and turned to me: 'And what's our Jacky going to do, eh? Got yourself a job yet?'

'Not yet. I'm still looking about for one.'

'What did you do in Belfast?'

'I was a barman.'

Harry absorbed the information silently. I wasn't sure how much the Whartons had told him about my reasons for coming to London, but there was a kind of crude grace to Harry. He didn't scratch around for too many difficult answers. I could see he was mulling over my predicament.

'A mate of mine is a chef at a flash place in the West End. He said they're always needing barmen, and they coin it in tips. Do you want me to ask him for you?'

'That would be very kind,' I said. I meant it. Rollo and I were really beginning to get on each other's nerves. It was becoming clear that if we stayed in the house together any longer, things would come to a head — and although he was smaller than me he had a nastier temper and sharper teeth. I had even stopped baiting him, because I could sense that he was slowly building up to biting me properly, and I had enough scars as it was.

★   ★   ★

Delauncey's restaurant belonged to a wealthy, grizzled Australian man and a grizzled, wealthy British woman. They were a pair of ruthless old hippies who had married each other long ago on a beach in Bali, and probably regretted giving in to the dictates of bourgeois society ever since. They wore platinum love-beads, leathery tans and hand-stitched clothes that cost them hundreds of pounds from Notting Hill boutiques and then fell apart at the seams after two outings. His name was Delaney, but her maiden name was Price, so I never worked out where the Delauncey's came from. Pricey's would have been more appropriate.

It was the sort of restaurant that had a menu the length of your arm, and not a single thing on it that you unambiguously wanted to eat. Every simple food was mangled up with something mildly nasty or complicated. If you fancied chicken, it would arrive steeped in a mango-and-chive sauce. If you asked for a bowl of soup, you would find that the soup of the day was blood-orange-and-watercress. You couldn't have got a bacon sandwich in Delauncey's, but if you had, it would have been free-range bacon wrapped in warm ciabatta bread with a drizzle of chicken livers and a shredding of coriander. The customers were delirious with happiness. They would gladly have eaten their own spleens if it came served in a basil mousse with an ugli fruit twist.

Our customers were finger-snapping men from the City in charcoal suits and pinstriped shirts, who — to show that time was money — always made a point of ordering from the Express Menu, which took expressly seven minutes longer than the ordinary menu. We had tipsy, highlighted women, fresh from their body maintenance classes, pushing endive-and-squid salads through the automated gates of their bright white smiles into gym-hard stomachs. We had ladies who lunched, and PR girls who launched, and market investors, and business assessors. And I worked behind the bar.

My introduction to Delauncey's was Harry Smiley's friend, Francis the chef, a six-foot-four Molotov cocktail of bonhomie and menace. Long nights of excess had left a dull patina on his native robustness: he looked like a thinner, rain-damaged Luciano Pavarotti. Francis moved in a fug of flashing, yellowing teeth, baroquely foul curses and swishing knives. When the restaurant was full, and things were heating up in the kitchen, a vein on Francis's forehead would begin to bulge and pulse in a kind of samba rhythm as his huge hands flew efficiently and ominously in fifteen different directions.

The freedom which Francis afforded his hands had got him into trouble in the past. He had slapped the most junior of the kitchen staff, a pale-faced French boy who was too slow at chopping the parsley, and sent him reeling into a pan of bubbling water. The boy was only lightly scalded, but the rest of the kitchen staff had squeezed their shreds of courage up into a communal ball and made a formal complaint to Mrs Delaney. Francis was made to say sorry to the quivering boy, wearing a forced, ingratiating grin that was somehow more frightening than his expression of rage. He looked like a hyena about to savage a baby gazelle.

'I ap-ol-ogise for slapping you. It was very wrong of me,' he said.

'That is all right,' said the French boy, nervously.

They shook hands.

Mrs Delaney said, 'Well that's that over then,' and left the kitchen, satisfied.

'Next time use the little, sharp knife for the parsley, it will chop faster,' said Francis, in a cold, businesslike voice. Then he went over to stir a cream capers sauce for his fillet of sea bass.

He hated the kind of food he had to cook at Delauncey's, and often made a point of telling me so. Francis revered meat. When he ate out

141

himself, he went to places where they served pieces of an animal's interior that only surgeons and abattoir workers knew existed. He would have been happiest working in one of those New British restaurants, where they give claret-faced customers every known variety of offal, cooked in styles that are increasingly obscene to vegetarians. But Delauncey's was regular work with decent money, and Harry Smiley had slyly hinted that Francis's recreational habits were becoming expensive: 'The trouble with Francis is, he spends far too much time with his old mate, Charlie.'

I had noticed the same syndrome in Francis myself, a certain subcutaneous twitchiness, although I had been slow to put a substance to it.

14

There was consternation at the Whartons'. Rollo had killed a grey squirrel and then dragged it into the house. It was lying on the hallway mat, with one dead bright eye staring up at the ceiling. Two front paws were raised in supplication, a plump little friar caught up in an unexpected massacre. Rollo lay dozing some distance away, a crust of squirrel blood drying in the seam of his jowl. It was the first time he had killed anything, and the Whartons looked at the sleeping dog with suspicion and respect, as though after all these years he had become a fresh mystery.

That night I lay in bed at the top of the house, in the dark, wondering how it was that Rollo had managed to kill the squirrel. They were so fast: I had seen them shinning up trees like circus performers.

I didn't sleep well. The dream that kept troubling me came back, or a version of the dream. In it, I was looking out of the bedroom window in the Whartons' house. Below me, standing in the falling rain on the wet street, was a man in a dark hood. He was calling out to me, 'Jacky, Jacky, come down here, I have something for you,' and holding up the curled body of a dead squirrel.

'I'm not coming down,' I called out to him from the window. 'I can get the squirrel in the morning.'

'Then I'm coming up,' the man said. He

began to climb up the drainpipe towards my window, slowly at first. I felt myself filling with fear, like a flooding ditch. I was rooted to the spot.

The hood came waggling up the pipe until at last I could look straight into its eyeholes, but saw no eyes. In a panic, I picked up the lamp base from beside my bed and hit at the thing inside the hood over and over again. Then suddenly the hood fell off and the stunned face beneath it, with blood running down in a rivulet from the forehead, was Big Jacky's.

'Aw, why did you do that to me, son?' he said, in a voice soaked with an immensely soft and patient sorrow.

I couldn't speak. My hands were trying to press his bleeding head back together and make it well, but none of it would work.

'Why did you *do* that, son?' he said again, sadly.

When I woke up, my face was wet. My heart was beating at a hundred miles an hour, like a starling's ticker, and the sheets were damp with sweat.

★   ★   ★

How could you explain love and how it creeps up on you? How it slowly takes a grip, spreading across you like blight across an elm tree, shortening your breath, sneaking into your dreams, making your mouth suddenly foolish, ambushing your clumsy, stupid heart with stabs of jealousy and desire?

144

And how can you explain the illogicality of it: how you might say there's a girl there, who is certainly beautiful, and intelligent, and amusing, and if she were to be flattened by a bus tomorrow I would be very sorry, of course, for the loss of a life, but not that sorry? And there's a girl there who's not strictly anything that I can really convey, except that first I saw her laughing in a way that something in me understood, and then I thought I might love her.

She started as a waitress in the restaurant, about two weeks after I got the job behind the bar. She didn't talk to anyone much at first, because she was too busy trying to work everything out, with the managers shouting in one ear and Francis in the other.

She had thick dark, wavy hair that fell jaggedly on to her neck, as though she had taken a chop at it herself with the kitchen scissors. Pale skin, as pale as paper, and dark, watchful eyes. She was small and fine-boned, as if pieced together by an intelligent hand. At the beginning, she spoke to me only in drinks orders, and her name was Eve. The significance of her name wasn't lost on me, since I had already started to weave meanings around her. Eve, I thought, the woman at the start of everything.

One day, I tried a joke.

'Two small glasses of house white, a gin and tonic with ice and lemon, and a margarita,' she said.

'And a thimble of lemonade for the pixie on table twelve,' I whispered to her. She gave me a sceptical look, but I saw her glance over to table twelve, where a tiny man with a Florida tan and a permanently astounded expression, as though his eyebrows had been surgically tweaked upwards, was leaning forward into the monstrous bosom of his formidable blonde companion. A smirk crept up the side of her face before she could catch and kill it. I carried on quietly with my business, mixing drinks in the cocktail shaker, as though I had noticed nothing.

She had a six-year-old son, Francis said.

'Any husband?'

'*Husband*,' he said, mocking me for being old-fashioned. 'I don't think so. Why, do you want to marry her?'

'I'm not the marrying kind,' I said.

★ ★ ★

Phyllis sent me letters from Belfast. They fell on to the Whartons' doormat every couple of weeks or so: a page or two of blue ink, written in her painstaking, cramped hand.

There was one lying there this morning. I pictured her in the evenings in our front room, drawing the curtains and mulling over her account of events.

Dear Jacky, it said, *Hope all is well with you. The weather has been terrible here, clouds and drizzle so no surprises there. Mary and Sam came up to visit at the weekend, Mary looking very smart in a green suit she bought in Lisburn. Sam hadn't much to say for himself because the football was on so we gave him the remote and left him to it.*

Two men I didn't recognise came to the house looking for you last Friday. I said you weren't here, you had gone to live in Scotland and they should leave us alone now. The next day there were dirty words sprayed on our wall but I spoke to Mr Murdie and between us we have managed to get it off with the paint remover. Hopefully that will be an end to it, as I can't be doing with any more trouble.

I was round at Titch's house on Sunday for his mother's birthday. We had a lovely evening with a Chinese takeaway and white wine, and a coffee cake with candles in it. Titch is on much better form and is now going out of the house by himself a couple of times a week, although not in the evenings. He asks after you all the time. I am enclosing some snaps of us on the night, taken by his Uncle Joe. Titch got them developed in Speedy Snaps. Take care and give my regards to the Whartons, love Phyllis.

There were three photographs with the letter, of Titch, Phyllis and Titch's mother sitting round the kitchen table on the big night. Uncle Joe must have been on his tenth can of lager, because they were all slightly askew, as though the kitchen floor had suddenly sunk in just before his finger pressed the shutter. Phyllis was in camera mode: teeth graciously bared, eyes staring straight into the lens, hand lifting a wine glass in a determined, recordable gesture of celebration. She was wearing a blouse I hadn't seen before. Titch's mother was laughing with her eyes closed, a paper party hat slipping off the back of her hair. And Titch was smiling too, but there was the ghost of something fearful in his eyes.

I turned to the last picture. Titch had arranged his arm so that his fingers were making rabbit ears out of the back of Phyllis's unwitting, permed head. Good sport of Phyllis to have included it. She loved photographs. It made me laugh out loud. I slipped it into my wallet and went to work.

15

She was a good waitress, and I liked to watch her working. It pleased my eyes to follow her round the room, stopping only when she happened to look over in my direction. She could stack and carry heavy china plates like they were made of paper, and she could keep many different things in her mind at once: the menu for table twelve, the bread for table ten, the bill for table three, and the wine list for the man with the face like an aggrieved muskrat who was signalling at the table by the window.

She was friendly to customers almost all the time, but I saw her behave otherwise once with a man, a City type who had had too much to drink. He was with three friends at a table close to the bar, and all night they had been ordering successive bottles of a very expensive white wine. They had loosened their ties, and their voices became slightly slurred as they grew a little too loud. A jagged haze of noise surrounded them, the kind of noise that always set my teeth on edge.

As the wine flowed, they thought they would have a bit of fun with the waitress. Every time Eve brought them something they would quickly demand something else, 'Oh, and more bread!' or 'Another bottle of mineral water!' — stagily, like loud, capricious children with a powerless nanny.

With each demand, Eve's manner grew one degree colder: slowly she was retreating into herself, the way Murdie used to when there was trouble at the Whistle.

She brought them another bottle of white wine, in an ice bucket. 'Here comes the ice maiden!' one of them shouted, a tall, sandy-haired type, his face lightly mottled with drink and excitement.

Eve smiled, but her smile was a sliver of frozen water. She had endured enough of them over the course of the evening. Sandy Hair could see the put-down in her smile: he was quick to spot the offence, in the way that drunks are quick.

'What's your name?' he asked, in a bantering tone edged with aggression.

'Eve,' she said. She turned to go.

'Eve!' he said, loudly, and gave the abashed man next to him a little shove. 'This bloke's name is Adam. Really.'

'Would you Adam-'n'-Eve it?' chimed in a third man in a mock-cockney accent, his face shining at his own wit.

'No,' Eve said, still smiling thinly, 'I wouldn't.' She turned again to go.

'Will you bring Adam an apple?' said Sandy Hair.

'We don't have apples.'

'Not even an Adam's apple? It looks like *you* have one.' He peered showily at her throat, screwing up his eyes.

Two of the men laughed. One looked a little embarrassed. Eve stood there just staring at them, as though something had disconnected inside her. Sandy Hair perused the pudding menu, ostentatiously. Something in her reaction was disturbing and annoying him. He was struggling to keep his game in the air, to re-establish his authority.

'Well, could I have an Apple Strudel with Glazed Caramel then, Eve,' he said, sharply. She went to the kitchen to get it.

I watched her coming back with it: her body was stiff and her mouth was pinned into a tighter line. She set the strudel down in front of him.

'This looks wonderful,' said Sandy Hair. He took a spoonful quickly before she had time to leave.

'It tastes so magnificent, I think my friend Adam would like one of these as well now, Eve, so hurry up,' he said.

The exchange had lost all pretence of lightness. They stared at each other with hatred, like two battling cats. Somewhere along the line, with the 'hurry up', this had flared into war.

'I don't think he's going to have one after all,' Eve said, her face utterly impassive.

'Why not? I'm paying the bill here.'

'Yes, and you're going to pay the bill now,' she said with a terrible flatness, 'because you're ugly, and stupid, and rude, and there's only so much shit that I'm prepared to take.'

The surrounding tables fell discreetly silent, the diners' forks suspended halfway to their half-delighted, half-open mouths. But at Sandy Hair's table the men had stopped laughing. Their round eyes were jerking over to her, and then back to him.

151

'Get. Me. The. Manager,' spat Sandy Hair. His face was rigid with anger. Eve turned and walked away.

Mrs Delaney, to her credit, took Eve's part. She brought them the bill, and when Sandy Hair kicked up too much of a fuss she just knocked off the cost of a bottle of wine, but without conceding the point. Maybe some vestige of sympathy with the workers still clung to her from her hippie years. Or maybe she just knew how hard it can be to find really good waitresses these days.

★   ★   ★

It took me a while to work out what it was I liked about Eve, and when I did, I wasn't sure what that said about me. It was her air of dislocation, the feeling that the current of life had suddenly picked her up and swirled her off to somewhere out of her control. Most people had harbours, and anchors, and moorings, but Eve was floating on the sea with her eyes wide open, holding tight to her son's hand.

She brought her son into the restaurant once, because the childminder was sick and there was nowhere else for him to go. His name was Raymond. He sat in the corner of the kitchen and played solemnly with some dough that Francis gave him. I watched him making dough-pebbles and then some funny-looking dough-men, with big unwieldy heads and stringy arms and legs. Francis put them on a baking tray and stuck them in the oven to cook for Raymond to take

152

home, but a party of twelve people came in and we all forgot about them. We opened the oven when Francis smelled something burning, and there they were: a huddle of little burnt bodies, hapless midgets who had overnighted in Pompeii.

Francis was annoyed at himself and swept them into the bin with a snort of irritation as if to erase all evidence of his mistake. I saw Raymond's face fall. It wasn't the burning he minded, I think, so much as the discourteous disposal.

'I'll make you some more and send them back with your mother,' I told him, and he stared back at me with his oddly lucid, grey-green eyes.

'I made those ones myself,' he said, with the air of someone quietly stating an obvious fact.

When Eve was taking him home later, holding his hand, I saw something like a broken stick of charcoal hanging loosely from his side trouser pocket as he ambled out the door. He had fished one of the blackened bodies out of the bin.

There were times when I thought there wasn't much point to the life I had. I sat up in my room and looked at the squares of grey city sky through the dilapidated window frame. I missed Phyllis, for all her ways. I missed Titch and his mother. I missed my father most of all, and I thought sometimes that, now he was dead, there was no one in the world who my own death would really matter to, beyond casually saying, 'Oh isn't it terrible what's happened to poor Jacky,' no one who might lie awake night after night and ache for how big the darkness was without me.

That's how we measure out our own reality, through the pain that the absence of us will cause in others. That's what roots us and gives us substance. Without it we're just ghosts passing through a series of doors, river water running into the ocean and leaving no trace.

When she wasn't at the restaurant for a couple of days, I even found myself missing Eve. It felt good to miss someone I could see again.

16

It was getting colder. The leaves had rusted and fallen from the trees, leaving them spiky and shivering in the breeze. The days were shorter, guillotined by early darkness. I went up to Oxford Street and bought myself a heavy coat made from dark, thick tweed: it weighed me down and lent me substance against the wind. But London was choking me: the clotting of people, the taste of fuel in the air, the relentless voice in the Tube station that never tired of telling me, day after day, to Mind the Gap and Let the Passengers off the Train First.

Eve and I were friendlier now. We would sometimes share a cigarette out at the back of the restaurant, leaning against the wall beside the bins. I told her all about the Whartons, and she told me about Raymond, and her mother who drove her mad.

The mum had developed a habit of calling round, she said, and then passing the evening cosily lamenting the state of affairs that had left Eve working as a waitress with a six-year-old child to keep and no man to support her. Each time, the lamentation would take a fresh shape around familiar themes, a never-ending work of embroidery on life's misfortunes. Sometimes she would reproach herself for not forcing Eve to study hard enough at school. Or she would shift the blame over to Eve, for being — as she put it

— 'too easily distracted'. Often she would rail against the duplicitous character of Eve's former boyfriend, who left Eve a year after Raymond was born and got on a plane to Canada (never to be heard of again) but inevitably this well-worn path carried her straight back to poor, gullible Eve, and her now legendary inability to 'find a decent man'. Eve wasn't even looking, so far as I could make out, although I was looking at her all the time.

'Your father liked a drink, and God knows he was no angel,' the mother would say. 'But he would never have gone off and left his wife and child to fend for themselves.' Her outrage on Eve's behalf, enlarged by five years of repetition, had become a sort of quilt to be clutched around her at every opportunity. The trouble was, it was no comfort to Eve. Every time her mother walked in the door, she came hand in hand with the unwelcome spectre of Eve's feckless boyfriend.

When the mother at last cheerily waved goodbye, her conscience satisfied after an evening spent helping out her unfortunate daughter, Eve would creep into bed, defeated, and pull the covers over her head. It would take a couple of days back in the restaurant before her spirits recovered.

One day, Eve was quieter than usual. She didn't sing when she pinned up the orders, or tease me about being slow with the drinks. I asked her what was the matter, and she hesitated for a moment before telling me.

'My mum came round last night,' she said,

'and it started off all right. We were watching a film on TV, and Raymond was on the floor, trying to make a mobile, shaped like a football, to hang in his room. For once it seemed as if everybody was happy.

'Ray was making a bit of a mess with the football, and I was telling him to be careful about where he put the glue and only to use a little bit. That was what started her off: she couldn't bloody resist it.

''It's a pity Ray doesn't have a dad to help him out with that. Women can't really get to grips with footballs,' Mum said, with that wistful, grieving look she gets on her face every time she talks about my home life. She doesn't normally say that sort of thing in front of Ray, but for some reason it just popped out last night. It didn't even make sense.

'Anyway, that did it. Something snapped in me: I've had years of her going on and on like a stuck record, using the old more-in-sorrow-than-in-anger-Chinese-water-torture voice, about what a failure I've been. So I told her: 'I've had enough of this crap, Mum. The truth of it is I'd be pretty happy if I didn't have to listen, twice a week, to you telling me how bloody sad I am.'

'Then I went and got the notebook that sits beside the phone, and threw it so it just missed her head. I said, 'Next time you feel an observation coming on about how it's a desperate pity that Ray doesn't have a dad, or that I didn't work hard enough at school, or that I have a job carrying plates of food over to City bankers, don't tell it to me straight away. Just write it

157

down in there. Then I can have the joy of reading all your criticisms at once, perhaps on Christmas Day, as I carve the turkey that the strong-jawed, smiling man should really be carving in the family that I have failed to deliver. It can be my Christmas present from the Misery Club.''

Eve's face had taken on an expression of remembered anger and exhilaration. 'What did your mother say then?' I asked, awed by this sudden surge of eloquence. It was another thing I liked about Eve: the way that, once she was pushed to her limit, she would actually say the sort of things to her family that I would only dare to think.

'She didn't say anything. Her jaw dropped, and she looked shocked. But then I looked over at Ray. He was standing up, still holding that gluey football, with a wounded look on his face. 'I do have a dad,' he said, 'Everybody has a dad. But mine has gone away for a while.' Then he set down the football, and went out of the room. After that he wouldn't talk to either of us.'

The exhilaration had gone: she was upset now at remembering Raymond. I wanted to put my arms round her, and stroke her fallen face, but I thought maybe she wouldn't like it. I put my hand on her shoulder.

'He'll come round. His feelings were hurt,' I said.

She let my hand rest there for a moment, saying nothing. Then she went to take the order from the couple on table twelve.

★ ★ ★

158

I had been out with girls before, of course, in Belfast. I liked them well enough, but I was never very sorry to see them go. In fact, by the time they did go, it was a relief. I could sense that there was a whole range of emotions they wanted and expected me to feel: passion, jealousy, acute distress if they weren't available that evening and a keen excitement if they were. I tried to feel this way, if only to make them happy, but I didn't. The more I didn't feel that way about them, the more they felt that way about me.

They exhausted me, with their storm of inexplicable feelings. I could see them, like mime artists watched through a thick pane of glass, gesturing furiously, weeping with frustration because I had forgotten to phone them when I said I would, or tearful with joy if I had forced myself to make a special effort and bought them a bunch of flowers. It was a fake, though. I realised that they were happy with the flowers because they thought the flowers said 'I love you.' But I didn't love them, I only quite liked them, and so gradually I stopped buying the flowers because I knew that the flowers were telling lies. Then, after a while, my heart would slowly sink when the phone rang, with its irritable summoning. Brrrrrrring. I had briefly enjoyed sleeping with them and maybe kidded myself it could go further, but the weight of their disappointed expectations became a burden to me. I would catch myself guiltily yearning for long rows of evenings spent on my own, or just watching television with Big Jacky.

I had the hazy feeling that perhaps I was the kind of man who was discussed in detail in those articles in women's magazines with headings like 'What to do when he seems distant' or 'When he won't commit'. All that endless talk. I always felt a bit sorry for the men in those articles, the anonymous villains of complaining anecdotes. If you ever got to hear their side of things, perhaps they wouldn't have seemed so bad after all.

If a woman has a pretty face and a laugh just a wee bit like the buzz of an electric carving knife, for example, what should a man do? Should he be frank and say: 'I have slowly come to realise that if we were to spend thirty years together, the cumulative effects of your distinctive laugh — in spite of all your other virtues — might one day make me dream of going after you with an actual carving knife. It is surely better for us to stop seeing each other now before things get that serious'? Or should he just let longer and longer intervals lapse between his phone calls, until — wreathed in mystery and irritation — he finally disappears from view, a misty folk-memory of masculine disappointment?

Except that often he doesn't just fade away into nothing, as he might have hoped. The worst parts of him are kept hideously alive, simplified and distilled in a thousand feminine retellings, until at last he emerges as a creature of malevolent energy or pitiable confusion: the bastard or the useless man who just can't get himself together. Although they were really the same person, I always preferred to inhabit the latter character.

For a long time, I never thought that much

about the girls I had been out with. But after I fell for Eve, I felt sorry for all the unhappiness I had caused them. I hadn't really understood it before, but I did now. If she wasn't at work, for some unexpected reason, my day clouded over. If I saw her laughing too long with a flirtatious customer, I was seized with pain. Was this what they had been feeling about me, as I lay listening to the phone ringing and deliberating over whether to bother picking it up or not? Was this love, then, this busy, hungry rat let loose in my chest? If so, it was unbearable. Suddenly, I was on the other side of the thick pane of glass, watching her working and talking, and wondering if she had ever really noticed me.

If I woke up early, I took advantage of the extra time to do nothing but lie in bed and think about her. I thought about the obvious, of course, but that wasn't all. I wanted to run the flat of my hands all over her and feel exactly how she fitted together, to trace the line of her vertebrae with my finger and take account of each small bump. I wanted to cook her dinner and for her to fall asleep later on the sofa in the crook of my arm. When I caught myself yearning for things like that, I knew I was in trouble, because if nothing happened between us now after all, I might be hounded for ever by a sense of loss.

One day, I asked her if she wanted to come and see a film. I tried to make it sound casual, as if I could have easily asked anyone at Delauncey's, but she just happened to be standing there when the thought occurred. She looked surprised: what sort of film? An arthouse French film, I said, about a man who dreams of becoming a famous architect but who is locked up in an asylum by his scheming relatives, where he builds scale models of the world's most famous buildings from empty medicine bottles and packets of drugs. It sounded pretty dreadful, she said. I thought it did too, but I couldn't think of anything else to say.

'There's probably a bit more to it than that,' I said. 'Come on and see it, it's got great reviews.'

There was a silence while I stared uselessly at my futile shoes, with their veneer of city dirt. Then she thought for a while. She would come and see it anyway, she said: she would telephone her mother and ask her to look after Raymond for the evening.

Our shifts ended at six. It was a dry night, but crisply cold, and we were both wearing our winter coats. Her thin shoulders sloped under the heavy cloth, and an arc of her pale neck was exposed where the wind lifted up her dark hair. When we were walking down the street, navigating the crowds, I took her arm in mine. She turned towards me for a moment, with a question in her brown eyes. I looked back at her. Then she turned forward again and we carried on walking down the street, arm in arm.

In the cinema I reached for her hand, as we sat in the darkness and watched the thwarted architect build a teetering scale model of Notre-Dame cathedral out of empty packets of antidepressants. After he fixed on its clumsy spire, he raised his fists and pounded them in frustration against the asylum walls. It was a strange and slow-moving film, but nothing about that evening was boring to me. Her hand lay still and cool in my hand, like a sleeping bird.

⋆ ⋆ ⋆

Life had battered Eve a little bit already. Well, that was all right; life had battered me. I liked that about her. She had learned that happiness wasn't a right, you had to try and make some of it yourself. She didn't expect me to sweep her up on a white charger and carry her off to a big house with hot and cold running money flowing from gold taps, its rooms swarming with laughing, photogenic children. Even if I wanted to, I couldn't have. She just wanted me to love her, but she was suspicious of love, and therefore of me: she came towards me jumpily, like an animal that was once pelted with grit and hasn't forgotten the sting. Sometimes when she forgot to be suspicious and I forgot to be secretive, I was happier with her than I had ever been before in my life.

She wouldn't let me stay with her when Raymond was in her place, a square two-bedroom council flat in a block in King's Cross. It would confuse him, she said, and he had had enough of that already. But on the nights when he went to her mother's we would lie folded together in the dark, whispering to each other and doing other things too without my old urge to escape afterwards, but only to stay there always.

You could hear the wind and the traffic outside, and I loved her the most then. I can't remember all the things I told her: silly stuff to soothe her, about Big Jacky and the aunts in

163

Carrickfergus and the way the starlings swooped and shifted like thick black smoke above the Lagan river at dusk. When she finally mumbled words to say goodnight, and her breathing grew deep and regular, I would wrap myself tight around her sleeping back, her breasts like heavy silk beneath the weight of my arm.

With her there beside me, I found that I could remember things without so much pain. I never told her the truth, though, about how I got the scars.

★   ★   ★

'How did you get those?' she would ask sometimes, tracing the marks on my legs and face with the tip of her finger. 'What happened to you, Jacky?' she would say lazily. She liked the defective tracks left on me, the way a child is pleased by a patterned stone it picks up on the beach. Each time she asked, I gave her a different explanation: sometimes a car crash, sometimes a motorcycle accident, sometimes a love affair with a woman who had hands made out of can openers. The explanations were different on purpose, to let her know that I was lying, because I didn't like the idea of her being fooled. But I didn't want to talk about what had really happened. I didn't want her to feel sorry for me, or to see me the way I saw myself, lying on a patch of waste ground crying in a pool of blood and piss.

Every so often, though, the dream returned: the hooded figure advancing towards me as I filled with fear. Eve would tell me in the morning that I muttered and shifted in my sleep but she couldn't make out what I was saying. I was grateful for that much, at least. I said I had always had bad dreams, even from a child.

17

'You're a weirdo,' Raymond told me one day, as we sat on a wooden bench waiting for Eve to pick up some things from her mother's house. We were both freezing cold and his voice rang out in the icy air like a clear bell. He didn't say it in a show-offy way, the way children do when they playfully rehearse a whole singing string of insults in front of some frowning adult: 'You're a nerd, you're a prat, you're a big cowpat, you're a weirdo, you're a freak, you're a geek.'

No, he said it calmly, as though the thought had first occurred to him some time ago and he had pondered it carefully since, turning it over in his mind, and had finally assured himself of its truth.

I felt disappointed. I suppose we always hope that children will give us back the best sense of ourselves, the sense that the world has slowly rotted; that they will see us as capable people who can handle things more confidently than they can. Instead, just this flat assertion: 'You're a weirdo.'

I checked that no thick werewolf-hair had sprouted from the back of my hands; that I had not absent-mindedly donned eyeglasses with milk-bottle lenses or a mustard-coloured shirt with a hilariously large collar.

'Why do you say that?' I asked him.

He pondered a while longer. I stamped my

feet to keep them warm and blew on my hands.

'You say your words in a funny way. And you've got some funny lines on your face,' he pronounced in his little London voice.

'Is that all?'

'Yes.' He stamped his feet to keep them warm too. I felt a stab of affection as I looked at his ridiculously small feet, encased in scuffed brown lace-up shoes. One of the laces had unravelled. I bent down and retied it for him, then stood up again.

'You're a weirdo,' I told him, neutrally. He turned quickly towards me at my echo of his own phrase, with an expression of nervous interest in his eyes, but he didn't say anything.

'You say your words in a funny way,' I said, 'and you're extremely short. Your mother also tells me that you enjoy eating scrambled eggs, and that is the sign of someone who is badly weird.'

He sat there, watching me, not knowing if I was serious. I moved right away from him, towards the other side of the bench.

'You terrify me,' I said, wobbling my head from side to side in a fearful judder. That tickled him, finally: he began to laugh. His face creased up and he held on to the zipper of his green anorak with one hand to steady himself. His pale brown hair stuck up at the front like a hello.

'Maybe next week, if your mother says it's all right, I'll take you to the zoo,' I said, 'Would you like that?'

He nodded yes.

I don't really know why I hit on the zoo: that's

where divorced fathers take their Sunday children. At least it wasn't McDonald's, I suppose, But Eve liked the idea of me taking him to the zoo. Anyway, she said, it would give her a bit of time to herself: she wanted to get her hair cut, and have a look round the shops without Raymond clamped to her side quietly agitating to go home.

I arrived to pick him up on Sunday morning, and he was all dressed and ready in his green anorak, with a blue scarf round his neck and a notebook in his hand: there was an air of anticipation about him. I kissed Eve goodbye, and she waved us off at the door. Anyone watching us might even have thought we were a family.

It's daunting, taking someone else's child out for the day. You're worried that you might do something slightly wrong and set them off into a screaming tantrum or a sulk, and then have to hand them back to their mother, surly or weeping, with the defeated admission hanging in the air that, as things turned out, they didn't like you very much and (although you won't actually say this, of course) you didn't like them at all.

Raymond wasn't like that. He was easy company, if that is the right way to put it. It was as though there was something already old in his understanding of how life went. With circumstances being what they were, and Eve having to work, no one ever really had quite enough time for him, although Eve and her mother did their best. But instead of becoming a pain in the neck and clamouring for more attention, the way most children did (the ones you always see in the supermarket being casually smacked to the staccato tune of 'Shu-dd-up, Luc-as' or 'Put-it-back, Ti-na') he had absorbed the fact that attention was somehow rationed, and that you just made the most of it when it finally came round. The rest of the time he locked himself in a dream-world with his books or his toys. He must have decided that the trip to the zoo was a good thing, therefore he wasn't going to wreck it. Like Eve, he seemed to know that happiness was not a right. I appreciated this, and it made me sad.

A child's tantrum carries a kind of confidence, after all, the belief that everyone will love them no matter how badly they behave, that they'll be calmed down and carried home without conditions. Raymond should have been too young to know that love is a breakable commodity, but he sensed it anyway and it made him careful.

It was a cold, overcast day. I had forgotten the smell of zoos, the distinctive earthy whiff of llama urine and zebra shit wafting over from the pens. I bought Raymond a shiny souvenir map from the shop and gave it to him, telling him it was his job to direct us around the animals. He took his task seriously, squinting diligently at the pathways on the map. He wanted to start with the camels, and we walked over to where they were chewing sideways and sulkily, their drooping mouths trailing strands of hay. Their coats looked mangy and their humps had slumped to one side like deflated bags.

'They like to run in the sand,' said Raymond.

'That's why they're grumpy here.' He knew these things from the animal encyclopaedia Eve had bought him a month ago: I had seen him looking at it with a rapt face and open mouth.

Then we went to the gorilla enclosure. The massive silverback, the daddy of the troop, rose up on his enormous haunches and ambled towards us. Raymond reached for my hand. We stared at the gorilla. The little jewelled eyes set in his great, seamed mask stared back at us, impassive and dignified. He turned round, presenting the vast expanse of his silvery behind, and walked over to a darkened corner, where he sat in profile, eating a banana. His gigantic hands worked with a clever delicacy, peeling off the yellow skin. It was like watching a very fat man dance on nimble feet.

'He doesn't have enough space in there,' Raymond said. 'He should have more trees and things to swing from.'

He was right, of course, but I didn't want Raymond walking from enclosure to enclosure feeling sad for the animals cooped up inside. I could sense the dust of gloom settling on our outing. So I steered him instead towards the creatures that have the gift of appearing content anywhere, even Regent's Park on a grey November day: the frantic parakeets and the capering spider monkeys; the lazy, ornamented iguanas and the big-eyed lemurs that darted and scuttled through underground cages in an artificial half-light. He liked all that, and he started to laugh and chatter about the way they looked and point things out about their strange hands or curious toes.

The sun came out as we were leaving, cool autumn sun. It fell on the stout, piebald body of the South American tapir that was standing in an oasis of green grass, peacefully rooting in the soft ground with a head that tapered to a long, elegantly questing snout. I couldn't get over the strangeness of him. He was a joke and a miracle rolled into one, a patchwork pig stitched to an anteater. The more I looked at him, the more I started to laugh: not in mockery, but in a kind of amazement. I looked at Raymond, and he was laughing too. 'Look at him,' I said. 'Isn't he mad?'

'Yes,' said Raymond, his face contorted with happiness. I was happy too.

The moment you start loving someone, it frightens you: it's not just what they might do to you, but what you might do to them. I loved Eve, and now I was starting to love Raymond. But what was I? A barman, on not much of a wage, with a body full of scars and twinges and lies and a home I couldn't go back to. I could sense my own precariousness, and I was getting vertigo. They were two innocents who had invested their faith in me, and I was a con artist. I had walked towards both of them masquerading as a solution, but I was lugging a suitcase full of problems.

I had come to London by accident, only to escape. It had just been a stop-off on a flight to somewhere else; I didn't know whether I really wanted to stay there. What was there in London for me, but a room in a bedsit and a lifetime mixing gin-and-tonics for pink-faced business-men? I saw my future stretching out, the marathon evenings of the oldest barman in the big city. The thought of moving on filled me with exhilaration and sorrow.

Raymond asked Eve questions about me now, wanting to know when I would be coming round to their flat. That pleased me as much as it worried me. I feared disappointing him. More than anything, I feared becoming an echo of his idiot father, the boyfriend who had run off to Canada when Raymond was one.

The thought of that boyfriend bothered me. He was there, constantly knocking on a door I struggled to keep closed, leading to thoughts I didn't want to entertain. I couldn't understand how he could have left her, when I thought she was so perfect. Had he just been a fool, or was there something lurking in Eve that had slowly driven him away, something I hadn't yet seen? This was a cheap way for me to think, I could see that. They had been very young when Raymond was born, after all, and people left each other for all sorts of reasons.

But if he was such a fool, then why had Eve loved him, if she really had loved him — was her judgement really so bad when it came to men, as her mother was fond of saying? There was that feeling of disconnection about her that once reminded me of a woman floating on the sea. Did she just allow herself to be loved by anyone who drifted along and threw her a lifebelt? That's the problem with love: the thing that pulls you towards someone in the first place is the thing that slowly spoils them for you ever afterwards.

So maybe it was only chance that she loved me, maybe I just happened to be hanging around at the right time. If I had stayed in Belfast, who might Eve be with now: one of the slavering customers who kept coming into the restaurant to chat her up, or someone like twitchy Francis, with her hanging off his arm like a gangster's moll laughing at his jokes as he pushed her from bar to bar?

Perhaps if I went away for even a month I would come back to find Eve with someone else, looking at me as though she only dimly recognised my face and didn't care much anyway. It wasn't true, I knew that, but maybe it was true. And then I would look at her sleeping face on the pillow beside me, her mouth gaping half-open like a gormless child's, and feel a wave of pointless tenderness. Sometimes I would rearrange the duvet over her to keep her warm. Then I would shut my eyes and try to sink back into sleep.

Now and then I thought that, Jesus Christ, it had been much easier when I was on my own. With nothing to lose, there's much less to go wrong. You can hang on to the bare fact of nothing and feel a kind of security. Once you have something, you're always in bloody freefall.

★   ★   ★

Every so often I called Phyllis at home, although I usually preferred to write rather than talk: there were fewer unreadable pauses. I gave her my

173

work number for emergencies, but I didn't give her the one at the Whartons'. I had unspoken concerns, although I couldn't quite sharpen the thought, that someone might try to force it out of her.

She told me that she had bumped into Titch's mum, who said that a wee package had been left on her front step, wrapped in sparkly paper and with Titch's name written neatly on it. When she opened it up, inside were two boxes of Jaffa Cakes, and a floral 'With Sympathy' card in which was written, 'Get Well Soon Titch. Your 'friends' are thinking of you.'

Titch's mum had put it deep in the bin without telling Titch. Phyllis said Titch's mum couldn't get over the fact that it had been so beautifully wrapped, all the care that had gone into the cruelty. The story worried me. It burrowed deep into my brain, coming back now and then to give me the cold sweats. Then Phyllis mentioned that the glass in the front door of the newsagent's had been smashed in on Saturday night — probably by young hoods with nothing better to do on their way back from the pub, she said — and that gave me a bad feeling too.

★ ★ ★

'I've got a new job,' Eve said one night, when we were sitting on her sofa watching the news, her warm shoulder slotted under my arm. She was wearing a cone of newspaper on her head that Raymond had made her. I couldn't believe what I was hearing. She hadn't mentioned even

174

looking for a new job before, and now she was looking at me expectantly, waiting for a pleased response, offering me her departure like a present tied with a big flouncy bow on top. A flash of fury went through me, but I didn't say a word. I kept on staring at the screen. Some supermodel had just got on to the bestseller list with a cookery book. She was all bone and eyelashes. It must have been the kind of cookbook where you drool over the list of hard-to-find ingredients but never actually turn on the oven.

'Look at her,' I said. 'The last thing she cooked was probably a big slice of melon, followed by three hours in the gym.'

'Aren't you pleased?' Eve said. 'It'll pay much better money, and I can choose more of my own shifts.'

It was all I could do to sound civil. When my voice came out, it was choked and dry. 'That's good,' I said, the words emerging as half-frozen drips from a small, tight tap. Christ, how stingy can you get? I was aware of how miserly I must have sounded, but I couldn't help it.

'Where's the restaurant?'

She took the newspaper cone off, as though wanting to maintain her dignity in the face of an assault.

'About three streets away from Delauncey's,' she said, 'at a place called Harrigan's. The boss is Irish, and so is the head chef. You'd probably like it, they do a modern version of traditional Irish food. Champ and wheaten bread and all, but fashionable, dressed up with Chinese vegetables and cranberry jus and stuff. It's very expensive.

175

You have to wear a uniform, but it's a designer one all in black.'

It sounded rotten, soda bread and beef sausages with beansprouts on top, and fifty per cent added to the bill for the privilege of having your taste buds confused.

'That sounds nice,' I said, mechanically. I was dazed. So, just like that, she wouldn't be around any more for cigarette breaks and knowing looks exchanged over the bar. 'When did you decide to look for a new job?'

'Only a few days ago,' she said, 'Francis told me about it and said that he'd have a word with the manager there for me. He said that he knew I had problems working hours that suited Raymond.'

Francis! That big meddling bastard Francis, pretending to be sympathetic, sticking his fat chef's paws into everything. He'd never mentioned anything about the idea to me. And nor had she, for that matter. I looked forward to seeing her at work: it was the only thing that now made bartending at Delauncey's bearable. Without her presence there, all the point drained out of my day.

'What business is it of his where you work?' I said, sourly.

There were pictures of a Russian cat circus on television: a grey tabby was walking across a trembling tightrope while spectators cheered it on.

'For God's sake, Jacky, he was just being nice!' Eve shouted suddenly. 'I've gone and got a new job. When most women get new jobs, their boyfriend takes them out somewhere to celebrate. But I don't even expect that much. You could even just say something like 'I'm glad for you' or 'Well done' and I'd be happy. But you sit there, staring at the TV. You're locked in your own little world, with your mysterious scars and your own bloody secret thoughts. You don't care what happens to me, or if you do you don't show it. Tell me why I should care what happens to you?'

She stopped, a little shocked by the force with which she had spoken. I looked at her white face, still pale with anger. When she said that about the scars she had looked almost nervous for a split second, as though shocked by her own readiness to wound. For a moment I felt sorry for her, but the feeling was drowned in a fresh wave of rage. I did care what happened to her. The truth was, I cared too much. She could hurt me just with a slight inflection of her voice. I had bought her flowers only the day before: they stood in a tall blue vase across the room, with their stupid yellow heads nodding at my stupidity. The sight of them inflamed me with fury at what a fool I was to love someone so selfish, what a blundering clown to go trailing around after her with my absurd floral offerings. I might as well have worn a snap-on red nose and a greasepaint tear.

If she had been just a friend telling me about a job, I could have roared, 'Fantastic news', and bought drinks all round like the beery life-and-soul of the party she seemed to want. But not *this* sudden abandonment, from her, brandished without any warning.

'If that's the way you want it,' I said stiffly. I got up and picked up my coat.

'What are you doing now?' she said.

'I'm going home,' I said. 'Why should you care what I'm doing?'

As I turned to leave, I stumbled over a pile of newspapers. Raymond came stealthily out of his room, a watchful cat creeping from behind a row of bins.

'Where are you going?' he said.

'I'm going home,' I said quietly.

'Why are you going? It's early,' he said. 'We were going to play Monopoly.'

His reasonable voice made me feel sad and ashamed.

'I know we were, son,' I said. 'But something happened. We'll do that another day.'

Eve watched me from the sofa, her face stiff and cold, eyebrows raised. I shut the door behind me very, very gently, because I wanted to slam it so badly. No, not slam: I wanted to rip it off the hinges, smash it into tiny little pieces and set fire to the pile of broken shards that remained.

I waited at the bus stop for long enough to tell two beggars — both a few years older than me, one fat and boozy, looking like a rotten acorn in his beanie hat, and one with the stretched, hollow look of a heroin addict — that no, I didn't have any spare cash. Then I smoked precisely two and a half cigarettes, inhaling deeply and frequently, before the red double-decker finally trundled into view, travelling at the speed of a tricycle pedalled by a fat and lazy child. It took forever, winding through King's Cross and the pub-ridden thick of Islington and down into Dalston, with its African hair salons and Caribbean fruit shops.

It was one of those autumn nights when everyone looks pinched and sad, defeated by the city, as if the Tube delays and the exhaust fumes have nestled into every bag and wrinkle on their faces. The only places with any warmth were the African barber shops, still lit up for business. A barber was razoring a man's hair and telling him a joke at the same time: they were both laughing. There were a couple of half-full beer bottles sitting in front of the mirror. I thought how nice it would be to go in and get my hair cut and have a beer with them there too, but I felt too white. I looked every time I went past on the bus, but I'd never seen a white person in there yet.

Maybe no one would care about me being white, and the barber would just talk away as normal. Or maybe the clientele wouldn't like it much. No, there would probably just be a moment of silence if I went in, and then everyone would be very polite, waiting for the stranger to get his hair cut and leave so they could relax again. The more I thought about it, the more alone I felt.

I got off the bus, stopped and bought two Fruit Grain Crunch bars and a bottle of water in the all-night grocer's, and let myself into the Whartons' house. The television was going full blast and they didn't hear me come in. I walked all the way up to my room at the top of the house. It was cold here, but quiet. I took off my shoes, got into bed with my clothes on and lay there on the iron bed facing the wall, with its patches of cream paint peeling delicately like a child's sunburn. When I pressed my cheek next to the cool of the wall, I shut my eyes. After a few minutes I opened up one of the bars and ate it, breaking off chunks and pushing them in past my teeth. It was like swallowing little clods of crumbly earth, with seeds mixed in. I saved the other one for another time. It was almost good to be here, cocooned in sadness, answerable to nobody. There's no emotion so reliable as loneliness. It turns up bang on time and promises never to let you go. For the first time in a while, I felt safe.

18

I didn't see her for a month. For two days she was still working at Delauncey's, but not on the same shifts as me. Maybe she had specially organised that in order to avoid me: the thought made me feel sick. Then she moved to Harrigan's just as she had said. I didn't try to get in touch. Every memory of her was a knife turning: she had such soft skin.

'Are you still seeing Eve?' Francis asked one evening while I was organising the bar before the customers came in. He was hanging up his designer cashmere coat with the falsely innocent expression of a man who had just watched you back your car into a lamp-post and then walked over to enquire if the journey had gone well. I didn't really know what to say: a 'yes' or a 'no' could cause equal amounts of mischief, in their different ways. I stared at him as if I couldn't quite remember who he was.

He sighed sympathetically. 'Well, you wouldn't be the first to come a cropper there.'

I wanted to punch him so that the flesh on his complacent face went rippling in all directions. More than that, I wanted to know what he meant.

'A cropper?'

'I knew her boyfriend Steve, the one who went off to Canada. She used to do his head in with her moods. He couldn't make her out at all.

181

Once he put his fist through a plate-glass window, she had wound him up so much.'

I was stung on her behalf. 'Well, a fat lot of use he was. He was a headcase. He went off to Canada and left her in the lurch with Raymond to look after. Never writes or sends any money either.'

Francis answered in a conciliatory voice, like someone smoothing down an over-excited child: 'I'm not saying he was right, Jacky. Steve was a bit of a nutcase. Just saying that she wasn't Miss Easy-Going herself.'

'Yeah? Well you can fuck off,' I said, 'because it's not your business.' My arms were shaking: I went back to replacing the empty Gordon's gin bottle and didn't meet his eye. Francis looked exhilarated. He savoured an angry reaction like the first mouthful of one of his bloody juicy steaks.

'Still smitten,' he said, lighting up a cigarette as he walked into the kitchen, before breaking into a few bars of 'Who's Sorry Now?' I had to hand it to him: he was a wind-up merchant par excellence. He would have loved it if I'd really gone for him, and we'd had a big punch-up over his pristine stainless steel worktops, spilling blood on the chopping boards. That would have been his version of male bonding: sharing an Armagnac together afterwards as he gave me ice cubes for my black eye and lectured me about the best way to throw a right hook. My version of bonding would have been sticking his sagging chef's arse to his work bench with a medium-thick layer of superglue. I made a mental note to

182

do it on the day I left for good, with no forwarding address.

Maybe I would go home to Belfast for a week to think things over. I could stay in a hotel in the city centre, and get Phyllis and Titch to come and meet me. I would take them presents as a surprise: a couple of comedy videos for Titch, and a jumper from Marks & Spencer for Phyllis. She loved Marks & Spencer with a quiet passion, I had noticed, always speaking of it with an unmistakable note of reverence as if it were church. The company had kept a store open in Belfast city centre right the way through the Troubles, when others shrank away, and for Phyllis it had become a touch-stone of glorious normality. But I felt I didn't belong in its enveloping cosiness, like a mourner who had accidentally strolled into a wedding.

I thought of buying Eve some chocolates, but then I remembered that I was probably someone she would prefer to forget. I had a sudden picture of Eve's mum energetically lecturing her about getting involved with yet another bad bet, while Eve stared at the floor. I hadn't met Eve's mum yet, but Eve had told her about me on the way to the agonies of a formal introduction.

Still, there was a whole other reality out there, in which men washed the car on Sundays and talked passionately about the wisdom of upgrading their sound system. And they never seemed to question what the point of it all was — or did they, now and then when they had time to think?

When I watched television alone, once or

twice a week when the Whartons finally trundled out for a few drinks, the feeling would come to me during the advertisements that I was an alien in this society. I began ignoring the programmes, but I couldn't stop watching the ads, flicking back and forth between them like a spy absorbing the mysterious rules of another country. I was trying to work out how the wider world thought people ought to behave: innocently greedy for ever more stuff, it seemed, eager to inspire envy, touchingly exhilarated by a successful white wash at a low temperature. When I heard the Whartons fumbling at the door, I would quickly turn over and pretend I'd been engrossed in a film.

And what do you do if none of it applies to you: if you happen to look really odd — which I didn't at least, apart from a few scars — or there is just never anyone in an advertisement who lives even slightly the way you live, an adult orphan renting a single room with a funny old couple who like the television on too loud?

Books didn't make me feel the same way television did, and I read all the time, up there in the bedroom with the rain spattering on the windowpane and the distant hum of noise from two storeys down. There were plenty of men in books who lived at least a little bit like me, and even seemed to feel the way I did some of the time — drifting and half meaningless — men like that fella in *The Stranger* by Camus or Raskolnikov in *Crime and Punishment*. Once I had that thought, I immediately regretted it and wanted to chop it down as if it had never come sauntering into my mind, because the thing that those characters had in common of course was that they ended up murdering someone.

★ ★ ★

I would be lying if I pretended that I hadn't thought about killing McGee. I never forgot about him for more than a few hours, and then he would come sliding back into my thoughts like an eel disturbing calm water. At least a couple of nights a week I lay in bed with my arms neatly tucked underneath the blue-striped, fraying counterpane so I couldn't see the raised unpleasantness of the scars, and — just before I drifted off to sleep — I would think of all the different ways that I could do it. Sometimes this calmed me down, like a sleepy little lullaby of revenge, and sometimes I had to stop thinking about it because it inflamed my nerves too much.

I thought about tricking him into drinking a pint of beer full of crushed sleeping pills and then pushing him into the Lagan so that he sank like a stone and never came up; or monkeying with the brakes on his car and watching him go skeetering across the road slap bang into a brick wall; or binding his arms and legs together very tightly before turning on the gas in his kitchen, sealing the door and then walking out to inhale the clear, crisp, sweet air. That wasn't the way feuds were usually settled in Belfast: it was usually with a bullet or a pipe bomb, but I didn't have a gun and I wasn't a pipe bomb type of person. I didn't want to meddle around with explosives and wires and end up blowing half my own arm off. I preferred something sneakier.

There's something unsettling about looking into another person's dreams of revenge. It's like taking a peek into the friendly neighbour's living room and seeing all the rubbish from the previous year strewn across the carpet. Revenge squats there among the steaming entrails of unfinished business, a clump of the bad stuff in a corner of the human heart.

But I won't say sorry for it. What bothered me about those characters in *The Stranger* and *Crime and Punishment*, if I have to admit it — what made me want to button up my overcoat, check my watch and say 'thanks fellas, I've enjoyed your company, but I've got to be somewhere else in five minutes' — was that they killed people who didn't fully deserve it: that Arab on the beach who hadn't done much to Meursault yet apart from flash his knife, and that mouldy oul moneylender who was only trying to get by herself, scraping a living from one of those freezing Russian flats, not to mention her harmless half-sister.

I was contemplating killing someone who did deserve it, though. In fact, I couldn't really think of anyone who deserved it more than McGee. There were times when I thought that I could never really rest until he was gone for good.

Anyway, when I mused on killing him, I wasn't thinking about it quite in terms of cold-blooded premeditated murder and all the other ponderous phrases that you usually find hanging out on the street corner with the word 'defendant'. I liked to do it in the muscular, dispassionate words that I had culled from crime novels, descriptions that were abstract and humorously blunt at the same time. I thought about how I would just be rubbing him out, cancelling or erasing him, taking him down, and how — after he had gone — the world would be a better, cleaner place, like a page from which an ugly blot had just been delicately removed, painted over as if with Tipp-Ex. That could be his obituary, a headline in the *Belfast Telegraph* that read: McGee, One Of Nature's Worst Mistakes, Was Yesterday Cleared Up. Of course, I wasn't really going to do it, was I?

19

When people in films are having personal difficulties, they tend to throw themselves into their work. I tried to throw myself into mine, but it was too shallow: I kept accidentally surfacing. I remembered that fella who used to work in Murdie's bar, who went off and got a job on a cruise ship, and I thought that maybe if I saved up a bit of money as a nest egg I could do the same thing. In some of the dreams I had Eve with me, but those ones I crumpled up and threw to the corner of my mind.

Then in between cruise ship jobs I could go off travelling with just a few belongings to all those countries I had only read about in books: Mexico and India and Thailand and all the other sunny, busy, glittering places with temples and snake charmers and tricksters and carnivals, where you didn't need a whole lot of cash to see weird and stupendous things and have a good time.

The world was a whole lot bigger than Northern Ireland, I told myself, with its drizzle and cramped pubs and that dank little feud that has flickered for centuries like a soggy peat fire, filling the air with its damp, choking smoke. It was bigger than London too, with its traffic that never budged and its sour-faced, busy people and pocket-emptying prices and rip-off tourist pubs with indifferent roast beef dinners and watery drinks and women who pretended to like you and then didn't care if they never saw you again.

I began to work very hard in Delauncey's: I even learned how to make a string of new cocktails from a book that I had bought myself, and wrote their names up with chalk on the blackboard behind my head. I was bursting with initiatives, like one of those model employees from the how-to-get-ahead books who ends up owning the company. Mrs Delaney noticed how I was always bang on time for my shift — or even a few minutes early — and polishing glasses with a perky smile. She began complimenting me on my industry, and giving me little conspiratorial glances throughout the day as though she and I were the only ones in there who really under-stood the meaning of good old-fashioned hard work. Like most rich hippies, she had a staunchly authoritarian heart. Sometimes she complained about the waiters and waitresses to me — their lateness, their laziness, the stains on their white shirts, their 'simple lack of professionalism', as she liked to put it — but I made a point of never joining in. Nobody likes a snitch, not even the boss who's buttering the snitch up to be a snitch.

The tips started stacking up, along with the salary and the overtime money, and I wasn't spending much. I got paid in cash and kept it all in my suitcase at the Whartons'. Week by week, I watched the small pile of notes grow like a grubby but well-fed little pet. Then sometimes I would divide it up with elastic bands and chivvy selected bundles to different hidey-holes in the room. No one was going to steal it, of course: the

189

Whartons were honest people and unusually lacking in curiosity. They accepted me as a simple and unremarkable fact of life now, like the rain or muddy footprints in the hall. But I liked the administrative business of counting and hiding the notes. It was as if I were tied up in a secret conspiracy with myself. And I enjoyed just looking at the money, contained there in its squat packets. All sorts of possibilities were lurking in it, silently multiplying like good bacteria.

★　★　★

A month after I had walked out of Eve's flat, I bumped into her on the street on the way back from work. Something made me lift my eyes from the squashed Coke cans and sandwich wrappers strewn across the pavement and there she was, wearing a new black coat belted tightly at the waist, and a distracted expression. The shock of her quiet beauty hit me like a glass of ice-water in the face. She saw me out of the corner of her eye a second before she passed me by. We stopped and stared at each other. For a moment I forgot to be angry. What had I been angry about anyway? I couldn't really remember. Oh yes, I had been angry because she got a new job without telling me first. Was that it? Was that all? What an eejit I was.

It filled me with such elation to see her again that my head swam, and all the words floated away from me.

'Do you want to go somewhere for a coffee?' I said.

'I've got to be at work in twenty minutes,' she said.

My heart fell.

'But it doesn't matter if I'm ten minutes late,' she said.

In the café she ordered coffee and a slab of coffee cake from a sleepy-eyed waitress with two limp hanks of blonde hair. It arrived surprisingly quickly, and after a couple of mouthfuls she pushed the plate over to me.

'You have some,' she said, and handed me her fork.

I took a mouthful, and then another. It was fantastic cake, bittersweet and moist, with a fudgy buttercream that slid recklessly all over the inside of my mouth. I could have eaten that cake all day, and then fallen asleep with a wedge of it jammed in my mouth.

'That's the best cake I've ever eaten,' I said.

'I know,' she said.

'How do you know?' I said. 'I might have eaten a better one and forgotten about it, or I might even be lying.'

'I can see from the expression on your face that it's the best one,' she said. 'And it's the best one I've ever eaten too, so it's probably also the best one you've ever eaten.'

'How do I know that there isn't an even better cake out there in some pastry shop, waiting for me to go out and find it?' I said.

'There can't be,' she said. 'If this tastes like the best, now, then it just is the best.'

'Have you eaten a lot of cake?' I said.

'Not that much, but enough to recognise a

really good one when it comes along,' she said.

'Me too,' I said. 'I mean, I don't wake up in the night thinking about cake. I don't dream about cake. But when I taste a top-notch cake, I hope I have the humility to recognise it for what it is.'

She was starting to laugh. I took another forkful, then passed the plate back over to her.

'I feel sorry,' she said, eating, with sadly downcast eyes, 'for all the little people out there in the world who will never get to taste this cake.' Instead of crocodile tears, she wore two tiny cake-crumbs on her cheek like decorative moles.

'Those little people will go to their graves never knowing what cake could really be,' I told her.

While I was talking, she was nodding and methodically demolishing what remained of the cake. Finally, I looked down at the plate: she had left me a tiny, carefully crafted square, as if designed for an insect's birthday celebrations.

'That's for you,' she said.

'Is that all?' I said.

'Do you think you deserve more?' she asked. I felt a faint cooling of the temperature. She checked her watch and suddenly drained the last of her coffee in a businesslike way.

'No,' I said.

She started shrugging her coat on.

'Can I see you tomorrow after work?' I said.

'I'm working late tomorrow. I'll see you on Friday.'

'What time?'

'Eight. In here. If you're not here I'll know you can't be bothered.'

She leaned over and gave me a brief kiss on

the cheek: she smelled of lemons. I thought of all
the times she had kissed me on the mouth and
suddenly felt a sadness worse than anything I
had ever felt, apart from when Big Jacky died.

'I love you,' I said quietly, staring at the ant's
cake.

She looked at me with a funny, half-stern
expression.

'Good,' she said. 'Maybe I love you back.'

I watched her go out the door and turn right
into the dwindling afternoon, down into a
crammed street of expensive restaurants and
dirty-plush hostess bars, wincing against the
wind as she turned up her collar and then
disappeared from sight. I speared the ant's cake
delicately, on the end of one fork's prong so it
wouldn't break. It tasted briefly wonderful, like
swallowing the best split second you ever had.

★　★　★

I woke up so happy the next morning. The
autumn sunshine came through the curtain and
stroked my eyelids, wheedling them open. I felt
full of possibilities and second chances.

Ten minutes later, the clock-radio clicked on
and a familiar voice flooded the room. It was
Brian Nixon, the official spokesman for McGee's
lot. He was always on the radio and television
now since the ceasefires, blathering magnanimously about 'the two traditions'.

The English media loved him because he
made a lot of his Protestant working-class
credentials. He spoke in a bass voice using

193

too-complicated words stuck in slightly the wrong places, but they were prepared to give him points for trying. They thought they had discovered an authentic curiosity, The Talking Belfast Prod — a new thing, since most of us were reliably taciturn in the face of interrogation.

Nixon had regretful blue eyes and a heavy, blurred jawline, but then sometimes he'd get a bit blustery and muscular, just enough to hint that he was the sort of guy who hung out with hardened gunmen. You could tell that the interviewers enjoyed that even more. They went briefly malleable, like an East End glamour-bird offered a drink by one of the Krays.

He didn't sound that authentic to me, though: he had picked up his style of talking from the IRA spokesmen, who used it to remarkable effect, and the two sides were at it all the time, oozing their way across the airwaves, competing for who could sound the most emollient.

Liam Blake was one of the IRA men who organised that notable day of carnage in the early 1970s when more than twenty different bombs exploded right across Belfast, a sunny afternoon suddenly darkened by grey smoke, flying shards of metal and spurting crimson rain. Shoppers ran screaming from one explosion into the path of the next. A family friend of Murdie's was killed that day, and one evening at our house he started talking about it, normally enough at first, until he said: 'Och he was so funny, that wee lad. He could do these impressions of anybody, he could do — ' but the last word seemed to stick in his throat and he stopped very abruptly. He got up and walked quickly over to the window and stood there stiffly for a while, turning his head away from us and staring out at the street. After a bit Big Jacky got up and poured them both a drink and they began talking about the football. I had wanted to know more — in which part of the city, how exactly it happened — but I didn't ask him about it again.

Blake, however, now spoke almost exclusively in a voice polished with piety, a thoughtful social worker issuing case reports. It did my head in just to hear it. Between them the assorted paramilitaries talked so gently that everyone was thoroughly deafened, and hardly anyone could hear the swish of baseball bats up alleyways at all.

Forget all that, I thought. I turned the radio off and got up. I would take a shower, clean my teeth, go to work, see Eve, my heart sang. Tomorrow I would write to Phyllis.

Twenty minutes later, on my way out the door, I glimpsed a letter with my name on it in familiar handwriting, beaming from a pile of bills on the beige mat: Phyllis had written to me. I tucked it into my coat like a warm promise to read on the bus. It was a cold day, but the sky was a pale, icy blue and the sun bounced off the pavement. The leaves on the hedges shimmered. My coat was exactly thick enough to keep the wind from bothering my body, and I felt an uncomplicated joy in being alive.

Once I had sat down on the top deck, I scythed Phyllis's envelope open with my thumb and pulled out the letter. It read:

Dear Jacky,

I am sorry but I have some terrible news. Titch has killed himself. He did it two days ago, hanged himself in his room. His poor mother came home and found him and called the ambulance but it was too late to save him, he had already passed away. He had been very down as the weekend before there was a pot of paint thrown over their front door and he said to his mother he was sure they were going to come and get him again. His mother is in an awful state I have been doing everything I can for her, getting her shopping and helping to sort out the arrangements. He is going to be buried on Monday, don't you be tempted to come home, you have had enough trouble already, but we all know you will be thinking of him. He was awful fond of you as you know and never stopped asking how you were doing,
Love, Your Aunt Phyllis

Titch. I got off the bus at the next stop, and walked back to the Whartons' with my heart beating very fast. Titch dead. The enormous shot of pain hit me like the injection of a drug.

My course of action suddenly seemed very clear, as if a hazy world had become a place of pure, sharp lines. Two things were about to happen. I was going to go back to Belfast and kill McGee, and when I had done that I would go to Titch's grave and lay a wreath in front of his headstone. Then I would leave for good.

*   ★   ★

From the Whartons' house, I called into work. The manager, Hassan, answered the phone, and I heard my own voice saying: 'Hassan, I'm so sorry. My mother has just had a heart attack and the doctors say it's very serious. I'll have to go back to Ireland to see her, and I might be a week or so. I'm sorry about this but there's nothing I can do.' I sounded breathless as I spoke, but not for the reason I was telling Hassan.

I could tell he was dismayed: it meant a couple of days of difficulty for him, trying to find a suitable barman to stand in for that length of time. But he had courteous manners, and he was not the sort of man to take a mother's illness lightly. After all, I had never missed a day before. I had noticed that the well-being of his own large, extended family weighed unusually heavily on him. He seemed permanently oppressed by a father-in-law's medical bills or a cousin's interminable legal studies in Morocco. His face, above a forcefully starched collar of blinding whiteness, always looked crumpled and wearied.

'That's terrible news, Jacky,' he said, after a brief pause of reckoning. 'Don't worry, we'll sort something out here. I do hope your mother recovers. Give us a call in three or four days and let us know how she's doing.'

'Of course I will, Hassan. Sorry about this.'

'No, no, I'm so sorry about your mother.'

For a second, I felt bad for lying about my mother's life-threatening illness. I had never done that before: it was pretty low. But Titch was dead. And then I thought the reason that most people worry about using something so terrible as an excuse is because they fear that perhaps their mother really will die soon, as fate's punishment for lying.

My mother was already dead, however, and it had happened to me before I ever thought about lying. Any debt I owed to fate was pre-paid in full almost before I could talk. The more I thought about it, the more I realised that I could, with every justification, use the excuse of my mother nearly dying — or, indeed, having just died — again and again throughout my entire life, until I became far too old myself for it to carry any credibility. Fate had handed other people all the benefits that came from a real live mother, and coolly denied them to me, like some hard-faced cloakroom attendant who lost my only coat on a freezing night and never said sorry. Why should I also turn down the few famished advantages that could flow from bad luck?

I briefly wondered, though, what my mother would think of me killing McGee, and felt a pang of guilt. She had probably had high hopes for me: Big Jacky said she used to sing me to sleep every night. I pushed her out of my head. I had had a long run of bad luck. She had died, Big Jacky had died, and now Titch. My existence so far had been like some bloody Shakespearean play, littered with corpses.

That run would surely end with the eradication of McGee, and then a new, cleaner life could start for me, a lucky life with love in it and maybe success too. If I let the chance to end things slither away from me now, the thought of my own weakness would chafe at me for ever.

The thing was, I needed to do what must be done quickly, before the anger that gave me the energy ebbed and I started to think too much. The Whartons knew that my mother had died years ago, so for them it was Titch that I reheated and hauled back to the border between life and death. I scribbled a note that read: 'Good friend seriously ill, have had to go to Belfast. Back in a week or so.' I left it on their kitchen table, anchored by a coffee mug. Then I packed some things in a bag — underwear, toothbrush, a suit, and the majority of my worn, filthy-soft little bundles of cash — and headed out into the street towards the coach for Scotland. One thought thudded round my head, almost too big to be absorbed into my bloodstream. Titch was dead.

20

Belfast

How do you shop for a murder you haven't yet planned? I was sitting on the neatly made bed of a Belfast hotel room, a brightly lit people container shaped exactly like a box. The planners had fitted the maximum number of these small, profitable boxes into the enormous concrete box that constituted the building itself. In one hand I held a piece of lined paper and in the other a pencil. The only words written on the paper were: *rubber gloves*.

There were several cast-iron principles for carrying out a successful killing, I had decided. The first was obvious: that nothing I did should arouse any suspicion. Above all, I had to appear very normal, which was difficult because I was feeling so strange. I'd sort of lost perspective on what normal meant, but — seen dimly from a long way away — I thought perhaps it might manifest itself as a sort of cheerful blokeishness. If placed under any stress, I decided, I would try to exude a mild, friendly laddishness, the way a cuttlefish squirts out ink to blind its adversaries.

One of the chief obstacles to organising a murder is that you suddenly realise just how pointlessly nosey other people are about your most mundane business. Under ordinary circumstances their inquisitiveness would be tolerable, but when a dark intention is already planted in your brain every gasbag taxi driver or shop assistant is transformed into a potential police witness. You can picture them giving their statement to the investigating officer, swollen with self-importance at the drama of being asked, brow furrowed with the strain of remembering, until — from somewhere in the slop of their memory — they finally dredge up some nugget of detail to sink you for ever.

Still, I wasn't quite ready for an interrogation when I checked into the hotel and the girl at the wood-veneered reception desk downstairs suddenly said, with an expression of benignly professional concern, 'Here for business or pleasure?'

She was in her mid-twenties, rake-thin with resolutely over-plucked eyebrows and reddish hair swept back into a sleek ponytail. A laminated name badge identified her as 'Marie'. Why ask? I thought. It was the most anonymous of all hotels, surely, designed for the budget businessman and the economy traveller, bristling with trouser presses and stripped of room service. But they had probably told her at the training course to be bright, to ask customers perky questions in order to show that you cared. Part of me wanted to retort sharply 'Neither!' or 'Business!' but people pick up on irritation and it sticks in their minds like a sharp stone.

'Pleasure, I suppose,' I said. 'I'm over for a friend's wedding, and then I'm going to take a few extra days to see some relatives.'

She looked up quickly, more keenly interested

than I had anticipated, and said, 'Where's the wedding?'

Indeed, where was the wedding? What a stupid thing to say in the first place. I had forgotten that women love to talk about weddings. It's like casually mentioning to a gang of small children that you're going to visit a chocolate factory tomorrow and expecting that to be the last word.

I scrunched up my face and hid my eyes with my hand in mock-shame, buying extra time. Scatty me.

'I haven't looked at the invitation again since I came over,' I said. 'I think they're getting married in the City Hall, and then the reception's in a Belfast hotel, so it'll be within taxi distance, wherever it is. But I hope I've got the day right, at least.'

'Just as well I asked!' she beamed, buoyed up by my masculine disorganisation.

I gave her a smile as wide as Belfast Lough, and as icy cold inside: 'Just as well you did. I'll dig it out from the bottom of my case and have a look.'

'And will none of your relatives put you up?' she said.

She was getting a wee bit flirtatious now, as I stood there filling in some endless, detailed form about the room. Name, date of birth, residence, favourite colour, make and style of underpants, approximate rate of hair loss, last time you can remember eating tofu, views on the afterlife. I wrote in a fake name: John Mason. Christ, why had I done that: wouldn't it have been better just to be me, after all — officially, at least — I had nothing to hide. Too late. It would look weird if I scribbled it out now. John Mason, who the hell was he, what kind of name was that? How many more multi-headed questions were going to fly like rogue missiles out of that thin, magenta-smeared slot of a mouth?

'Och, no, the houses are all full,' I said. 'I've got a bit of work to do as well, and you know how it is if you try to get anything done in anyone else's house.'

'Get a bit of peace here, eh?'

Thank God she hadn't asked what kind of work I did. What kind of work did some eejit called John Mason do anyway? I had only chosen the name because it sounded solid.

'Yes, a bit of peace is just what I need.'

My nerves were pretty frayed when I finally hurried upstairs with my bag, and closed the door behind me. I stared for a while at the sickly reproduction of Monet's water lilies that was hanging on the wall in a blue plastic frame. Poor Monet, I thought, endlessly shrunk and copied into such blandness.

Then I got out the paper and started to write the list of things I needed, beginning with *rubber gloves*. After a few minutes, I crossed out the word 'rubber' twice, and wrote in 'leather' instead. I didn't want to leave any fingerprints for the police to find, but I wasn't going to kill McGee wearing a pair of yellow Marigolds, as if I had popped in to do the washing-up and then changed my mind and suddenly murdered a man because the water wasn't hot enough yet to really get the grease off the pans.

Underneath 'gloves', I wrote: *find out where wedding reception is.* I knew she would ask me again. She'd dug up her wee bit of information like a terrier, and she wasn't going to let up until she'd tugged out some more. Tug, tug. Who was the bride? Was there a decent buffet? I bet she even knew someone who was going to the very wedding I was going to pretend to go to.

Maybe I'd have to murder Marie as well, I thought, and flatten her in the trouser press. I laughed for a bit at that, and I started thinking about how best to destroy the list once I had written everything down and memorised it.

Some time later I called Hassan's mobile phone, knowing he wouldn't answer in the evening rush, and left a short message telling him of my mother's death. Then I ate a banana and a stale bread roll I had in my bag, cleaned my teeth and fell asleep.

★ ★ ★

In the middle of the night I woke up with the sensation of falling through the pitch-black air, and I remembered that I was supposed to meet Eve in the coffee shop at eight o'clock the night before. I pictured her sitting waiting for me, the cast of disappointment slowly settling on her face as the waitress circled the pickings of the dead evening like a skinny blonde buzzard.

Eventually Eve would have requested the bill and walked out. How long would she have waited for me — half an hour, an hour? The knowledge that I'd let her down kept stabbing me, but I suffocated the regret with the thought that she was better off without me, even if she didn't know it. I could never go back to her now anyway, all messy and blood-stained after what I was about to do.

★　★　★

On the coach that dragged itself out of the grey, clogged suburbs of London and way up to the fields and craggy heathery patches of Scotland — punctuated with tidy wee flowerbedded towns and stone kirks — and on to the wind-battered, salty ferry port of Stranraer and over to home, I had thought about Titch. He was the closest thing to a brother I'd ever had. You don't choose your brothers, after all, and I hadn't ever chosen Titch. He was just always there.

After my mother died, Big Jacky had got friendly with Titch's mother, through chatting at the newsagent's, I suppose. As the two jagged halves of broken couples, they had sometimes helped each other out with looking after one another's children. I don't think there was ever any romance between them — certainly, the thought had never occurred to me at the time — but then there were vast tranches of Big Jacky's interior life that were unknown to me.

I used to go to Titch's house after school, or whenever Big Jacky had to be somewhere else, and we'd mess around together in the yard for hours with toy cars or magic putty or anything Titch's mum could come up with to stop us from yowling that we were bored. Sometimes I'd stay the night at his house. She'd put us in the room with the big double bed, mumble the protective incantation of the Lord's Prayer and then kiss us both good night. I always loved the bit when she tucked us in and whispered 'sleep tight, don't let the bugs bite' before switching off the light and plunging us into darkness. For that, I was even willing not to make a fuss about Titch snoring as he lay on his back, starfished in his blue pyjamas, although sometimes I would close in his arms and shove him hard over on to his side.

The thing is, I knew him so well. I knew that he was lazy, and that he sometimes stole things he fancied from shops, although he never took so much as a piece of chewing gum from me without asking. He had been very greedy since he was little. By the time he was three his mum had to put all the biscuits up in a cupboard high out of his reach, because otherwise he would wolf them all down when she was distracted with cleaning the house. She told me that she used to come back downstairs to see a trail of empty packets and the telltale pink pastel crumbs of Fondant Fancies on the floor, and Titch sprawled out on the sofa quietly enjoying some kind of monumental sugar rush.

It was only later, when he was about twelve, that he started the shoplifting, and even then it wasn't because he really wanted the things he took. It was the only real grab for independence that he had. He was a lot slower than the rest of us, and a little part of him knew that he was never going to join the Foreign Legion, or go hitchhiking round Ireland on his own, or chat up beautiful girls on holiday in French campsites and lure them laughing into his tent. He would never have put it exactly like that, of course, but he sensed it all the same. He was so close to his mother, so dependent on her bottomless love for him, that if he hadn't occasionally practised some minor subversions to proclaim his difference from her he would simply have melted into her and ceased to exist.

The stealing grieved his mum, who was so honest you could have given her a million pounds in cash to look after and found it untouched a year later. She tried hard to stop him from doing it, and eventually — after tears and recriminations — she realised that it wasn't going to stop, and came to a practical arrangement with the understanding Mrs Hackett, whereby Titch's mum regularly paid off in full whatever losses Titch incurred. And so even Titch's secret rebellion became part of a scheme quietly regulated and operated by his mother, although it was rarely spoken of at all. I sometimes wondered if that was why he had tried to nick stuff from old McGee in the first place: to start his own game afresh.

He could be generous too, though. There was the time he had saved up his pocket money for weeks to buy me a birthday present, a personal stereo I had wanted so that I could listen to my music tapes without bothering Big Jacky. I remember opening the parcel, badly wrapped in blue shiny paper with about half a roll of Sellotape securing it. It was my fifteenth birthday, and Titch was watching me closely, his pale blue eyes moving from my hands opening the parcel to my face and back again, as though he couldn't choose which to settle on. The second the paper fell away, and I glimpsed what was inside, he said breathlessly, 'I bought it I didn't nick it,' because he wanted me to understand that it was a proper present, which had involved planning and self-sacrifice on his part, the very qualities that his mother and I were regularly berating him for not having.

I couldn't even bring myself to think about Titch's mother. Her grief was too vast to contemplate, a Milky Way of pain. He was the only one she had. I could think about Titch, though, so long as I didn't dwell on the dull mechanics of how he must have patiently planned his own death. It had shown such efficiency and determination, qualities his mother and I had never suspected he had. How much fear and despair had it taken to forge this strong, alien capability in him? How long had these emotions burned away in him, unremarked or smoothed over with phrases about him being 'still a bit down'?

He must have realised in the end that his protectors couldn't shield him, that the forces outside were stronger than either of us. He must have understood that when his attackers shoved his frightened mother to one side to drag him out of the house, and again when he saw my battered face staring up at him from a hospital pillow. When he thought they were coming back for him, I suppose the only thing left for him to do was to go somewhere they couldn't reach him.

I hadn't been able to protect him, no. The next best thing was to avenge him. He was going to be buried on Monday, and I knew I couldn't go. To create some fitting symmetry, perhaps, I had decided that the night before his funeral I would murder McGee.

★ ★ ★

Once, when Big Jacky had been to some church jumble sale, he brought me back a job lot of Agatha Christie detective stories. I was about twelve years old, and I started working my way through them very methodically. I used to try and guess who the murderer was shortly after being introduced to the entire cast of characters. It took a lot of will-power not to flick through to the end and find out straight away if I was right.

At first, I would always guess the most obvious person, the one with the creepy smile and a long-held grudge and a touch too much brilliantine on their hair. Then — once I realised that it was never them — I started guessing the least obvious instead, the real trouper who was busy making all the funeral arrangements and had been a loyal friend to the deceased through thick and thin.

It usually wasn't that one either, though. She was sly enough, Agatha Christie, and the killer was mostly some character who had just wandered in stage left, someone you actually hadn't thought about that much but considered pretty okay if you did.

In real life, of course, the killer often really is the most obvious person, the one with a motive the size of a skyscraper. That's why most genuine murder hunts end up catching The Last Person to See The Victim Alive, or the Person Who Stands To Gain Thousands of Pounds From The Life Insurance Policy. Most fat-bellied, case-hardened detectives already know that life is much simpler and killers are more brutishly transparent than in an Agatha Christie novel.

I pictured the police interviewing the Whartons, and realised that they would say about me, with no ill intent, 'Well, he mostly kept himself to himself.' I really did. That wasn't good: I was already a case-notes cliché, and I hadn't even done anything yet. Perhaps I should have invested more energy in appearing friendly and outgoing when I had the chance. It was too late to change now. It would seem very odd if I returned to London from my good friend's hospital bed having been transformed into a compulsive extrovert. It would look incongruous, as though I had been elated by the misfortune of others.

It wasn't ever going to get as far as the Whartons, though. If you imagined McGee's murder as an Agatha Christie novel — briefly overlooking the fact that she preferred to write about the destruction of retired English colonels and genteel lady librarians rather than psychotic Loyalist paramilitaries — then the character I wanted to be was one who never appears in the book at all. He is never talked about, he is never graciously introduced to the house party in the drawing room, and so he never figures in any of M. Poirot's magnificently complicated Belgian calculations: he can't, because he's not there.

That would mean, of course, that the murder is never solved. It couldn't be, because the readers never saw the killer, or if they did, they didn't even register his existence. It's as if at the end of the Christie novel the murderer should turn out to be a petrol-pump attendant who was never actually mentioned, but who filled up Lady Motterly's chauffeur's tank during that journey to London which merited one line on page 153. It would never happen because it would make for a rotten book, and Poirot could never explain why he had alighted upon the petrol-pump attendant in the first place. That's why it would make for such a successful crime.

The first thing I had to do was learn how to stop looking like me. The person skulking around near the scene of the murder had to appear quite different from John Mason, the cheerful, forgetful guest at a city centre hotel. I had once read an article in a Sunday supplement about how easy it was to change your appearance just by altering the shape and furniture of your face. The man pictured in the article had begun by stuffing cotton wool into his cheeks, to give himself jowls and pouches where none had previously existed. In the before and after photographs, he had turned from a trim, distinguished man to a bloke who had let himself drift to seed via the time-honoured route of readymade TV dinners and value packs of lager.

I got up early on Friday morning and crossed the hotel lobby in a hurry, to avoid any contact with nosey Marie. In a city centre café, I ordered their biggest mug of tea and a bacon and soda-bread sandwich. The tea was powerfully strong and hot, and the springy bread melted down at each bite to hit the sinewy crunch of salty, crisp bacon. For a moment I almost forgot that something terrible had happened and another was about to happen. If only I could have frozen that wonderful moment with my mouth full of bacon sandwich and hung suspended in it like a doughy chrysalis for a month. But then I remembered McGee, and the bread jarred in my fast-drying throat and made me cough.

It all looked so achingly familiar. I had missed Belfast, with its broad avenues and crammed shops full of earnest girls out shopping arm-in-arm with their mammies. I watched them in stores in Royal Avenue as they mulled over clothes intensely for minutes at a time and then rejected them with a small, haughty turn of the head, letting the scorned cloth fall back into the hanging rack.

I had missed the wee fellas on the corner near the City Hall, hawking the *Belfast Telegraph* by yelling 'Telly' in a long, strangulated howl, as though the word had been first stretched and then plaited. I had missed the bespectacled assistants in the handsome bookshops, who took enquiries very seriously and all looked as if they attended Leonard Cohen appreciation conventions in their spare time.

I couldn't enjoy the city with the same confidence I used to, though. I felt like an ex-husband tiptoeing back into the house where his former wife now lives with her thuggish, heavily armed lover. One clumsy move, one broken vase or clatter of falling cutlery, and my unwelcome presence would be advertised to all. I didn't want to bump into anyone I used to know, and have to struggle through ridiculous explanations. The sooner this business was concluded, the sooner I would seal it off tightly, like a dirty parcel headed straight for the bin. If no one else knew anything about it at all, it would be that much easier for me to dump.

★ ★ ★

I was working on a disguise, so I started off in Belfast's best joke shop, the one I used to plague Big Jacky to take me to as a child in search of plastic flies and smoke bombs. The line-up of rubber masks featured the usual suspects, Dracula and Dolly Parton, with a sprinkling of more recent favourites, Tony Blair and Bill Clinton, along with Gerry Adams and Ian Paisley as an appeal to home-grown waggery.

I chose the Clinton, because it was the only one with a tight enough elastic strap to sit right. With its red blobby nose and symbolic topping of ridged grey hair, it didn't look altogether unlike Mr Wharton. The face was creased in permanent joviality, revealing a generous spread of rubberised American teeth. I felt good when I had it on, wobbling my head from side to side like a giant puppet. It made a start.

Then I selected a wee black metal gun entitled 'The Spud Gun', designed to shoot out raw potato pellets at high speed. When I picked it up it had a surprising and pleasing weight in my hand. There was also one moustache — a luxuriant dark brown thatch — that matched my hair colour, and with some trimming it could be convincing enough. I was hunting for the moustache glue when the assistant padded up, sporting a light veneer of friendly concern on top of a well-entrenched expression of solid boredom.

'Fancy dress party?' he asked.

'Yes, tomorrow night,' I said, without elaborating. He took the items to the till and started totting up the cost. How the lies piled up. As I paid and walked away I could see him fussing over the masks with a slight frown on his face, re-hanging the Dolly Parton one at the front.

★ ★ ★

At the end of the day's shopping, I had a canvas rucksack that contained the bones of my alternative identity: the Clinton mask, the moustache and the potato gun.

In a second compartment was a baseball cap, a dark blue canvas bomber jacket, a grey sweatshirt, a pair of trainers, some balls of cotton wool, and brown-rimmed reading glasses from Boots. There were also two small cushions from the home section of a department store.

In the third was wide brown masking tape and a pair of fine leather gloves from an old-style gentleman's outfitters. The gloves were especially nice: supple, stretchy black leather, lined with silk. I caught myself regretting that they would have to be burned later on.

In the late afternoon, I stopped off at the bar of the Miller Hotel near Botanic Station and ordered myself a pint of Guinness. The barman's face had long ago settled into a comfortable grouchiness, but his manner was friendly. An idea struck me.

'Do you have many functions on here?' I said, jerking my head towards the rooms behind me.

'A couple of things every weekend,' he said. 'Weddings and work dos, stuff like that. Never ends.'

'Got one on tomorrow?' I said sympathetically.

'Aye, a big wedding reception, about 120 people. They're setting up some of the flower arrangements for it over there.' He sighed: 'The crazy money people spend on flowers.'

In the corridor outside the lounge bar I could dimly see some uniformed women reverentially carrying around small pyramids of lilies and greenery. A board outside the 'function room' bore the gold, stuck-on words 'Conway and McManus: Sat: 3pm'. That could be John Mason's wedding party, a sop to throw to Marie if necessary. I started walking back to my hotel through the late afternoon throng of chattering schoolchildren. As I was about to pass the Whistle, I ducked down a side street and took a diversion. The last thing I wanted was to bump into Murdie, or — worse still — any of his regular clientele.

★   ★   ★

I often found myself wondering whether McGee ever regretted what he had done to me and Titch. Here I was, having thought about McGee nearly every day since the beating. It seemed odd to think that I probably never entered McGee's head at all. This was a hate affair, but the dynamics were pretty much the same as those of unrequited love. As time passed my rage had fermented and thickened while McGee was free to carry on without a backward glance.

I tried not to brood on it, but I fiercely regretted the way I had lied and begged to him when I was frightened. Since a beating was coming anyway, I might as well have hung on to my dignity. The memory of how I had acted burned away at me, when I let the thought resurface. I hadn't yet realised that one of violence's slyest tricks is to make you feel dirty for having been on the wrong end of it.

I resented my preoccupation with McGee. I had never wanted someone like him in my thoughts at all. What did he think happened to us afterwards, the people he left cringing and bloodied on the ground, curled up like smashed hedgehogs? He didn't think about us, of course. We were done deals, finished business. The idea that one of us might come back to destroy him would have seemed absurd.

I pictured him sprawled out on a cushion on his living-room floor, relaxing after his gym session, watching mafia films back to back surrounded by half-drained cans of tepid beer and empty takeaway cartons as the light died outside. Over-muscled stock phrases must sit

216

around in his head, I imagined, ready to club to death any puny dissenting thought. 'That wee shit had it coming to him', 'He should have shown me some respect', 'Nobody messes with me or my family', 'Let that be a warning to any other wee fuckers trying to take the piss'.

This last phrase was the precise point, in my imagination, at which I usually walked through the door and shot McGee dead.

Except that I wasn't going to shoot him. It is difficult to get hold of a gun in London unless you hang around with gunmen, and I didn't. Any such attempt would mean involving at least two other people in my plans.

I imagined asking Francis casually, for example, 'Hey, where would I go about getting a handgun?' His nostrils used to flare excitedly at any whiff of illegality like a horse's snuffling above a ripe apple. He wouldn't have been able to get me one himself, but among his so-called 'underworld connections' he probably knew someone who could.

I couldn't bear the thought of being united with Francis in any kind of conspiracy, though. It was in his nature to blab. First he would gab to his coke buddies, excited for once to have some bona fide tale. Then, if he found out that I had actually used the gun, he would try and shed responsibility like a tight, itchy suit. One sharp query from an interested police detective and he would flood the room with wet confessions. It was clear that a real gun might create all kinds of unnecessary mess. So that's how I had ended up with the Spud Gun, and the rudiments of a plan.

21

When I got back to the hotel I hurried through the lobby in case Marie was on duty, alive with questions about my evident shopping trip. Each time I shut the bedroom door behind me and flopped on the bed I felt a rush of relief. But this time as I lay on that bedspread, staring at the Monet print, the plan was beginning to take more detailed shape, like a small, dark cloud thickening on the horizon.

It started with a dog.

I remembered a story that Big Jacky once told me, about a fella who used to bet on greyhounds, and a wee scam he had going to fix the races. The owners of the greyhounds kept their prized beasts in the backyards, monitoring their diet carefully in the run-up to a race, coddling them like fragile plants in a frost.

But the night before a race this fella and his friend would go around chucking steaks over the yard wall to the dogs they wanted to lose, and the hungry animals fell upon the gift of meat with slavering joy. Come the big day, to the bemusement of their owners, these dogs — normally flashing miracles of muscle and rippling grey silk — would toddle out of the enclosure with all the urgency of a bloke offered his third helping of Christmas pudding after the Queen's Speech.

And I remembered, too, that McGee had a

dog: a sleek, densely powerful Alsatian called Major in which he took palpable pride. Major was tethered in his yard, apart from when McGee took him on parade round the streets, inspecting the sites from which he and his da collected 'donations'.

The dog wasn't mistreated — McGee was too meticulous about it for that — but it didn't have much of a life: it was all hard, cold angles and short leashes, between the yard and the street and the outside kennel, and God knows there wasn't much warmth emanating from McGee. The animal doubled up as a security guard. No one would dare attempt to get into McGee's house through the backyard when the dog was there. Major was ferociously alert. Sometimes you could hear him barking at the milk van or the postman.

That's the thing about a dog: when you have one, you start to rely on it. It's human nature to trust a dog, even among those who show very little humanity to speak of. I read once that Hitler had his dog Blondi with him in the bunker, and he appeared to be utterly devoted to her right up until the moment when he ordered his cyanide pill to be tested on her, watching as the capsule was forcibly crushed between her long, elegant jaws to make sure that it was fatal.

The dog served him until its sudden end, and then — after Hitler and Eva Braun took cyanide themselves — their dog-handler shot each one of Blondi's puppies. That's where loyalty to a headcase gets you.

Still, a person who made as many enemies as

McGee shouldn't rely on anything or anyone.

It came to mind that Phyllis had a packet of sleeping pills that she kept in the bathroom cabinet. To get hold of the pills, though, I had to get back into my old house.

★ ★ ★

It's complicated to kill someone, even when you are doing it with an organisation behind you, which I wasn't. It takes a lot of planning. Think of all the work that used to go into those multiple demises that the IRA and Loyalist paramilitaries regularly arranged for us in Northern Ireland: the industrious collection of information on the target, the spying and strategising, the agreed division of roles, the justification for the attack, the overcoming of doubts, the squashing of compassion, the rush of adrenalin, the cleaning of a gun, the priming and planting of a bomb, the cool anticipation of the aftermath, the finalising of the press statement, the shooting or the explosion, the shredding of flesh. And after that came the strenuous maintenance of self-righteousness in the face of the screaming, the weeping, the disbelief.

There's so much to get right.

★ ★ ★

The people who were the softest targets, usually, were those who had a routine. In most places a routine makes a life easier, but in my country it helped to finish it off. People settled into patterns, the shapes that fall naturally in a week. They opened their grocery store at the same time each day, or locked up after work, or went to church or Mass on Sunday. And then right in the middle of the irreplaceable ordinariness, instead of the next polite greeting to a customer or the anticipated lull of the afternoon tea break, instead of the short drive home, just as the leg of lamb was spitting hospitably in the oven or the kettle bubbling towards tea, what on earth oh my God what on earth should come walking purposefully towards them but Death?

Here's a routine: Sunday night was Phyllis's bingo night with her friend Julie. Off she went, lipstick on, wee bag zipped and clamped to her side, bit of excitement sure, wouldn't miss it for the world. From a distance, I watched her leave. I wore a baseball hat tugged low over my eyes, glasses, and the stick-on moustache, with cotton wool jammed in the pouches of my cheeks. I sported a little pot belly from a small cushion I had taped around my middle. I moved differently, slouchily, as though my stomach was already pushing forward in expectation of its next can of lager. I carried the rest of my kit in the backpack, along with a packet of cooked cocktail sausages I'd bought in Marks & Spencer downtown.

I slipped into the house with my old key, looking quickly around to see if anyone was watching, and shut the door sharply behind me. For a second I stood against it and closed my eyes, breathing in the sweetish, wood-polish smell of the house. It was my house — all those years here with Big Jacky — and yet it didn't feel like mine any more. You go away even for a short time and things shift irrevocably. I had become a burglar, nervily tiptoeing around the furniture of my own life.

I took it all in: the flaking paint, the sideboards suddenly full of knick-knacks — she'd got them all out of the cupboard and put them on parade. She'd got rid of the sofa without even asking, the forgiving old sagger with the wooden frame where Big Jacky and I had been so happy, and replaced it with something squashy, floral and horrible from one of the sofa shops in town. I felt a surge of fury. As I turned to see what else she had done, the corner of my jacket caught one of the ornaments — a grey, glazed pigeon — and it crashed to the floor, shattering with surprising force and scattering little fragments across the room.

I found a dustpan and brush under the sink, swept up the pieces and put them in one of the plastic bags Phyllis kept compressed in a drawer. The handle of the pan felt sticky in my hand. I was beginning to feel overheated and tense. No point looking for a bin outside now. I went up to my old bedroom, and shoved the broken pieces far back under the single bed, into a light grey snowdrift of undisturbed dust. She wouldn't come across them there for a while.

Under there too was a small box of my old toys, including just the item I was hoping to find: a pair of police handcuffs, complete with keys, that Big Jacky had long ago unearthed at some charity shop or other. They had once been my most prized possession. I knew precisely how they worked, because at the age of nine I had played cops and robbers all around the house for weeks on end with an extraordinarily forbearing Big Jacky, and at least fifty per cent of the time I got to be the cop.

I carried on, encouraged now. Phyllis's stuffed little packet of sleeping pills sat in the bathroom cabinet, exactly as I had pictured it. Best just to swipe one whole metallic sheet, I thought, and that way she would think it had fallen out somewhere. Anyway, I might need them all later. Down in the kitchen, I took a sharp knife and made a small, deep incision in the end of a cocktail sausage: I pushed a pill inside, and watched the puckered meat close back over it, like a tiny arsehole obediently receiving a suppository. Three pills into each sausage, three sausages in total, wrapped in foil and put in my pocket. Oh, and the keys for the cellar to Big Jacky's shop. All done.

Then I started watching the clock.

Phyllis usually came back from bingo just before eleven, after a couple of drinks with Julie. It would be disastrous if she saw me. I would get entangled in the sticky web of her panic and never make it anywhere near McGee. I went through the house, setting it straight, carefully eradicating any clear taint of my presence, and stepped out into the cold night. There weren't that many people about now, as the pubs hadn't closed yet. The authorities had scaled down the British army patrols, with their jolting cargoes of jumpy young soldiers looking out warily from the back of Land Rovers, and the darkness meant that the disguise could pass with less scrutiny.

22

About half an hour after I threw the sausages into McGee's yard, the dog stopped moving around. I could see it, if I jumped to look over the wall. It was lying down with its eyes closed but still breathing, giving little snorts, its side gently rising and falling.

I climbed over the wall, jumped into the yard and squatted near the kennel, just beneath the windowsill. It stank a bit there, of dog hair and rain and old scraps of forgotten food. I had time to think of what I was getting myself into, to acknowledge the anxiety slopping around my stomach. I now wished I had a real gun, but there was no going back. I had been crouching there about fifteen minutes, with small pains starting to quiver through my ankles and knees, when I heard voices coming closer as the lights went on in the living room.

Oh Jesus no, more than one of them, I thought. Please don't come out into the yard. I raised my head a bit, looked in, and saw McGee. Next to him was Marty, in a wee black bomber jacket. He looked suddenly older. I ducked again and pulled on my Bill Clinton mask under my baseball cap, inhaling the smell of rubber and my own souring breath. From above my head, I could hear far too clearly what they were saying.

'Sure you won't actually be doing anything,' McGee said. 'You're just the lookout. You're lucky enough to be let into an operation at all at your age. Beer?'

There was the crack and hiss of a can being opened. First one, then another.

'Anyway, you're too wee to go to jail. You're underage,' McGee said. I got the feeling that he thought this passed for reassurance.

'But who is it you're doing?' Marty said. His voice sounded high and shaky, a little breathless, as though he had accidentally slipped into waters too deep for him to swim in confidently.

'Who said we were doing anyone? Anyway you don't need to know. Better if you don't.'

'Are they in the Provies?'

'Does it fucking matter? You don't need to know. They're trouble, just like the Provies. But just remember, if you squeal about this to anyone, ever, I'll have to come after you.'

A silence.

'Don't worry, son,' McGee carried on in a more avuncular tone, as if he had been kidding: 'I know you're going to be okay, and you'll get a few quid towards that skateboard you keep going on about. Top lad. Okay?'

'Aye.'

'Aye well, come back here tomorrow after school and I'll give you the plan of where you've to be at what time.'

'All right. See you tomorrow.'

'Are you not going to finish your beer?' McGee called after him. But the front door closed as he was still speaking. He was slurring a little. With some relief, I realised that he was properly legless.

★ ★ ★

I could hear the sound of humming, breaking into words. McGee was singing a country and western song to himself — *'I go out walkin' after midnight, out in the moonlight, ju-st like we used to do'* — and rooting about in his fridge for the makings of a snack — *'I'm always walkin' after midnight, searchin' for yo-u'*. Then he remembered the dog. 'Major!' he shouted. I tensed myself. The dog made no sound, no ragged, gratifying, anticipatory panting and scrabbling. 'Major!' he yelled again, stung, and opened the back door. The dog was lying there, a long slab of fur spread flat out in a haze of soft rain. McGee started walking towards it: 'What the fu — '

And he didn't get any further then because I hit him hard on the back of the skull and jumped on his back and we were into a tussle on the slippery, cold ground. I had to be quick before he recovered himself. He kept twisting and jerking his head round to see who I was, but I forced his hands behind his back while he was still reeling and snapped them into handcuffs before he could yank off my mask. The gloves made my fingers a bit stupid but I got it done anyway.

I could confirm even from the smell of him that he'd had a load to drink. It was slowing him down.

Still, he was sinewy and vicious, working well with what he had left, trying to knee me in the groin and headbutt me at the same time. 'Why

227

the fuck are you wearing that mask?' he spat out, slurring again. I knocked him to the floor with my fist. His feet skidded on the wet ground, and he fell over awkwardly on his shoulder.

My mask was tugged awry. For a second I couldn't see anything at all but white rubber, but I jerked it back into place and got the toy gun out of my jacket pocket while he was still down, quickly, so he couldn't get a good look at it. I pressed it to the back of his neck, put my face close to his ear and whispered very deliberately, 'Come quietly with me or I will shoot you in the head.' I had thickened my accent, and the cotton wool in my cheeks made my voice sound sludgier.

He stiffened slightly then, became calmer and more alert, as though I was finally talking a language he properly understood.

'Where are we going?' he said. Not so much of the swagger now.

'Somewhere to talk.'

'Who are you?'

'Bill fucking Clinton,' I said.

We went inside the house, me still pressing the gun into his neck. I had to watch him like a hawk. He was fast and tougher than me and looking for a way out. Any moment, even with his hands tied, everything could turn around.

'What kind of gun is it?' he asked. I could hear him calculating.

'One that kills people,' I said. 'Now shut the fuck up.'

It wasn't a good position to be in, threatening a fella like McGee with a fake gun. It was like going into a showdown during the Cold War with an Airfix model of a nuclear bomb. He could sniff out weakness. I was worried he was going to push it so far that in normal circumstances I'd have had to give him a warning shot, and all he'd get would be a soggy potato pellet.

So long as he could only feel it and not see it, I was probably all right. If you're a drunk hard-man and a cylindrical metal object is pressing into a vulnerable spot, you tend to make the most obvious assumptions.

'What the fuck did you do to my dog?'

'He's all right.'

'He's dead.'

'No he isn't. He's still breathing.'

'He looks dead. What did you do to him?'

I didn't like to see the dog there in the rain getting cold. I wanted to put a blanket over him but I couldn't let go of McGee. It would be a fatal signal of soft-heartedness. The whole thing was losing momentum anyway. There was too much chat. The action was starting to sag. Any minute now we'd be sitting around in a circle crying and discussing what went wrong in our childhoods. I had to up the ante. I shoved the gun hard into his neck again, so hard it must have really hurt. I could feel a bead of sweat running down my back, a fingertip's trace of liquid panic.

'I'm going to put your coat on you with the hood up, and walk out the door with you next to me. Don't say anything,' I said. Then I had a brainwave.

'There's someone wants a word with you,' I

said. 'Nothing's going to happen to you. He just wants a word.'

That eased it. A 'word' was something he could handle. The waiting presence of a shadowy third party made sense. It felt like business. The scenario fell into some kind of imaginary order. I was no longer his weird nemesis, just a brusque escort to a deal. This had happened to him before, in one form or another. Through the fog of his drunkenness, he could start to weave links back to that protection racket, this drugs supply, create phantom strategies, foresee a future. People always want to imagine the best.

'Calm down,' I said.

He was chewing it over.

'Is it over that deal on the building sites? I made sure everyone got their cut.'

'I don't know,' I said. 'He just said to get you over. He's got some new racket. The sooner you go, the sooner you'll be back home. He just wants a word. Got your keys in your jacket?'

Nice touch, I thought, the implication that he would need them again in the near future.

'Aye. Why the handcuffs?'

'Don't know,' I said. 'That's what he said. But don't make a big song and dance or someone will call the peelers, and that won't be good for you or me. If you start that carry-on I'll have to shoot you and run.'

I draped his coat across his shoulders and started hustling him out the door. On the way I quietly took his spare house keys off the peg and slipped them into my jeans pocket. I'd come back later maybe and sort out the dog.

I pulled my hood down over my mask, and we walked together to the end of the street. It was a wet night, late now, and the pavements glistened. No one passed us. They were all in their houses with the curtains drawn, sticking the kettle on for one last cup of tea before bed. If anyone had seen us, sure we were just two tipsy messers going off to a fancy-dress party. I stopped outside Big Jacky's shop and took out the keys I had borrowed from Phyllis.

'Why are we stopping here? This is a newsagent's,' he said.

'He's waiting downstairs,' I said, and I shoved him through the door and hustled him downstairs into the cramped, gloomy cellar where Big Jacky used to keep the cleaning supplies and the extra stock. I saw Phyllis had been keeping it in order, full marks to her. It was crammed with stacked boxes of Tayto crisps and Kit-Kats.

'He'll be in here in a minute,' I said, 'but he wants you to wear this across your eyes.' I took out a long, clean rag from my pocket, to use as a blindfold.

'I don't fucking want to wear that,' he said, furiously. He started shoving his shoulders around again, roaring and kicking boxes at me, trying to trip me over and knock off my mask. I knew exactly why he didn't want to put it on. It's the kind of thing they make people wear before they get shot.

'Shut up,' I hissed at him. 'He's bringing a friend from England. The fella doesn't want you to see his face before you hear what he's got to say.' I threw in some more flannel for his drunken logic to tangle with: 'He doesn't want a witness before he's got a deal. If you can get through this, there might be some decent money in it for you.'

He quietened down then and let me tie it on him, knotting it tightly. I guided him to an old brown chair in the corner, a recliner with padded, threadbare cushions, and pushed him back on to it: he sank down almost gratefully. I remembered sitting on it as a child, as Big Jacky did the accounts. If you leaned right back on it a footrest zapped out, and it felt a bit like a bed. Or a boat, or an aeroplane, or whatever I wanted it to be. Today: a little prison, maybe.

⋆ ⋆ ⋆

'Cup of tea?' I said.

There was a kettle and a mini-fridge at the back.

'Take off this fucking blindfold,' he said, shaking his head. Now he had it on he hated it even more.

There was something in the arrogance of his tone that angered me. I sprang towards him and hit him very hard and quickly then with my right hand across the side of the head, enough to send his brain bouncing off the inside of his skull. The force and exhilaration of the violence surprised me; how easy it would have been to carry on. But I stopped there. Not yet. I needed time to think. His nose started to bleed, with some of the

232

blood soaking into the edge of the blindfold, blooming like a poppy across the white material. I saw him freeze. He knew he had miscalculated.

'Don't swear at me again,' I said quietly.

'Okay,' he said.

I went to the small sink in the corner and boiled the kettle. Two small cups, a teabag in each one. I put a lot of milk in his so it didn't scald his mouth, and mixed it nice and strong, mashing the bag against the side of the cup with my spoon until the tea came pulsing out in dark-brown clouds. Then I stirred in a good few of Phyllis's little pills, with sugar to mask the taste.

I walked back and held the tea to his lips.

'Tea,' I said, gently. 'Have a wee drink. He'll be here in a minute. I'm having one myself.'

He hesitated for a minute and then started drinking. It was cold in the cellar and the tea was warm and sweet. I watched him gulping sloppily and gratefully, the skin on his jaw shaded with dark bristles, the smell of stale alcohol rising in waves from his pink mouth. A disgrace of a human being — but still, in all his little machinations, a significant piece of work. He was more bearable with the blindfold on. You could conjure him up some humanity.

When he had finished, dribbling the last bit on to his T-shirt, I took the cup away.

'He'll be here in a minute,' I said again.

I sat on a hard chair next to him and drank my own tea.

Then I picked up an old blanket from the corner of the room and put it over him. He didn't move, except to cough now and then.

The room was quiet, with that sour hint of damp that clings to cellars. A light bulb with a rosy, floral shade over it hung incongruously from the ceiling, as if a little girl had tried to decorate a nuclear bunker. Phyllis's doing. As the period between his coughs lengthened, I took a walk around, checking what had changed. It was tidier, certainly. Phyllis had a fussy gift for personal organisation that Big Jacky had never demonstrated. There was a pillow in the corner. She kept a small canvas holdall down here with clean underwear, clothes and a face towel in it, and a make-up bag decorated with sprigs of flowers, in case she had go out and meet her friend straight from work. Phyllis loved all that stuff. Too much boredom in her life had led her to make a mild cult out of preparedness.

McGee was asleep now, snoring, full of stewed booze and rotten convictions. His mouth hung half open, a skinny line of congealed blood snaking towards it from his right nostril. A slim gold chain with a miniature dagger on it dangled from his neck. I thought of him carefully picking it out in the shop and handing over the money.

I sat and looked at him. If I were going to smother him, now would be the moment. That pillow would do, held down with sufficient force. There would be a brief, gurgling struggle and then it would be over. What was left of Titch would be lowered into the ground tomorrow, to the sound of his mother's sobbing. McGee deserved this. It had a finality about it. I got out the thick roll of masking tape and wound it round his legs several times, tying them tight

234

together. Then I did a few more loops to fix him to the chair.

I picked up the pillow and stood beside him, staring down at him.

And then what? How to dispose of him? I hadn't quite thought that bit through. I couldn't just leave him here afterwards for Phyllis to find, stiffening among the coupon stacks. If I could keep him here for a day it might be possible to come back in the night with a wheelie bin, cram him in and wheel him far away.

I began to feel very tired. You might think that killing someone you hate will free you, but unless you plan to make a habit of it and rack up so many you can't count, it just bonds you to them for ever. Looked at that way, murder is a stronger glue than sex. I don't suppose you ever forget someone you kill, unless you're in the thick of war and can't even tell who it was. This stuff soils you, becomes difficult to scrub off. With each ebbing breath, they will etch themselves on your memory.

I was lousy at covering my tracks. I could end up doing time for McGee, mouldering in jail for the main chunk of my life, watching as paramilitaries got early release while I — classed as what the police used to call an 'ordinary decent criminal' — was held in for the full stretch, enjoying the blocked toilet in the tiny cell and the boiling sugar water thrown in my face by McGee's resentful fellow-Loyalists.

I had thought that the destruction of McGee would make me feel exultant, but now I could actually touch the possibility it just felt squalid, the mental equivalent of getting dog shit on your shoe. I wanted him out of the cellar. Even in his stupor his presence was leaking potential harm. I knew with sudden certainty that I didn't want to kill him. But if I didn't kill him now, how was I going to stop him killing me?

By the time he finally came round, he would be beginning to puzzle everything out about the place he was in, about ways of punishing me by threatening people I loved. So far this whole exercise had been the equivalent of flapping a cloth at a killer hornet. If I was going to let him live I had to disable his capacity for revenge.

A few hours passed. I was in a fix. I had to go with anything I'd got.

★   ★   ★

Suddenly I had a thought: I went over to Phyllis's wee cosmetic bag and dug out her lipstick, a surprisingly lurid shade of poppy-red. There was an eyeshadow in there too, and blusher. The lipstick went smoothly on to McGee's half-open mouth. I kept it very neat around the edges, as though he had applied it himself with furtive pride. I didn't want him to look like he was dressing up for a hearty masculine laugh, like a rugby player on tour. It had to look sincere.

After that I smeared a bit of blusher on to his cheeks, and gently scissored off the blindfold before dusting blue eyeshadow all over his eyelids with a wee brush. I took the blanket off him, slowly so as not to wake him up. Then, with a few decisive snips of the big scissors Phyllis kept for cutting newspaper twine, I sliced down the middle of his T-shirt and carefully set Phyllis's cream lacy bra across his chest, over the pallid skin with the bulldog tattoo, the pimply forest of chest hair.

I braced myself and pulled his jeans and underpants down so that the tops of them hovered on his thighs. What was exposed was unedifying. A line had been crossed. Several lines.

He started to stir a bit, so I stepped back, waiting. He moved some more and then let out a long, wounded roar, like an animal pinched awake in pain from its den. His eyes opened and stared ahead of him into space, with a dawning consciousness that was slowly filling up with rage. He tried to move his arms, but they were still tied behind him, so he began to shake from side to side, roaring again in purest frustration. In the midst of this frenzy, his gaze came to rest on me. I was no longer wearing the Clinton mask or the other layers of my disguise. Immediately he became still, as though absorbing the full implications of my presence. There was a pause.

'You wee fucker,' McGee said, quietly, as though confirming something he had always known.

I said nothing.

'Why am I here?' he yelled, jerking the top half of his body off the chair. The suddenness of his movement made me step backwards.

I let his question hang in the air for a second or two. It was almost too big to answer.

'Why do you think?' I said.

I felt sick but exhilarated, to have him on the spot.

'I don't fucking know.'

McGee was still groggy, but I thought he could do better than that.

'Have a think,' I said.

'Because I beat up your mate and you?'

'That's a start,' I said. 'Beat up? That's a nice way of putting it.'

'What are you going to do now, then?' he said.

'I was going to bump you off,' I said.

'Why didn't you?' he asked.

Then he answered his own question: 'You haven't the bollocks.'

'Bollocks have nothing to do with it. I still might if I feel like it,' I said. I let out a stray hoot of laughter at seeing his mouth working foully through the clown's lipstick.

I fancied a smoke so I lit one up and sat down further away on a wooden box, watching him.

'What the fuck's so funny?' he said.

'Look at the state of you.'

He squirrelled his chin down on to his chest to try and see himself and caught a glimpse of the bra and the misplaced jeans. At that he started howling and struggling all over again.

'You fucking pervert,' he said. 'What have you done to me?'

A pause for thought.

'Did you touch my dick?'

'Nope,' I said, and took another draw on my cigarette.

The inhalation made a gentle burning hiss, fraying the fine paper. I loved that sound, the controlled fizz of the little flame. I felt tired and peaceful. A big cloud of blue-grey tobacco smoke came floating out of my mouth.

'Nice make-up,' I said.

He glared at me. He looked like a cross between Mata Hari and Desperate Dan. He started trying to crunch his mouth up so he could see it if he looked down. He must have seen a smear of something red, because he started to struggle again.

'Why are you keeping me here?' he shouted.

'Because I want to talk to you.'

'About what?'

I stuck the blanket back over him. His cabaret weirdness was too overwhelming otherwise and I couldn't concentrate.

'Why you kill people. Why you beat Titch. Why you hammered me.'

'You hammered me first.'

'I hit you in a bar. You hammered me with three mates and a bat with rusty nails in it. And before that you beat Titch into the hospital for a packet of Jaffa Cakes.'

'It wasn't about the Jaffa Cakes.'

'What was it about?'

'Respect. Order. Somebody has to keep order. Without it the entire place would fall apart.'

'Look around you. What order? Why did it have to be you?'

'What the fuck am I supposed to do? Let him nick from us every day? Let him shove my da over while people laugh? He's lucky I didn't stiff him.'

'You did stiff him. He killed himself last week, because of what you did. Didn't you know?'

There was a second when he looked surprised.

Then he just stared blankly back at me, the bloodshot eyes glazed with drink.

'You killed him,' I said, flatly.

I wasn't going to let it rest there: 'Just like you killed all those other people who didn't deserve it.'

'What does that mean?'

I felt a flash of anger at him even asking.

'You know damn well. Your outfit. Going around shooting wee Catholic lads walking home at night. Going into pubs and shooting oul fellas when they're drinking a pint and watching the World Cup. Is that what you're proud of? Is that the 'war'?'

'Nobody asked you to do it. When the IRA murdered Prods, the families came on TV and begged you not to do it to anyone else. You didn't give a shit. You just went on doing it.'

It was true, what I had said. I remembered the time they had shot a young Catholic workman while he was in his car eating his lunchtime sandwiches. His mother was on the television news, propped up by relatives. She had a dazed bleakness in her eyes that was hard to forget.

McGee remembered something he had heard from the people who made theories to hang around the corpses. His voice took on an air of self-importance, like a child at a recital.

'We had to make the Catholic population turn against the IRA. It was a necessary strategy.'

'How long before you decided your strategy wasn't working? How long before you decided it was wrong?'

Silence. I kept on.

'Why don't you just admit that killing Catholics gives you a buzz and spare us all the fucking pretence?'

I realised I was shouting. Better tone it down. Still, that riled him.

He sat up and hissed at me: 'If you want to wring your hands over dead Taigs, go ahead. I won't. The Provies killed my uncle, and he was never even into anything, just meeting his friend in a hotel when one of their bombs went off. They had to scrape him off the walls to have something to put in the coffin.

'If it wasn't for us defenders the Provies would already have murdered all of youse in your beds, like the cowardly wee shites that you are.'

'Defenders? My friend is dead because of you. Why would we need the IRA to murder us, when we've got you?' I yelled.

He glared back at me and said with slow deliberation, 'I didn't murder you or your big fat mate. More's the pity. Wish I'd whacked you both.'

'You don't get it, do you?' I said. 'But sure what chance did you ever have, growing up with your vicious oul da and that looper McMullen?'

'Leave my da out of it,' he said. 'He brought us up the best he could. And don't talk about McMullen.'

'Where'd your ma go?' I asked. I meant it to sound harsh, but for a moment my tone faltered into normality.

'What's it to you?' he said.

'I just want to know.'

'She pissed off and left us. I was seven, brother

241

was nine. Probably off to Scotland with some fancy man. Covered her tracks. Didn't want to be found, Da said, but he kept trying. That's all. Happy now?'

'Did you love her?'

'She was my ma. But she left us. So I don't love her now. What are you, a therapist? Shut the fuck up and let me go.'

'What are you doing with that wee fella?' I asked.

'What wee fella?'

'The one in your house. I could hear you talking. You're planning something.'

'D'you know him?'

'No, I've just seen him around. So you're getting kids to do your dirty work for you now?'

'He's doing nothing. Just keeping an eye out for us.'

'What will you do if I let you go?' I asked.

The silence stretched out taut, and then pinged back with a low, hoarse: 'Kill you.'

'If that's the way, don't you see I'll have to finish you off now myself?'

Nothing.

'That's one idea. Here's another. You leave me and my family alone and in exchange I don't make the photos of you public.'

His eyes snapped open. 'What photos?'

'The ones I took when you were asleep, when you were wearing all the make-up and the bra like it's your special thing. I gave the film to a friend who came to the door when you were knocked out. If anything happens to me or anyone I know, he'll get them developed at

Speedy Snaps, and send them to your da and all his mates. Then later I'll come back and kill you anyway.'

'You wouldn't do that.'

'I would. I understand they do posters too. Great big posters for the gable walls.'

'I'll burn Speedy Snaps to the fucking ground.'

'Which branch?'

He glared at me with his red, blue-shadowed eyes.

'Let me out.'

'I don't take orders. That's the deal. Do you want it?'

A moment's contemplation.

'Aye.'

'I'll be leaving today. Remember what I said.'

'Where'd you get the gun you had last night?'

I didn't like that question. With his nose for violence and its hardware, he had started to scent something not quite right about the gun.

'Never you worry,' I said. 'Rest assured it works.'

'Okay. I agree. Just let me go.'

I looked at the clock. It was only just gone six in the morning. In an hour Phyllis would be arriving to unlock the shop. There was the whole day ahead.

There's a point sometimes where you take a risk, not because you actually think it's a good or clever idea, but just because you're so very tired. I had exhausted the possibilities of the situation. I had realised now I wasn't going to kill him, and I suppose he had too.

I went and got the Spud Gun and put it in my

243

pocket, fumbling so he could see just enough of the movement but not the item itself. Then I ran a facecloth under the hot tap, wrung it out, and gently scrubbed Phyllis's make-up off his face. He shut his eyes. I got most of it off, but his eyes still looked faintly exotic, as if stained by woad. A swollen, purpling bruise was spreading next to his nose.

The make-up stuff and the pretend camera hadn't been very classy, I had to admit, but they plugged into his screwed-up values that stuck pride and shame in all the wrong places. Fellas like him fear mockery more than pain. I didn't want a reconciliation with him. I just didn't want him squatting in a corner of my conscience for the next fifty years.

★   ★   ★

I went behind him and unlocked his hands, and then started sawing through the masking tape on his legs. He opened his eyes, and for a second his gaze flicked across the scars on my arms as I hacked at the tape. When it finally came loose, he moved his arms and legs tentatively, wincing a bit as the feeling came back.

He got up off the chair with difficulty like a wretched old man, tugged up the jeans and nearly fell down again because his legs were so stiff. I stood at a distance and watched him as he righted himself. The expression on his face was hard to read. I had thought that maybe he would take a run and try to belt me one, but he didn't. I threw him an old T-shirt in place of the rag that was hanging off him, and he put it on, and then found his coat. Phyllis's bra lay, appallingly, on the floor. The whole thing felt embarrassing, like the morning after a costume party in which everyone present was out of their nut on drugs.

'So that's it, then?' he said.

'Aye.'

I walked beside him to the foot of the darkened stairwell. When he finally reached the stairs he groped for the rusted handrail, still disoriented, taking a moment to steady himself. As I watched him I imagined that he understood now that this incident had evened up the score, that after this we could leave each other alone.

'Remember what I said,' I murmured again, waiting for him to go.

At that he wheeled around sharply, as though some fresh energy had suddenly surged in him, and lunged for my neck. His hands clamped tightly round my throat, pressing hard, and I began fighting to breathe. There was a shocking amount of force just in his fingers and though my own hands quickly came flailing up to prise them off he held his grip. As my field of vision started shrinking and blackening I thought dumbly *so this is it now this is how it ends* and for a fragment of a second I was furious and then despairing at having fallen so stupidly into my own trap.

Then he let go just as rapidly. The assault had established what he needed to know: during it, I hadn't reached for my gun. While I was still gasping for shreds of air he brought his face closer to mine, stinking of sweat and beer, and

245

said with a small smile I didn't like, 'Watch out for yourself, Jacky. Sure I'll be keeping a good lookout for you.'

He began walking slowly and jerkily up the stairs. On the fifth step he turned round with a sarcastic grimace of mock-terror and added 'you, and your wee gun' — and then carried on.

The upstairs door clanged shut. I went to the bathroom and washed my hands in the sink. They were shaking very badly as I turned on the taps and I noticed that my legs had involuntarily followed suit, buckling and trembling like those of some blitzed accordion player. I caught a glimpse of my face in the mirror above the bowl: the red, exhausted eyes, the drawn, sick face. On each side of my throat was a livid puce impression of McGee's thumbprint. I started to wash my face, lathering up Phyllis's pink, flowery-smelling soap.

He hadn't wanted to kill me here. It wasn't a venue he had thought through himself, and maybe the crazy threat of the photographs had worked as some restraint. Still, as the warm water coursed down my aching neck it was dawning on me that from whichever angle you looked at things, he was out on the loose again and I had made yet another of my serious mistakes.

★   ★   ★

When I finally got some balance back I started tidying up the scene, stuffing everything into a black bin liner before Phyllis got in for the early morning deliveries. It took a while, but not half as long as if I'd had to fold McGee in there as well. I tied up the bag and carried it with me as I locked up and walked out into the cool air, gulping the oxygen down like ice-water. Along the way, I shoved it all — the torn clothes, the bloodstained rag — into a public rubbish bin. As I walked away I felt a small jangling in my pocket: McGee's spare house keys. I hesitated for a second and then hung on to them, just in case. In case of what, I didn't know.

★   ★   ★

Back at the hotel, as I went to get the key to my room, Marie was waiting for me on reception, alert as a terrier, ears cocked, fresh up from the rabbit hole.

'Big night last night?' she said. 'Was the wedding good? I noticed you didn't come back.'

Her face wore a roguish expression I didn't care to engage with. My scarf was looped to hide my sore neck and even to look at her mouth moving around as she talked made me weary.

'Aye,' I said hoarsely. 'What a wedding.'

'Did the bride look nice?'

'Beautiful,' I said.

'And the bridesmaids?

More banter. I thought of McGee, trussed up with the mad smear of red lipstick on.

'Quite something,' I said.

'I bet you're not feeling too chatty today,' she said, knowingly.

I widened my eyes in humorous assent. Speech was, increasingly, beyond me.

I had a sleep and called Phyllis later from the hotel room, to ask about Titch's funeral. She thought I was phoning from London. For once she didn't give me too many details, except to say that Titch's mum was so deep in grief that she had seemed not to be fully there.

His mum had brought along Titch's brand new puffa jacket which they had bought together in the city centre the week before he died. She stood at the graveside clutching it tight as he was buried. Phyllis said it almost looked as if Titch's mother was holding the warm jacket for him because she thought he might need it again later on the way back to the house, but of course no one mentioned that, they just tried to make sure she got through it. The da turned up half-cut with an enormous floral wreath that said SON and made an exhibition of himself caterwauling and crying my poor boy, my poor son, again and again until everyone wished he would give over and go home.

23

It felt like a relief to be back in London. The air was dirtier, but the life was cleaner and easier. Work was a pleasure in its simplicity: you did this thing, washing glasses and mixing drinks, and people gave you money and left you alone. I somehow felt as if, just by having made it out of the cellar without killing McGee, I had been handed a new lease of life. The day I came back there was a sympathy card on the bar, signed by my fellow workers — including Francis, in his loopy, flamboyant hand — to say they were sorry for the loss of my mother. I felt briefly guilty, but then I told myself it had just arrived post-dated by decades.

'Thanks,' I said to them quietly, still a wee bit bruised and downcast.

Mrs Wharton, who knew nothing of this lie, nonetheless met me with tear-filled eyes. She broke the news to me that Rollo had been 'put to sleep' while I was away. He'd been irritable and walking strangely, and then he'd finally gone berserk one night and buried his teeth in Mr Wharton's left leg. Tests had discovered a large growth pressing on the dog's brain. 'It was the kindest thing,' Mrs Wharton kept repeating of the euthanasia, as though she wasn't at all sure that it was. The house felt calmer without him but different. Even a small, malign presence punches a hole in the air when it leaves.

There were times, though, when I woke up in the dead of night and couldn't get back to sleep, when my anxieties sprouted claws and destroyed any possibility of rest. The loss of Titch, the heartbreak of his mother, and that weird circus with McGee in the basement all wheeled around my head in some nightmarish mix.

One other thing worried me, too: what if that photograph threat simply slid off McGee, and he went after Phyllis anyway? Fears have a way of shrinking over time while resentments sprout muscles. Phyllis was well liked locally, and if McGee's lot harmed her openly it might go down badly, but I knew things didn't have to be so clear-cut. He only had to wait until a feverish patch of the year when for some reason there's a bit of mayhem on the streets and then one young hothead among many happens to chuck a petrol bomb through a ground-floor window in the wee small hours and whoosh a middle-aged woman sleeping upstairs is burned or asphyxiated.

Then the talk will start. Isn't it awful, what happened? Och it is indeed a dreadful tragedy, just a nice lady alone in her own home, not an enemy in the world, clearly he got the wrong house, what on earth is this country coming to, even the leadership is furious apparently and they issue a stern disciplinary warning against these young bucks who get over-excited, there's to be no more of this carry-on, but in a place like this with our difficult history sure tempers run out of control now and again, it seems the fire spread unusually fast, must have been the foam in the soft furnishings, but it isn't an official breach of anyone's ceasefire thank goodness for that, as even everyone in the government agrees so there's some consolation at least.

Far away in another city, however, one person will understand very clearly the precise nature of what sailed through that ground-floor window, exactly as he is meant to. A message in a bottle, addressed to me. Was any of this likely? It was hard to tell any more.

I fell into the habit of ringing Phyllis at home every couple of days to gauge the temperature around her. She was delighted with the calls, of course: it seemed to her as if I was finally behaving almost like a son. I'd kick it all off with 'How are things?' and then she'd be straight out of the starting blocks, telling me that prices had rocketed at the local butcher's now they'd smartened the place up, and how the doctors had cut a tumour the size of an orange out of her friend Julie's husband just in the nick of time before the thing seeded itself all the way through him.

I had developed the art of listening on one level while letting my mind roam freely on another. Along the way at intervals I had learned to throw in 'Aye' and the odd incredulous echo — 'an orange? Jesus' — and the technique served me well. The trick was to keep an ear out for key words and interrogatives, and respond to them like a sharp tug on a harness, otherwise you could come badly unstuck. This particular evening Phyllis was talking on again, and meanwhile I was thinking with a mixture of remembered pleasure and encroaching sadness

251

about the time when Eve and Raymond and I had walked through Chalk Farm and bought ice-cream cones even though it was bitterly cold outside because this one shop had flavours we had never tried before. Pastel-coloured, sharp-sweet sorbets that chilled the flesh inside our cheeks. And then Phyllis suddenly said down the line: 'Well, is there anyone in London you've got your eye on?'

The question brought me up short. What had prompted this? Maybe I'd mentioned Eve in passing and she'd somehow picked up on it. My love life was new territory for Phyllis, as something self-consciously bold in her tone suggested, and I didn't want her to make herself comfortable there.

'My eye on?'

'Yes, your eye on.' She was unusually persistent.

As my situation stood with Eve, it was poor timing for romantic confessions, like admitting to someone you had sat an important exam just as the news came in that you'd failed. It was best to be evasive.

'Och well, you never know.'

She correctly interpreted my equivocation as assent.

'Well if there is and she's important,' she said, 'don't let her get away.'

When she said that I briefly recalled the image of a snarled car on a damp country road, and what Phyllis knew about someone getting away.

'I'll keep that in mind,' I said more gently. 'Thanks for thinking of me.'

After that she went back to talking about her difficulties with the business bank account for the shop, and I returned to thoughts of the ice-cream parlour. I couldn't remember which flavour Eve had chosen that night, although she had talked about how good it was. It seemed terrible that in such a short time already I couldn't remember this little thing, and I realised that many more details about Eve — all the tiny facts that, massed together, made up her full reality — were destined to slip away from me now, one by one, with no chances to replace them. And then another sentence drifted over from Phyllis that ended with the words 'burned down the photo-shop'.

A small electric shock, transmitted through the ear.

'What did you say, Phyllis? It's a very crackly line here.'

'I was just saying that somebody burned down the photo-shop nearest us where we used to get our films developed. You know the one. Speedy Snaps, it's called.'

'Who would do a thing like that?'

'No one knows. I forgot to tell you earlier. It said on the news they think it was started at night with petrol-soaked rags pushed through the letterbox and then whoever it was threw in a match after it and up it went. I bumped into David who manages the place, poor fella, he was all through the wreckage of it the next day trying to salvage anything that was left. The police don't know who did it, he says, in fact they're looking into former employees.

253

'David's a lovely fella, he says what torments him is the thought of all those customers who trusted them with the films, their baby pictures and wedding pictures and whatnot, all those precious moments up in flames. He and his wife have only just had a new baby themselves so they know how it must feel. I said to him, 'David you must remember that it's not your fault, nobody will blame you. Sure it's awful if photos get burnt but thank God at least it wasn't people.''

'Aye,' I said. 'At least it wasn't people.'

'And here's a funny thing because David never mentioned it at the time, but a couple of days later I got a nice wee letter in the post from Speedy Snaps just saying 'we're deeply sorry that your photographs were destroyed in a fire at our premises, we know that some images are irreplaceable'. It was addressed 'to the Occupier' but I don't remember putting any pictures in there lately — did you before you went?'

'No,' I said, 'I don't think I did.'

'Maybe I did have something in there that slipped my mind, I'll have to double-check. But it gave a number that you can call if you want to be compensated and they'll send someone to the house to drop off a complimentary package — '

Oh God. A complimentary package with wires and nails in it, maybe.

'Don't ring that number, Phyllis. That letter's not from Speedy Snaps.'

'Well who else would it be from?'

'It sounds like a scam. Trust me. I've heard about this kind of thing before. The fraudsters hear about an incident in the news and then they send out letters on the back of it to steal your details. Are you on your own at home tonight?'

'No, I've just been *telling* you all about it, Jacky, Julie's coming to pick me up at seven and I'm going to stay with her for ten days to help her out while her husband recovers from the operation. They have a lovely spare room.'

Ten days. I made her promise again she wouldn't ring that number. I had ten days when at least she wouldn't be sleeping in our house. And after that I'd have to get her over to London where I could explain things to her in person and put together some kind of plan. What then? I hadn't a clue. If she left the house she couldn't return to live with Mary and Sam, not after how much she had come to enjoy her life in Belfast. It would be like shoving her back into a living tomb. Maybe she would have to come and stay with me in London.

I had a sudden, horrifying vision of Phyllis and me twenty years hence, living together as the odd couple — Eve having long since vanished — with me as one of those middle-aged men, neutered by duty, who wears his clothes too neatly pressed and can never ask a woman back to his tiny flat because his elderly aunt is always pottering about, watering house plants and snuffing out erotic possibility. It's strange how saving someone from a living tomb so often seems to involve climbing into one yourself.

It didn't matter, I told myself. I could deal with that later. Just the business of now mattered. Something about the erratic, panicky way I had begun to weigh up risks and decisions told me that I might not easily get through another tragedy in which my inaction played a part. I needed to buy some thinking time. Before the week was out I'd sort out someone to mind the shop and then send Phyllis a ticket to London for a surprise holiday when her stint at Julie's was up. The idea would thrill her, a picturesque treat, a story to tell her friends.

In the meantime I rang the head office of Speedy Snaps in Northern Ireland to check whether they had indeed written to their customers to offer compensation. They had no idea what I was talking about. Regarding the fire in the Belfast branch, they said, they were still in the very early stages of working out what had been destroyed. They hadn't yet tried to contact any customers at all.

McGee had known I'd hear about the incident and the letter. He was clever that way. I don't think he thought that my photos of him really were in Speedy Snaps waiting to be developed, if he even believed in their existence. He'd just torched the place as a signal that he was ready to do anything. The letter was to remind me that he knew where Phyllis lived.

★   ★   ★

I thought about Eve all the time, too: what she was doing, if she was thinking about me, whether Raymond missed me, whether he played Monopoly with anyone else now or if the board just lay untouched in the corner.

I knew that after I'd left her alone that night in

256

the café, if she saw me now she would just walk away before I could say anything. She had that ability, once someone finally crossed a line.

One day I sat down at the battered little wooden desk in my room back at the Whartons', the legacy from one of their long-departed sons, and wrote her a letter. I explained it all: the death of Big Jacky, how I had got my scars, Titch's death, and even — in abbreviated, codified form — my run-in with McGee. I felt better for it, whatever happened. The secrets between us had begun to corrode our affection, rusting it with patches of mistrust.

When I had finished describing what had happened, I wrote plainly at the end: 'I'm sorry. I love you and Raymond and I want to be with you and stay with you. I hope you will let me. There will be no more messing around.'

I meant it. I never liked those adults who were in and out of children's lives, schmoozing them and then disappearing, returning with great fanfare like Santa Claus and the Easter Bunny rolled into one and then buggering off again, stopping only to explain with stumbling, mealy-mouthed phrases that things were 'complicated'. I had been that person to Raymond, and I didn't want to be like that again. Big Jacky had never mucked me about. He loved me steadily and without question, in his own way.

I posted the letter and tried not to hope too much. Eve might have met someone new, and who could blame her?

★ ★ ★

257

The following days merged into one another, mined with different varieties of unease. At night I took consolation from picturing Phyllis in the warm company of Julie, who thankfully lived in another part of town. I kept the thought of Eve and Raymond at bay. It was too highly charged to hope for or even think of, like a package just outside a pub that might explode if you touched it. I thought sometimes about how to construct a life around their absence, one that didn't have them in it but somehow ticked on successfully anyway, and I couldn't quite make it work.

Everywhere I looked in London, I could see people who had fallen out of a life that almost worked into one that leaked malfunction from every small action. They fell so far that their shadow-lives became invisible to everyone else, even in the full glare of daylight. They laid out beds in stone corners of the city, using doorsteps for mattresses and straining plastic bags full of grubby possessions as pillows. They pestered passers-by for cash with stories as crumpled as the back of their shoes, and I wondered what had brought them here.

Different things, I supposed, the small mysteries of failure. The thousand ways you can descend. The bonds of love that glued people in place — the mother, the father, the brother, the sister, the lover, the friends — had melted away from them, or maybe they had dissolved those ties themselves: soaked them in drink, or drugs or disappointments until finally there wasn't even a thread left to hang on to. And then life becomes painful but simpler. You have nothing, you need everything, you have to work all day for the little something that will vanish again overnight.

Your feet hurt, you're cold and your crumbling teeth are aching, and you have to think about that. You can sometimes blot it out, and the deeper stuff too, with a portable anaesthetic of your choice. There is more and less to manage at the same time, and all your negotiations are with strangers, which at some blurred point in the past became less wounding than the ones with friends.

Every day I walked past the same man on the way to the bus that took me home from work, and — with a tiny jab of nameless guilt, which I usually ignored — shrugged off his hopeless muttered lie of 'spare some change, mate, for a cup of tea'. Funny how they always named the need for tea, as though it was the one confident English right no passer-by could decently deny.

But today I stopped and briefly took him in as he stood in the dingy doorway: the watery, expectant, pale blue eyes, the matted hair, the stubble and the loosely belted trousers. The grime-seamed, panhandling palm. He must only have been about thirty. I didn't want to give him cash. It would hasten his wreckage. I nodded towards the fluorescent light of the convenience store.

'Can I get you something from in there?'

'I'd rather just have the money, mate.'

'No, but I'll get you something to eat from in there.'

He looked at me with a lurking truculence. Something was better than nothing.

'Sandwich then, mate.'

Under the strip-lighting of the shop, I tried to assemble a package for him: a chicken sandwich, satsumas, a chocolate bar, some toothpaste and a toothbrush.

I handed him the thin plastic bag swaying with the weight of its contents. He peered into it with mild interest.

'Thanks, mate,' he said dully, like a child with a dud Christmas stocking. His eyes slid away. He would have preferred the cash, which could have bought him some crackle and pop and forgetting, rather than all this dreary nourishment and fluoridated dental care. Fair enough.

I walked on and waited for the bus. It wouldn't be so hard at all, I thought, just to slide down to where he was. It was so easy that the thought of it frightened me, like tiptoeing to the edge of a cliff and peering over, and feeling — just for a split second — your head starting to spin and your knees giving way beneath you.

★　★　★

They used to get all the daily papers at Delauncey's and stick them in a rack at the café section of the restaurant, in the pretence that it was some kind of Left Bank joint where customers could sit thoughtfully and ponder the day's political events. At the end of the day, when I remembered, I would take them home in my bag. Nobody else wanted them. Francis had probably never sat down and read an entire newspaper in his life, although he was always blathering about mind-blowing books he had read while often, I had noticed, getting the titles slightly wrong. He was prone to wittering about Jack Kerouac's *The Karma Bums*. I savoured his little errors: they gave me a brief sensation of superiority.

But I felt at home with it, this feast of tiny print. It reminded me of my childhood in the newsagent's, tying up the remaindered copies with Big Jacky, absorbing the electricity of events from all over the world, plugging into the stronger voltage of those near home.

Something happens to you when you grow up in the midst of bombings and shootings, with the possibility of someone's agony always in the air like the coming of rain. It's a secret that nobody really talks about: you get hardwired to the news.

The question of 'will it happen to me?' and 'will it happen to anyone I love?' and 'will it happen to anyone I know?' slowly becomes a reflex, almost a professional interest. You look at photographs of the aftermath of an explosion, say, in Iraq or Sarajevo, and you feel that sickened, sneaky tug of familiarity, the little quickening of recognition. They have it so much worse, you think, but still it's something you already know, the intimacy of chaos.

In London, I still kept track of stuff at home. Delauncey's didn't get the *Belfast Telegraph*, so I sometimes read the *Irish Times*. In between its own stories of soaring house prices and political scandals it reported Northern news like a form letter tersely mentioning the latest doings of a regrettably delinquent cousin.

The day of Phyllis's scheduled departure from

Julie's house was creeping nearer, and the Whartons had seemed okay with the notion of her visiting in exchange for a dollop more rent. As I boarded the packed bus home I decided to go to the travel agent's in my break the following day and book her ticket. I found a cramped seat on the top deck, where the air smelled of damp woollen coats, and inched open my copy of the *Irish Times*. Two stories in, my eye fell on this:

KILLING CONNECTED TO INTERNAL LOYALIST FEUD, POLICE SAY
A man shot dead in the Sandy Row area of Belfast had close connections to loyalist paramilitaries, an RUC statement said yesterday. Witnesses said that Ronald 'Rocky' McGee, 28, was sitting in a parked car when he was approached on foot by two masked gunmen, one of whom fired several shots through the window of the driver's seat, killing Mr McGee instantly. The men made their getaway in a nearby car which was later found burned out in a nearby estate. It is thought that the shooting is linked to an ongoing internal feud which has claimed several lives, beginning with the car bomb attack which killed Kenneth Bates, a father of two, in Bangor last January.

McGee was unmarried and lived alone in the Village area of South Belfast: he had a seven-year-old son by a previous relationship who lives with his former partner.

The victim's Alsatian dog, which was in

the back seat of the car, was unharmed
after the attack.

I read it twice. I was shocked, I admit. It was
such a stark form of resolution, the fact of his
death.

I couldn't deny the deluge of relief. If a desire
for revenge had been warming in him regarding
me or Phyllis it would never now get the chance
to boil over. Just like that, a flick of fate from out
of the blue, a wee tap from God's finger, and I
was rid of him.

Except that it wasn't out of the blue. His end
just came flying in from another direction, one I
hadn't considered. I wasn't the only player in his
drama. He had been planning something, that
night with Marty. Perhaps his intended targets
had got to him first.

I felt dizzy, as though the news had rushed too
fast into my system. When I got off at the bus
stop the glittering lights and sounds of the city
seemed to swim and reel around me. I stumbled
from the kerb to cross the road and a black cab
gave a long, furious blast of its horn.

I put my hand down deep into the pocket of
my overcoat. McGee's spare keys were still there,
tucked into my wallet. I wondered had he ever
noticed they were missing. Part of me was
reluctant to let them go. It felt risky still to have
them on me, though, so I pulled them out and
dropped them down a nearby drain.

That night, I woke up in bed in the dark and
thought about what McGee had left behind. His
legacy, if you want to call it that. A trail of

misery, certainly. I was sure, without knowing the names of the victims, that he had been involved in murders. He left behind the grief of sundry relatives of the dead, the pain and death of Titch, the nagging ache in my bones, the braille of scars on my arms.

There were only these stains to remember him by, and then slowly history would close back over him like the surface of a river over a drowned man.

After his funeral he'd fade perhaps to a name on a gable wall, an incidental footnote in a history of the Troubles, an occasional nostalgic late-night mention from those fellow paramilitaries who still held him in their dubious esteem. The rain would fall down as it always did on the grey street where he had died and soon almost no one would think of him at all.

He had believed in his violent vision of order, until somebody else's version of it required him to be destroyed.

He left behind him a small, empty, tidy house, with bills on the doormat and cans of lager still cooling in the fridge.

He left behind him an Alsatian dog, to whom he had perhaps been sporadically kind. I was glad the dog was still alive.

He left behind him a father, hard and mean of spirit, who had brought up his son in his own image and seen him crumble to dust.

He left behind him a son, about whom I had not known, and a woman who maybe once felt something strong for him until the feeling grew complicated and sour.

He left behind him me, damaged but not dead. I had managed to survive him now, and I supposed I would remember him.

The second time I woke up, near to dawn, I thought about him at the age of seven when his mother went missing, and how he must have hunted for her every day like a hungry and abandoned pet, until finally he accepted she was never coming back.

And then I thought about his own seven-year-old son, being told of his death, the child's mouth falling open in surprise and his face turning pale as the telephone kept on and on ringing and the funeral preparations gathered force around him.

★   ★   ★

The minute I had proved unable to kill McGee, he had begun to despise me all over again. He couldn't comprehend the language of mercy or conscience, or even ordinary squeamishness. He only spoke the local dialect of power. I wondered what emotion he had felt in his car, in the few seconds between seeing the gunman and the emphatic arrival of the bullet. Had he perhaps thought, in that instant, that I was the gunman? The notion brought me an unexpected flicker of pleasure, followed by a jolt of shame.

★   ★   ★

The next evening, about an hour after I got back from work, I heard the thin whine of the doorbell. From my room at the top of the house I could hear Mrs Wharton answering it, and a muffled conversation before she called up the stairs for me: 'Jacky, visitors!' in a voice slightly breathless with excitement. No one ever visited me there. I came downstairs warily. I suppose I half thought, against all logic, that it might be something or someone linked to the business of McGee's death.

There Eve stood on the chilly doorstep, her pallor framed by the darkness, looking at me steadily but with some kind of suppressed nervous pleasure in her decision to come. I knew she was serious because she had Raymond with her, his hand linked tightly in hers, his greenish eyes also fixed expectantly on me.

I stared at them both for a minute, frozen by the weight of joy that had descended on me, and then I opened my arms.

Part Three

24

I flew back to Belfast for Murdie's funeral, under grey skies baggy with the threat of rain. They had just renamed the City airport after George Best, and I couldn't be sure whether it was because he was such a brilliant footballer or such a hopeless alcoholic, or both. In Belfast we have a weak spot for glittering wrecks. Steady, reliable success isn't memorable enough for us.

I took a taxi from the airport. Through the back-seat window I could see Samson and Goliath, the yellow Harland & Wolff gantry cranes, our two biblical giants looming over what was once the world's biggest shipyard. The crowds massed along here in 1911 to watch the dazzling bulk of the *Titanic* slide on greased slipways from her building yard into the waters of Belfast Lough. Big Jacky's granny was there as a young woman, he told me — she was always so nosey, he said, she'd turn up to the opening of a can of corned beef — and when she was old she used to tell him how it was such a scorcher for May that she got sunburned on the back of her neck, and everyone on the quayside waved hankies and hats in the air and roared with full-throated pride that Belfast had built this unforgettable ship.

No one could have imagined on that blazing day that within the year disaster, not triumph, would hammer the ship's name into history. But the thing is, who would talk about the *Titanic* today if she hadn't sunk?

When I arrived at the church, a little ahead of time, Phyllis was already in a pew, red-eyed and smart in her best navy coat. Mrs Murdie, never the biggest talker, hugged me for five seconds longer than she ever did before, resting her head lightly on my shoulder. Even Gavin was in evidence, stouter and less chatty, his natural windbaggery deflated by the gravity of the occasion. He greeted me with every appearance of deferentially controlled pleasure, in a long black coat with his hair neatly combed. He seemed to be making himself useful, having a prudent word with the funeral director, steering Mrs Murdie gently towards the next stage of proceedings. Not a bad oul stick, in the end.

I did my bit: helped to shoulder the coffin from the church into the car for the crematorium, with the six of us — including Gavin and a solemn trio of Murdie's nephews — sweating discreetly as we quietly struggled to adjust for our difference in heights without visibly buckling or letting Murdie slide. That's the pallbearer's job, to uphold the dignity of the occasion. It's the last chance you ever get not to let someone down at a bad time.

The coffin was surprisingly heavy. I wouldn't have thought that dry wee man would carry such weight. Still, he did have weight for me: he looked out for me, always remaining alert to trouble coming my way, watching over me from a distance like a tough, chain-smoking guardian angel. Lung cancer finished him off almost as soon as the news leaked out that he had it, the final bill for all those years in bars breathing in the smoke from other people's cigarettes and his own.

He was the one who knew everything about my family, and when he was cremated a piece of my own history burned up along with him. It was just over ten years since he'd stood at the airport and solemnly waved me off to London. Now it was my turn to say goodbye. When I saw the curtains closing around the coffin — it happens so quickly, that final mechanical conjuring trick — I put my two hands over my face and wept.

Soon after, I found out he had left me money in his will, a sum that he had carefully set to one side and grown over the years. The solicitor told me that Murdie had attached a note to it: 'For Jacky, the son I never had, and in memory of his father, the best friend I ever had. To be spent on happiness and security. May your school never burn down.'

★   ★   ★

I run a café now, partly started up with Murdie's money. I would rather have had Murdie than the money, but I didn't get the choice. I was managing Delauncey's by that time, on a decent enough salary, but I knew the business well enough not to come a cropper on my own. I added Murdie's cash to a bank loan and poured it into a coffee shop down a side street in Soho. I didn't have any fantasies about floating about the place, graciously playing mine host. That's where people usually come unstuck in this game: they have a certain image of themselves.

The café's been running for nine years, turning a good profit, enough to pay for the usual heart-stopping London mortgage on a bigger flat with high ceilings and a handkerchief of garden just off the Holloway Road. Your own place means security, everyone sagely repeated as I signed the forms, but security's a maw that needs feeding. It turned out I had a keen instinct for business, maybe something that had passed down in the genes from Big Jacky: a knack for ordering the right stock, negotiating with suppliers, driving a hard bargain on prices but not being so stingy that they walked away or hated you. I knew how to defuse any residual tension with a joke, sensing what the customers wanted out of a place even before they could articulate it themselves.

I keep an eye on the shifting choices people crave. There are fashions in coffees and pastries like everything else, and in London people always want a new thing to tell their friends about. I'm naturally a jumpy person, keenly aware of others and their multiple urgencies. London suits me, with her surging crowds and speeding Tube trains. I understand her song.

A battered white statue of King Charles II stands in the middle of Soho Square, the patron saint of fun and decay. In the summer I check him out when I take a walk around there, and give him and his crumbling ruffles a wee nod. Now that I'm older, weighed down with necessary things to do, I respect fun more than ever: it's a dwindling stock, grab it while you can. And I like this area, with its quaint seediness, the old dirt still doggedly whispering through the thick lick of new gloss.

Behind the counter I work fast, collecting and returning cash, making the coffee quick and right. But when collective motion suddenly stalls on the shoulders of a single customer deliberating on a cake, bovine with indecision as a queue builds up all the way to the door, I can feel the tension bubbling in me. I start doing this little thing with my fingers, rubbing the tips of them back and forth very quickly. The thing is, though, you have to stay civilised here. You have to press the anger down and keep a tight lid on it.

★ ★ ★

I'm the coffee expert at our place, the resident caffeinated snob. I grew up in tea country, the Belfast brew made hot and strong, always ready to soothe a place that lived on its nerves. You could have a coffee, sure — an instant one, usually, insipid and faintly bitter — but it wasn't the national medicine that tea was. Coffee gave you the jitters, and we already had jitters coming out our ears. We medicated ourselves, swinging relentlessly between alcohol and tannin.

Now, in London, I like coffee even more than tea: I seek out the jitters, packaged into strong little bursts throughout the day. Short, sharp shots. I know about the countries it comes from, the beans, the roast, the grinding process;

enough, at least, to satisfy anyone who wants to have that conversation at length, and it seems quite a lot of people do. Customers want to be subtly flattered on their discernment. I buy therefore I am. From their footwear to their lunch-time sandwich, they are the sum of their choices. Who am I to sneer at that? It's what they have left, now that for so many of them God's a busted flush and a family is either falling apart or yet to be acquired.

I can play that game if they need me to. From the way I talk — fluent and considered — I can seem to care more about it than I really do. That's not to say I don't care at all.

Still, something's changing here. I can feel it in the air, even while I open the curtains and bat the thought away each morning. The beast that circles the shadow of the campfire is dragging closer. I know its smell. When I first moved to London I felt lighter, carefree. Just then, it was a place that was gradually getting clean of fear, not counting the restless electricity that haunts any city, that stirs and flashes in gang fights and criminality. But the old IRA terror, the fractious marriage of nationalism and Marxism, was fading away.

Then this new terror began, a fresh zeal jerking into life in fits and starts, hijacking the name of Allah. It's gradually hitting its stride now, mouthing fire and destruction on the Internet, trailing a metal stick across the railings and wakening up all the pale thugs on the other side. Yoo-hoo. We hear on the news now and then that the country is on high alert in expectation of an attack, even while our own thoughts slip quietly back to work and what's for dinner. Sometimes when I walk down Oxford Street I wonder to myself what it would be like if someone opened fire, which object I might choose to crouch behind.

Twenty years ago, leaving Belfast for London felt like saying goodbye to a mesmerising nutcase and going to live with someone calmer who knew how to hold down a job and keep her flat clean. London relaxed me: you could float at ease in its great mix of people, its cooling civility. Now I'm not so sure. Sanity is drawing down the blinds, mania is on the march.

What does the new terror want from us? More than a broad green slice of land, soaked in rainwater and bitter longing. It wants everything, so much it can't even explain. More than anything, it wants the pleasure of watching the rest of us in fear and flailing confusion, ripping up the best of ourselves.

★　★　★

I have something else to worry about now besides myself: a family, the nuclear proliferation of anxieties. People talk about love in quantities. 'How much do you love her?' they ask, as though it is always the same product in differently sized containers. They never talk about its shapes and distillations, selfish or self-sacrificing, all the wily forms in which it can present itself.

This family slowly grew on me. Over time it has rooted and pinned me in place, thick ivy round a wooden post. Now I couldn't extricate myself from it without snapping. If I think about it too much, sometimes, I get breathless, as if it is a weight pressing on my chest.

There's Eve, of course, the first to tighten her hand around mine. She's older now, calmer too, still slim but somehow stiffer and more solid than she was. We bicker about the bureaucracy of our existence, who forgot to pay the phone bill or used up the last of the milk. We don't argue about the big things. We know we are lucky first to have found each other, and then to have had the sense to stay together.

She asked me the other day: 'What would you do if I died first?' and I told her that I'd make a shrine to her just above the recycling bin, so I'd remember her every time I chucked out an empty bottle. The truth is I can't imagine what it would be like dragging on through the long days without her. Our friends — showily lamenting their silver hairs and solidifying paunches, glancing at us to see if we agree with them too easily — are realising that mortality is not quite as distant as it used to be. It never felt too far away from me anyway, always shadowing my family like a hungry dog, casting me sneaky looks.

Raymond is grown up, in his twenties and taller than me. He's chopped his name permanently down to Ray to travel lighter. He's got a degree in economics, a room in a shared flat, and a good-looking brunette girlfriend with an eyebrow piercing and a tattoo of a star on her shoulder, who laughs a bit too eagerly at all his jokes. When he gives me a hug I can feel the wiry energy in his arms.

They have new rules for each other now, his generation, ones that I don't really get. When I was growing up, sleeping with a girl was still a bit like grocery shopping in the old Soviet economy: there was more demand than supply. You had to do a stint in the breadline, but while you were shivering there at least you had a little time to dream. I'm romanticising it of course. I wasn't exactly a strolling troubadour. I wasn't even very nice, because the only one I could be bothered with was Eve.

There was more longing to it than this lot has, though. Now they go browsing in a hypermarket of infinite choice, ordering each other up on their smartphones like pizzas, tap-tapping with their little apps and Tinders, hooking up and hanging out and getting bored and drifting apart and swiping right again. They don't even take the time to dislike each other properly.

Still, who cares? Every generation messes things up in its own way. I loved Raymond, and still do, with the steadiness of an older brother. He turned me into an adult. Through those early years I woke him up on the dark winter mornings when getting him out of his warm bed was like tugging a wincing snail out of its shell. I walked him to school when Eve couldn't, listening as his harmless gossip about his classmates puffed out along with his breath in the cold air. When he was lying sick in bed with a temperature I brought him hot-water bottles and tea.

Now he's moved out I'm still doing that stuff for our daughter. She's ten now, and from the moment when she suddenly unspooled from Eve like a long, wild hare, I had only one prayer: that I be allowed the grace to live long enough to see her grow up and then to die before her. She clutched at my heart so fiercely I didn't think I could survive a world without her in it. That's my secret. It hurts to know or say it.

Her name is Elsie. She looks like a younger version of Eve but with my eyes, blue with black lashes. They're better on her, more optimistic. Children mash the pair of you up to make some newly minted thing of their own.

It strikes me as odd that somehow my accent wasn't coded in her genes: her short London vowels can still knock me back. It's as if a wee Eliza Doolittle had crept in, pinched my eyes and tricked me into cooking her dinner. Sometimes she tries to copy my voice, concentrating on getting the words right, but it comes out as a dragging parody — 'get yewer coat ohan' — like someone at home from Ballymisery who can barely count the cows and thinks that Belfast is the big smoke.

Now Raymond's moved out she lives a bit like an only child, drifting around the house with lined notebooks she writes in but won't let us see. Her best subject is English. Maybe she'll go to university one day and see it through this time, the way her da didn't. When she writes she sits very close to her pet hamster, darting glances through the cage at his stuffed golden cheeks. I sometimes wonder what travels through his tiny brain: a series of urgent requirements, impulses and images, like flashcards on a projector. That's not so bad. I know some people who can scoot

278

through an entire life like that.

When I pick him up I can feel his ticker beating frantic time against my finger, his bulging black eyeballs as shiny as caviar. He only has a handful of years, a slim bunch of days to throw into the air before the lights go out, and yet he spends so much of it just racing round in circles on his wheel. Maybe that's what God thinks of us, whatever shape God is in these days.

★   ★   ★

I keep company with the past, but I only stop and talk to it now and then. Until recently there hasn't been time. Between running the café and the demands of home, Elsie's early years felt a bit like being trapped inside the spin cycle of a washing machine. If there was a moment's pause, it was all you could do to catch your breath.

I'm mostly stuck over here in London now, ordering my coffee supplies, putting the bins out and doing accounts, but still I keep an eye on things in Belfast. I read the news online and follow the politics and I'm back and forth to help out with the shop. People over in England ask me sometimes, eagerly, 'What do you think of Northern Ireland now, what do you think of the peace?' I say: 'It is what it is' and their faces fall a little, as if they had handed me an expensive birthday present and I had said sulkily, 'I would have liked it better in red.'

Sure I like peace, I say, because peace is the

absence of killing. You would be an eejit not to want it. The real question is who do you pay for it, how much, and for how long? You get it on hire purchase. It doesn't float down from the sky.

McGee's bunch didn't do so well out of it. They got let out of prison but they didn't scrape enough votes to make it as politicians, to get a leg up into the big house. Gradually they melted off the political scene, back into the bars and the streets, clubbing together now and again to brood fondly over the long string of horrors they called their war.

The IRA guys moved on and up, though. Those same men that cranked up the death toll in the early 1970s in their donkey jackets and jeans, coolly giving orders for bomb blasts and shootings, are grandfathers and government ministers in suits now. They pore solemnly over lunch menus, and give the double thumbs up on charity fun runs for the disabled. They meet up to commemorate dead comrades and then go home to reminisce on Facebook.

Raymond follows Liam Blake on Twitter: that kind of nutty stuff makes him laugh. Blake's got an official account for himself, and one for his pet llama, which he also manages. He calls the animal Lliama O'Rama and photographs it in a series of funny hats, with a tiny tricolour stuck rakishly in the brim on special Irish republican days. Sometimes the creature moans on about the rain or says hooray it's looking forward to Christmas. The whimsy can spook you when you think of all the people Blake's calmly directed below ground. I've never seen a man who oscillates so wildly between genres, mixing blood and baby-talk without even a gasp of self-consciousness.

His mind has so many compartments now that it must look like the Palace of Versailles, with some dark wee rooms, built very early, that never get opened up at all. Through its long corridors, some ghosts get paraded with full honours and others are shut away in locked wings.

The IRA men of the 1970s heard the ghosts of the 1916 rebels whispering: the voices that said those who still dared to fight, kill and die would gain the true, whole, pure Ireland. The voices that said that there was still the North to be won, waiting for those with enough passion to seize it.

The ideal of purity screwed us all. All that passion meant in the North, in the end, was a weeping widow or a husband disembowelled with grief, a schoolgirl with half a leg, a dead teenage soldier, a buried policeman, a kid caught in cross-fire, a mother without her son. It was a dream that burned itself out in zigzagging paths of pain. Ireland was susceptible to the whispers of ghosts, and so we made more of them.

25

The stuff we've all found out now, you wouldn't believe. There were secrets concealed within secrets, leaks and surprises. Whether you're planning on killing or trying to stop it, you need to suck up wee pieces of information. Someone needs to tell you all the little things that someone else doesn't want you to know.

Official fingers became unofficially busy in paramilitary pies, encouraging an informer here, protecting another one there. The British made decisions in which means and ends formed knots that proved hard to untangle: information sometimes came from the best of people, sometimes from the very worst. Later these stories started to drift up from history, bulging and distorted, lost toys stirred from the bottom of a stagnant well.

★ ★ ★

I picked up a London listings magazine about six months ago; flicking through it for a film to watch, I came across an article about a guy called Gerry Maguire. It was publicising a club night he was running: 'This week the legendary Belfast-born DJ returns to Free London, spinning his celebrated mixture of trance, funk and house until the early hours.' Belfast-born. I looked more closely at the photograph: a good-looking fella a bit younger than me with light brown hair and a carefully shaped wee beard, wearing a T-shirt with a logo of something fashionable I didn't understand on it. He looked vaguely familiar.

I read on, noting that the interview was conducted in a style faintly breathless with respect, as if the journalist had pressed his face against the window of a more desirable life. There was talk of summers in mega-clubs in Ibiza and Gerry being flown halfway across the world to DJ at private parties. What music, the journalist asked, did Gerry himself like to get up and groove to? Gerry replied: 'I don't dance that much myself, because I injured my leg in a childhood accident. But it's definitely my job to keep everyone else up on the dance floor.'

Then I got it. It was a long time since I had last seen that face, but I was pretty sure now that it was the adult incarnation of bleached-blond Gerard, my neighbour from the hospital ward.

I went back and reread his quotes. A 'childhood accident'. You can say that again, with baseball bats in it. I felt a surge of pride in him, for tying a bandage over his past and carrying on, armour-plating himself in success.

Who would have thought he'd get so far? It's the fashion now to applaud people who publicly confront their old tormentors, dragging them through court cases and giving the spectators in the gallery a good show. That takes courage, sure, but it's not for everyone. Sometimes when you've looked hatred in the eye you just want to sprint away, far enough to stop it from ever touching you again. You don't want to say its name out loud, even softly under your breath, in case it somehow hears and suddenly bounds back towards you, fast and fierce as a cheetah. You have to get your own back just by living.

A bit of me wanted to contact Gerry though and say: hey, remember me from back then? Well done you, the pair of us didn't turn out so badly after all. I worried that I would just be poking about in the past, pulling apart his carefully tied bandage, but on the other hand I really wanted to see him. So I looked up his agent's address online and wrote him a note marked 'personal'. On the way to the café one bleak morning I threw it into the mouth of the postbox like someone pitching a bottle into the sea.

I had thought about the note carefully. It didn't say too much, just in case anyone else read it.

> Dear Gerry, I read an interview with you the other day and I was wondering if you are the Gerry who was in the bed next to me in the Royal Victoria Hospital in Belfast way back in 1995. If so, I'm glad you've done so well. If you ever want to come by and say hello I own a café called Two Shots in Noonan Street in Soho and I'm usually in there in the daytime. If I don't see you then all the very best and keep up with the music, Jacky.

I put my address on the envelope. It wasn't like me to seek someone out, but all at once I missed him. Maybe once or twice in your life it suddenly gets lonely when you have no one to talk to about all the stuff you thought you wanted to forget. Weeks went by, and I wondered if the letter had got lost in the post, or if he'd got it and winced a little and quietly crumpled it up. A bit of me felt like an eejit for having written.

Then one afternoon who but Gerry himself should walk into the half-empty café, looking around for me. I had someone else working on the counter. 'I'm over here,' I shouted from the back of the shop and when he finally saw me his face snapped into a wide smile. He came over and we gave each other an awkward hug — years in London had chipped away at our early reticence — and I stepped back to take a good look at him, at all the new ways he'd put himself together. He was wearing dark skinny jeans and a nifty wee trilby like a travelling jazz musician. When he moved towards the corner table I saw that he had learned to carry even his faint limp elegantly, a trace of damage that he now wore as nonchalantly as a scarf.

'Look at you,' I marvelled. 'Like a hipster Frankie Sinatra.'

He thought I was taking the mickey.

'Look at *you*,' he said, smiling. 'You called your café Two fucking Shots? What's that about?'

Close up I could see that his white, even teeth were not of the sort ordinarily bequeathed by our native city. They had clearly undergone some subtly expensive dental work.

'It's a reference to coffee,' I said. 'Two shots of coffee.'

'Yeah, better be,' he said. 'Make mine three. I'm fucking knackered after last night.'

He swore the way I remembered, rhythmically and without any malice, but there was an international patina to his accent now, a softening drawl buttered across his Belfast vowels. I had trained myself not to swear in front of Elsie. Cursing came unnaturally to me, but to hear him at it again felt relaxing, like he was rolling us a cigarette to share.

We sat down and he told me all about the DJ-ing and how things had started to go right when a promoter spotted him playing trance music in Belfast and offered him a gig in London and before long the jobs were trickling and then flooding in, even from outside the UK. His constant music references — dubstep, downtempo, breakbeat, hardcore — were all gobbledegook to me. For myself I liked live soul nights in down-at-heel old men's pubs, but it did me good to see his face all quick and bright at how life had panned out for him. He was still eating up his success like a ripe peach, with the juice of it running down his chin. There were no kids yet, he said, but he had met a woman he liked and I got the feeling that procreation had become a dangling possibility. The fine lines around his eyes signalled it might be time.

He went back to Belfast now and then to see his parents, he said, and recently in the city centre he had bumped into a fella who — the week after he'd finally come home from hospital, shakily bolted back together — had stopped to holler at him from across the street: 'Ye got what ye deserved.' But the fella must have forgotten all about that because now he came up to Gerry like an old pal, saying he'd seen him in the magazines and as a favour would he think about playing a wee birthday gig downtown some time in a particular club the fella had in mind.

'What did you say to him?' I asked.

'I told him in no uncertain terms to fuck off.'

In no uncertain terms. I enjoyed that. Gerry asked about me and briskly satisfied himself that my life was in good shape, like a clear-headed doctor checking up on the people who are still walking around after a train crash. He still pulsated to a fast beat.

And then, after all that, he suddenly started talking about Frankie Dunne. I suspected there weren't that many people he could talk about Dunne with. Maybe that was the real reason why he had come. It had clearly been sitting on his mind.

'Do you remember the fella I told you about once in the hospital, the Provo that beat me for joyriding?' he said.

'Yes.'

'Do you remember his name?'

'Aye,' I said, 'Frankie Dunne.'

'Well, it turns out Frankie was a tout,' he said. 'He was one of the IRA's chief inquisitors, and a very busy, chatty tout. He went around interrogating and stiffing people left right and centre for supposedly squealing to the Brits while he was doing the same himself, non-stop. For years he was one of the juiciest sources they had, the gift that kept on gabbing. It's all come out.'

He took a large bite out of his custard tart and rocked back in his chair, cheeks bulging, to see my reaction.

'Where is he now?'

'Nobody knows,' Gerry said. 'Vanished. Incommunicado. I don't think it's in anyone's interests to hear that bastard singing in public.' He gave a sharp laugh: 'Although I'd fucking well like to hear it.'

Gerry looked at his watch, made an alarmed face and quickly downed the last of his strong coffee.

'Good coffee,' he said. 'Look him up. A bit of it's got out already. There'll be a lot more where that came from.'

He gave me another wee half-hug: 'Well, sure I know where to find you now.' With all the gigs and the travel, he'd got good at leaving gracefully. He was off to eat sushi with his manager, he said. I watched him as he walked out of the door and into the soft promise of the summer evening in Soho, navigating the clogged pavements full of outdoor drinkers as he checked the messages on his phone. I wondered if I'd ever see him again.

⋆   ⋆   ⋆

I did indeed look Dunne up, and the more I read about him, the more I thought that as a teenager Gerard had a very near miss. It seemed that for Dunne the decision to cross the line between a maiming and a murder could depend on something quite trivial, like how he felt about the

288

quality of his lunch. There were pictures along with the news stories and, later, some longer feature pieces.

Dunne was a burly man with reddish, receding hair, a human pit bull who zealously sniffed out treachery against Irish republicanism wherever he imagined it was lurking, with the exception of his own interior. Those with experience of him told reporters that beneath his superficial conviviality lay a terrible coldness. Some people felt the chill too late to get away.

Dunne's sniffing went on all the time, setting nerves on edge, but the sniffing and the edginess became so constant that sometimes people almost forgot it was there, like the rain pattering on the roof. Then a thin trace of something would come floating on the air towards him. A rumour, a nervy laugh, an operation gone awry. Something that didn't quite sit right, something that snagged on the consciousness.

Something that snagged. It passed across the pit bull's flared nostrils. Sniff, sniff, and Dunne was on the scent. He conducted his enquiries with energetic capability, exuding the heavy musk of intimidation. He followed betrayals, but what he was really after was the exhilarating stench of fear. That came next.

It trickled out over the next few months, like a line of blood from under a locked door, the story of Dunne and his friends. They had abducted men, and women too. Some captives were fathers or mothers, some were kids hardly out of their teens, some were in the IRA and some weren't; they were taken up alleyways or driven away in the dark, down hopeless, nameless little rural lanes, on and on until finally the car stopped and they were shoved out faltering and afraid. Their tormentors would play wee tricks and jokes, kidding people they were about to be freed when in fact they were seconds from death.

There were much the same ingredients in every story, doled out in different measures. There was extreme pain, dispensed with ingenuity, or the intimate threat of it. Sometimes those held were in trouble because they had spoken out of turn, or lost the plot momentarily and punched a more senior IRA man. Maybe, with youthful folly, they had ignored the organisation and tried a small-time crime spree of their own. But most often the charge against the prisoner — the one that could turn bowels to liquid — was that he or she had been touting, passing on information that helped the British Army or the police.

Tout was a bad word. It stank of shame and brutal retribution. It sprawled obscenely across gable walls, inviting trouble, turning nods and smiles to cold glares of suspicion. Tout could stick to you like wet tar.

The enforcers kept to due process, all right: their own version of it. They would often compel the captive to make a tape recording admitting alleged crime, a stuttering confession which was retained as evidence that IRA justice had been done.

The process could take hours or days. The prisoner would cling to the dwindling hope that there was still a way out, a narrow tunnel through violence or shame or some as yet unspecified bargain which would permit them to crawl on their belly back to life. It had happened before to others, maybe it would happen again.

I keep pondering the moment when they finally realised that there was to be no way back, when they understood that this petered-out country road or that particular room, with its stained mug of tea and the nondescript blanket on the bed, was the last one they would see. The fine drizzle that flecked the windowpane would be the last rain: there would be no more of anything. The thought of them trapped there in that condition of knowing haunts me, their loneliness drifting across the decades like smoke on the wind.

And when I think of that I also sometimes think of McGee leaving the newsagent's cellar that grey morning, walking stiffly back out into the short portion of his life that was left.

★   ★   ★

Dunne wasn't alone in executing his duties. He just added some extra spin to the game. Even before his era, back in the 1970s, the IRA had killed local people who offended them and left the bodies by the road as a warning to others. At times they took to burying the bodies at night in the bogland. Then the captives just disappeared, gulped down by the soggy earth.

Their relatives never knew where they had vanished to, or even why. The disappeared existed only in hushed talk and creased photographs showing them with awkward smiles, in haircuts and clothes from the decade they had died in, sideburns and perms, flares or drainpipe jeans. Time dumped them there and ran on without them.

One was the widowed mother of ten children. After she was seized from the family home in West Belfast one night, her youngest children huddled close together for weeks like frightened puppies, with their fifteen-year-old sister struggling to play the role of mammy. The authorities were eventually alerted to what was going on, whereupon they promptly separated the children from each other and dispatched them to various institutions.

★   ★   ★

For many years Dunne was one of the prized British sources at the heart of the IRA, tipping them off as to who was planning what, when and how. He saved lives with his information and took others with his gun. As his story came out, I became fascinated with this man. Inside him, pulverised by his contradictions, what kind of dust was left, what smear of essence?

Dunne was different from other informers, not least in the enigma of his motivations. He was never touched or harmed by anyone. There was a good reason: for the longest time he gave everyone above him exactly what they needed. For the IRA he was the cheerful enforcer of internal discipline, the whistling butcher who was endlessly willing to roll up his sleeves and plunge into stomach-churning tasks that others avoided. For the British he held the key to the IRA cupboard of secrets. Either master could potentially have destroyed him, so he dutifully served them both.

So Dunne wasn't a psychopathic zealot after all. He was a psychopathic pragmatist, the poster boy for everything the Troubles became once the last of the fantasies dribbled out of them. He took care of business. He sucked up the cash. He played the ball, in all its intricate moves. He stayed on his feet until the final whistle blew. Dunne's hidden away somewhere now, hardly anyone knows exactly where. The main thing is, he's still alive.

26

Phyllis flew over to London with Titch's mum a couple of months ago, on a trip to see us and go to a musical in the West End. She had wanted to catch *The Phantom of the Opera*, which sounded a bit corny to me, but she was excited about it and had been reading up all about it on her iPad and egging Titch's mum on too. She kept saying, 'And I believe the bit where the Phantom appears is *amazing*.'

The pair of them were sleeping in twin beds in the spare room, which made me glad we had one, and when I passed by at night I could hear their muffled voices through the door, giggling at some joke like a couple of girls.

I wanted to say that the Phantom had been haunting the West End for so long now he was probably falling apart at the seams, but I kept quiet. It cracked me up to hear Phyllis going on like she was some kind of theatre buff — 'the Phantom is *amazing*' — with Elsie watching her wide-eyed, her mouth ajar, as though this great-aunt was the font of all theatrical knowledge.

She's in her seventies now, a bit tottery at the joints, but when I asked her if she would be okay leaving the newsagent's she answered me all airy like a superannuated Holly Golightly: 'Oh don't worry, Marty has it all under control.'

Aye, Marty.

Shortly after McGee was killed, all those years ago, Phyllis was back on the phone. In the course of the conversation she said that 'a wee lad called Marty has been calling round to the shop, asking for any odd jobs on Saturdays. He says he knows you.'

When she mentioned his name and his recent proximity, I had felt the prickle of wariness. What's that shivery line from the old play? *Something wicked this way comes.* That might seem a strange thing for an adult to say about a young boy, but there it was. My instinct was to tell him to stay away. I didn't know what that slippery wee fella would trail in the door behind him.

'Tell him no for now, Phyllis,' I said. 'I'll have a chat with him when I'm over.'

That night I lay motionless in bed and thought about him: his permanent air of twitchiness, the restlessness in his bones. From the first time I met him, I could sense he was out searching for a wing to creep under. We both knew it, but my wing had so few feathers on it at the time. And then he wandered into the path of McGee, a bird of prey.

It must have scared him, McGee's murder. From what I had overheard out in the yard that night, he was already getting frightened before it. He understood right from wrong; not enough yet perhaps, but a bit at least. I thought about his pale face the night he had tried to warn me to get out. He had taken a risk for me, that night.

If I left him alone there I knew it was only a matter of time before someone else found him, someone built along the same lines as McGee.

The next time I went back to Belfast I didn't see him around at all for a couple of days. Then I spotted him one evening hanging out alone on his wall as the daylight died, hunched in his bomber jacket. I sneaked up behind him.

'Hello stranger,' I said.

He jumped and turned around to look at me, surprised for a second before he remembered to seem blasé.

'I thought you were in England.'

I vaulted over the wall. He wasn't smoking, but there were two squashed cigarette butts on the ground directly beneath his dangling trainers.

'Well, not at the moment,' I said, 'or I wouldn't be here talking to you.'

'Aye,' he said.

'How's tricks?' I said.

'Okay, I suppose. Jeanette's gone off to college.'

'D'you miss her?'

'Now and then. When she's not here I've got her room, though.'

'Come on and I'll buy you a plate of chips and a cup of tea in the café.'

He liked the sound of that: although his shrug affected indifference, he was down off the wall in a jiffy.

The café combined a general air of decline with a brisk trade: its paintwork was peeling, but its deep-fat fryer was rarely out of action. Once we were sitting opposite each other over the scarred Formica table top, I got down to business.

'I heard you got a bit too close to the action not long ago,' I said.

He looked at me warily with his light, narrowed eyes, trying to work out what I knew and how.

'McGee,' I said, and took a slurp of my tea, watching him.

There was a silence, as he fussed about with the salt and vinegar on his chips, buying time.

'Who told you that?' he said.

'A wee bird.'

He paused for a second, then dropped his voice.

'Was it you that shot him?'

'Now why would I do that?' I said.

'You know why,' he said.

He sat back in his chair, staring.

'I suppose I did have a reason,' I said with a minimal smile. 'But you know I'm not really that kind of person.'

I wasn't worried that anyone in charge would actually think it was me. From what the news reports said, his death had Loyalist feud written all over it in indelible ink. Their interminable power struggle was still grinding on. Only the week before, wee Tommy's dad had been gunned down outside a pub.

But I stared calmly back at him until he got uncomfortable and shifted his gaze. You'll notice I didn't deny his suggestion flat out. I told him the truth, but with enough space there for him to imagine that I really might have had something to do with McGee's death.

I didn't do that for me, but for him. It's what he needed. It was a feature of his personality that he could only respect someone older if he was a tiny bit frightened of them.

'Phyllis told me you wanted to help out in the shop,' I said.

'Aye,' he said.

He kept his eyes lowered, but his body was tensed and alert, his head cocked to one side like a listening bird. He had only just turned twelve: he said his birthday had happened while I'd been away, and his ma had given him money to take a couple of friends to see a horror film with a 15 certificate.

I didn't understand how the ushers could have let him in, with him looking so small, but he wore a cynically streetwise air around town. Strangers give up early on shielding kids like Marty. They figure the likes of him have seen it all already.

'I need to make one thing very clear,' I said. 'Everything that happens in that shop has to be above board. No nicking stuff, no so-called 'donations' to anyone who might be collecting, no tip-offs about when the cash register is left unlocked to any special friends.'

His eyes widened in indignation: 'D'you think I would do that?'

'I don't know,' I said. 'You might. But if you ever do, I will find out. And if anyone approaches you, tell me. As it is, the shop makes one big donation from Phyllis every year, and in public too. To yon wee disabled club.'

He nodded. I snaffled one of his chips. It was best to be honest.

'One more thing,' I said. 'Your first Saturday's money, take it down to Mrs Hackett and give it to her in exchange for all the Walnut Whips you nicked. After that it's all yours.'

'I'm not going to do that,' he said, insulted.

'Fine. I was going to give you a chance. But go back to sitting on your wall. Go back to being a top lad. Maybe one of the hoods will bring you into one of their wee schemes so you can scrape together just enough for a fancy skateboard. Then one day when you stop being useful to them you'll see what happens.'

That stopped him in his tracks. The barbs were too sharp and specific. They stung and they were disorienting him. He couldn't figure how I knew about the skateboard.

He glared at me and stood up in a fury. Then he got up and walked out the door. I didn't follow: I pulled his plate over towards me and sat quietly polishing off the rest of his chips and enjoying my tea.

Two minutes later he walked back in and sat down.

'Okay,' he said, sulkily.

I pushed the plate back towards him and smiled.

That's how it started. Now he's a grown man, with a girlfriend and a baby on the way and a stake in our newsagent's. He never got that tall but he keeps in shape: he's a wiry, quick wee nut and he knows everything and everyone and how to dodge trouble. He gave up the fags when he turned fifteen, and got into kick-boxing and Thai cookery and later a part-time business degree. Phyllis loves him, and even says so occasionally, like the sap she's always been. I suppose I do too, although it would freak him out if I ever admitted it, so I just get him a present on his birthday and see him right with his Christmas bonus and leave it at that.

He didn't ask me about McGee again. I respected that. It takes intelligence to know when it's better to keep a box locked. I've never had a reason yet not to trust him, but after all these years I still keep half an eye on him. Okay, a quarter of an eye. The thing is that in some ways he's very like me.

★ ★ ★

Mrs Hackett got her Walnut Whip money — which according to Marty she accepted with good grace, even insisting he took half back — but she's been dead five years now. McGee's shop closed down when the old man retired. It's turned into a chemist's, and Phyllis goes there for her prescriptions. Belfast has changed, too. Everywhere you turn there are fellas with rampant facial hair sucking on giant sippy cups of warm, coffee-flavoured milk. The place is hiving with restaurants, with new eateries competing for awards every week. It's as if after all those long years of constant arguing people now can't get enough of stuffing their faces.

We came late to the recreational possibilities of

food, although those of drink had been heavily explored. I can remember back when the city, wrapped in the drab shawl of the Troubles, had only one Italian restaurant, Luigi's, run by a middle-aged owner who was a perfect caricature of an excitable Neapolitan. It was as though — in the absence of any other prominent Italians in Belfast — he was determined to give us our money's worth in terms of gross stereotyping.

His customers were a willing audience. Deep in our parochial wrangling, we were thirsty for a taste of the exotic. In our city many people were permanently incensed over history, politics, borders, insults, threats, killings, and the simple fact of one another's existence, but we'd never seen anyone get so worked up about food before. It was an enthralling novelty.

Luigi once chased a customer round the restaurant with a knife in a dispute over the quality of his monkfish. The fella on the other end of the knife had rashly suggested that the monkfish was past its best, and Luigi was determined to bully him into attesting otherwise. That was a high point, but there was some form of incident in there most nights. People used to pack out Luigi's, settling in amid the red-checked tablecloths just to shovel down spaghetti and watch the owner work himself up into that evening's rage, his gelled ringlets springing in indignation away from his contorting face. Even when Luigi was in a good mood, his jollity was as unnerving as his tantrums: it was potentially on the turn.

As time went on the food — which had often

been tasty, at least — began to veer consistently towards the inedible, to the point of blatant provocation. It was as though Luigi, who used to swing so dramatically between moods, was jammed on anger. Maybe he'd caught it from us.

His delicate balance of theatre and culinary unpredictability began to tip against him. Other restaurants opened and gradually drew customers away. Even his tempers lost their cachet. The taxman circled. Luigi's famous yellow Lamborghini vanished from outside the restaurant. I can't remember now how it all ended. There were so many stories in Belfast at the time, each one more pressing than the last.

★ ★ ★

I can see it now among people my age from home, the struggle in their different ways to make sense of everything that happened. They'll never manage it, because sense had so little to do with it. From the very start, the Troubles created their own logic, the crazed logic of opposition, like when you're in the thick of a blazing row and you hear yourself smashing a glass and screaming in a high-pitched tone that isn't normally yours. In the midst of so many voices urging you to weigh in, it was a fight just to stay half decent.

Here's the funny thing, though: after I left, I never cared so deeply about any city again. It was Belfast, with its broad streets and narrow furies, that held all the poetry for me. It enraged me and clasped me close like a family member.

Even after everything that had happened it was still home, the only place in the world where I didn't talk with an accent. I approached every other city with the politeness reserved only for friends.

Sometimes I think that maybe now I'll only go back for good in an urn, and whoever cares enough can spoon me out like instant coffee and sprinkle me over the Lagan. Or if Eve should die first, and I'm old and alone, perhaps I'll leave London behind and let Belfast drive me crazy one more time.

The city does that: it sits and waits patiently for its émigrés to return, and sometimes they do. When the world-famous snooker player Alex 'Hurricane' Higgins was ruined with cancer, he came back to Belfast, to the same streets where he first started out as a wee lad playing truant in a local snooker hall called the Jampot.

He fell into a small council flat in Sandy Row. There was nowhere else for him to be. His crackling wire of electricity, that made sparks fly off the green baize every time he walked towards it, had worked loose and reduced everything in England to ash: his stacks of prize money, his cheeky street-urchin's face, his marriage, his health. When he played in the world championship final in 1982, Big Jacky and I had sat jammed together on the sofa, eyes glued to the screen, and cheered at the television when he won the title for the second time. Away from the lights of the tournament halls, though, the little sizzle beneath his skin wouldn't let up.

Higgins couldn't get the hang of time, the way

most people learn to. He couldn't handle the way it slowed down without asking. When he was playing snooker, he could bend time to his will, letting it hang suspended in the air, or blasting balls round the table faster than an intake of breath. Out there in the world, though, the minutes moved too sluggishly for his internal beat, so he drank and brawled and head-butted to kick-start them somewhere in the chaos.

Back in Belfast in his final days, he haunted the pubs and streets, a six-stone shocker of a body hauled around by a tiny, gaunt head with burning eyes and a rasping voice, still smoking and drinking beneath a raffish fedora hat. Marty saw him a few times in the bar opposite his flat, reading the paper and sinking Guinness. By then a pint of the rich, black stout was often the closest he came to food. His loyal friends in the snooker fraternity, many of whom he had insulted in his cups, raised cash in an effort to buy him new teeth. He had none of his own left, but a skein of cockiness persisted in him like a live nerve.

The city still loved him and was soft on him. It prized even the husk of his charisma, and tolerated his explosive, sentimental qualities as similar to its own. It craned its ear in bars to hear his hoarse stories and stood him drinks, waiting for the day when it would wrap him up in legend and carry his coffin through the streets on a horse-drawn carriage. There's a painted mural of him now in Sandy Row, wielding a cue in his flashy heyday. He died alone in his flat.

Higgins came home to Belfast when he was

wrung out, looking for a last bit of comfort, but not everyone finds it there. Now that things are quieter, we tiptoe back to the old places where pain is tangled up with the past and unpick the threads and try to comb them into some kind of order. And there are certain people who can't seem to get anything in order, because their threads are lost or too densely matted, because they still don't know what happened to the people they loved, or who was to blame.

27

A month ago, in July, I was back in the shop, going over some of the stock orders with Marty. The pair of us were down in the cellar, surrounded by cardboard boxes of Tayto crisps, instant coffee and basmati rice. We had branched out into a small selection of groceries. Marty had a notion to bring in a line of Thai and Indian curry paste. He was grumbling that they weren't anywhere near as good as doing the real thing yourself entirely from scratch, but that most people were too lazy. This was rich, I thought, coming from someone who once subsisted almost solely on nicotine, chips and diesel fumes. Still, he's good that way, keeping an eye out for new stock.

As he was lugging the boxes, he suddenly paused and said:

'Och, did I not tell you — '

'Tell me what?' I said.

He looked at me hesitantly for a second, as though not sure whether to proceed, wondering perhaps if he was breaking some unspoken pact about territory that wasn't to be ventured into again.

'They arrested McMullen.'

For a moment I thought 'who?' and then I remembered: the sleekit looking heavy that used to hang about with McGee's dad. I'd always avoided him, with his half-smile and the creased

T-shirt clinging to his belly like the rumpled skin on boiled milk. There was a look in his eyes that intimated that any form of closeness would end badly.

'McMullen? Why'd they do that?' I said.

He looked at me again.

'Och get on with it, Marty,' I said, exasperated.

'They found a woman's body in a disused quarry down near Kilkeel and it was McGee's ma.'

I couldn't take it all in at first.

'His ma? How did they know it was her? How did they know where to look?'

'They were told. A wee fella who was brought along that night to help McMullen bury the body has terminal cancer. Said it was wrong what happened and he needed to get it off his chest. He gave a statement to the police. No one can do anything to him now, he said, he's going to kick the bucket and he doesn't give a shite who threatens him — '

'But why did they do it?' I interrupted.

'He didn't really know. Said McMullen had told him she was out of control and posing a problem for the organisation. But he seemed to think it was personal. Maybe she'd had an affair and the da found her out.

'There's a relative in Glasgow, an old woman now, who says that before McGee's ma went missing she called her up from Belfast and said she was coming to Scotland with the two boys. Then she never did. The oul doll said she told the police about it years ago but nothing came of it, the ma was just noted as missing. Sure everything was going crazy back then.'

'Did McMullen admit it?'

'Nope, denies it all. But the forensics confirmed that it's definitely the ma all right. After all those years in there. The stuff they can find out these days is incredible — ' Marty broke off for a second to contemplate the sheer science of it — 'And the other guy gave a full statement so they've got that.'

'What does the da say?'

'Can't say anything, he's in the nursing home, totally banjaxed, doesn't even know what day it is now. The older son goes up to visit him every other Saturday.'

'They told everyone she'd run off to Scotland,' I said.

In those days full of smoke and rage no one really questioned rumours of a solo flight.

'Aye,' said Marty, going back to unpacking the boxes. He took a pair of scissors and sliced decisively through a strip of parcel tape. 'Some Scotland.'

I went upstairs to get a breath of air. This news, after all these years, had stunned me. I thought of McGee tied up down there on that chair, a grown man still imagining the ma had walked out on him when all the time she was stiff in the grey cold quarry, entombed in that industrial grave. The sun was shining very brightly and it strained my eyes and made a seam of pain dance jerkily behind them.

I shouted down: 'Marty I'm just going for a dander' and then I started walking.

I kept on the move, out of the streets where I was born and then on, up past the boxy behemoth of the City Hospital, across towards the university area and into the Botanic Gardens. When I got there I briefly sat down on a wooden bench, just like old times, but after a minute or so I could feel a kind of nameless panic rising in me so I walked twice round the gardens fast with none of the old pleasure and then out past Botanic train station and towards the city centre.

I walked past the Crown Bar and Robinsons and thought about stopping in for a pint but I knew the restlessness would be too powerful again if I sat down in an enclosed space, so I carried on up through the wide streets past the City Hall until I made it to the waterfront at the edge of Belfast Lough, where the wind wheeled around the monumental new buildings that had risen near the water after the ceasefires. Eventually something about the churning movement of the grey sea allowed me just to keep myself still there and stare into it.

It's not even that I felt guilty about McGee, especially when I remembered what he did to me. By the time I knew him he had already hardened into what he was. Still, it knocked me sideways, the pity of it. Time had yanked back a tarpaulin and exposed a filthy secret curled in there, a knotted weed that throttled the hope in him when he was small and had possibilities.

Ten minutes or so passed, and gradually I started to breathe more slowly. I saw a stone lying next to me, part of a little decorative border, but large enough to be significant. I picked it up and threw it down into the shifting water and waited with my eyes closed for the faint report as it clipped the surface and disappeared.

★　★　★

You dig down into the past and finally your spade comes up against rock. There's no way through. Sometimes you need just to set the spade to one side. The thing is, I started remembering again recently. When I heard about what they found in that quarry near Kilkeel it churned everything else up too.

I'm watchful — that much has become a habit — but without always knowing what I'm looking out for. Something that doesn't sit right, I suppose, that sets the alarm bells ringing. When I walk into a room the first thing I take note of, still, is the exit.

I can feel it in the air. It's coming at us again, this time in England and beyond, another time when the rules are shredded, when unreason starts to swagger. Voices are aggrieved and growing shrill, slicing through the old wrappings of courtesy. Everyone yells that no one else can understand them. Everyone talks more than they listen, staking out their place on Twitter and Facebook with swear words in capitals and bellowing self-righteousness. I don't think they'll stop it now. It's all too exciting, until it isn't any more, and by then it's too late. Back home we found that out the hard way.

There may be bombs again at some point and maybe shooting. I hope not. I don't know what form it will take but it's hard to stop my mind from making strategies for it. Even in the immediate absence of flies, a spider still spins its web.

The secret is to be able to remember just enough about what happened all those years ago, but not to let it rush over me. I swallowed a little piece of darkness back then, and it lodged deep. I have to keep the remembering under control, tightly hedged about with the here and now, or I might suddenly become so aware of the fragility of things that I couldn't even step outside the door. How smashable we all are.

And then, safe at home, sure I could accidentally slip off a stool while changing a light bulb, bang my head and fade away like that instead while destiny sniggers in the corner like a rotten imp.

So I go out again and again into the city, pushing myself through London's thickened arteries to work and sip my drinks and sit on park benches in the sun. I keep watch only from the corner of my eye. We all disappear in the end, somewhere in the human dance of exits and entrances. That thought used to torment me, but now it helps. All you can do is try to be kind along the way, try not to disgrace yourself. There's no point fretting. You have to lie back and let the river shift you downstream as far as it goes. I can say that for me, of course, but not for Eve and Elsie and Ray. My worries still track them silently, barefoot on the riverbank in the dark.

Whatever happens, unless you seek it out, it won't be your choice. We can fight the drift of our times, but we can't always escape it, even now that we think we know so much. When I consider the sum of my life so far — the little family, the busy coffee shop, the modest stack of achievements — I know that I am not eminent in any way, and never will be. That's okay. Even eminence withers. Even tall sunflowers will droop and rot. In any case, I never even thought to get as far as eminence. Survival and love have been windfalls enough.

★   ★   ★

The day after I heard about McGee's ma I went up to the care home on Arnold Street where old McGee was incarcerated. On the way I walked past the waste land. It was bigger now, the nothingness spreading out like a stain after they bulldozed half a street for regeneration and then neglected to build anything new. Nonetheless it was occupied: the young lads were building a bonfire there for the Twelfth of July celebrations, to commemorate when the Protestant forces of King William of Orange routed the Catholic ones of King James in 1690. In our streets, news from the seventeenth century was still hot stuff.

In recent years these pyres had grown steadily taller until now they were twice the height of houses, preposterous turrets of wooden pallets, subject to sabotage from rival gangs. Confronted with these hazardous miracles of engineering, the city authorities wrung their hands and backed away. This one was studded with Irish tricolours, and an effigy of Liam Blake dangled precariously from the middle, awaiting the coming flames on the Eleventh Night. A trio of trainee hardmen were hanging around guarding it, shooting me watchful looks. When I was small I would sometimes come out with Big Jacky to witness the ceremonial lighting of the bonfire, but I stayed away from it now. The atmosphere around it had grown edgier. There was a wildness among some of the teenage lads that I could do without. When lit, the fire was so intense that you ran up against the wall of heat the moment you stepped out of your house. Last year a nearby bonfire had set a couple of houses alight.

The care home was two streets away, a low-roofed, red-brick, purpose-built structure whose architects clearly valued utility far above charm. From a distance, it looked as though it had been assembled from giant blocks of rust-coloured Lego. I knew McGee's surviving son was unlikely to be there because it was a weekday morning, but I had borrowed one of Marty's baseball caps anyway and tilted it low over my eyes. The older son wasn't even connected to the paramilitaries, from what I had heard, but I thought the home would have a camera outside it and I had never fancied guest-starring on closed-circuit television.

There was a heavy door and a buzzer you had to press to be let in. The young blonde woman at the desk smiled at me and I smiled too broadly back. It was the least menacing of settings, but when the door thumped shut behind me I felt the tolling of an irrevocable decision.

'Is Billy McGee here?' I said. 'I was told he was. I'm on a visit.'

'Are you a relative?' she asked — then, as if wanting to soften the bluntness of her question — 'He doesn't get too many visitors.'

'No,' I said. 'Just an old family friend. I mainly live abroad but I'm back in Belfast and I just wanted to pop in and say a quick hello.'

'He might not know you,' she confided, 'but I'm sure he'll appreciate the visit. Just up the stairs and turn right at Room 12.'

I walked up the green-carpeted stairs to the first floor. The whole place was hotter than a hospital ward, and the windowsills were studded with shiny vases of fake flowers fanning out air freshener. The scent of disinfectant hovered just on top of the smell it was meant to purge, the one that issued from small leakages of dignity, the body's faltering obedience to the will. In the background was the constant muted drone of a vacuum cleaner.

I found Room 11, and the door next to it was open. Inside, near the window, a middle-aged care worker in a white coat was patiently spooning the pale pink gloop of what looked like strawberry yoghurt into an elderly man's mouth. The man in the chair was old McGee. He still had his solid thatch of greying hair and vigorous brows. I paused for a moment in the doorway to look at him there, vacant and pliable in a navy-blue sweatshirt and a pair of sagging elasticated sweatpants. Before, he had favoured polo shirts and jeans. He had always stayed in decent enough shape, for an older guy. I remembered when, to a boy at least, his physique had carried the possibility of threat.

His carer looked up and saw me. She smiled through her thick pink lipstick and her gold earrings caught the light. Little splashes of decoration in all this carefully managed despair.

'Hello,' I said, by way of explanation. 'Just here on a wee visit.'

She turned back to old McGee and said with exaggerated cheerfulness, the sing-song way you would talk when buoying up a tired child: 'You have a *visitor*.'

He didn't turn his head, but opened his mouth reflexively for the yoghurt that had stopped coming. His jaw hung open, while she dabbed around his mouth with a napkin.

She looked apologetically at me: 'Is it a while since you've seen him?'

'A wee while, yes.'

'He's gone downhill in the last few weeks,' she mouthed in a stage whisper, preserving decorum. 'He might not know you straight away, but I'm sure he'll appreciate the company.'

I pulled up a leatherette chair next to her and sat down. A sudden wail of indeterminate anguish came from another room. The carer looked quickly from McGee to me and back again. The wail came again, with an added note of urgency.

'I wouldn't normally ask but we're so short-staffed today. Would you mind feeding him the rest of the yoghurt while I see to another resident? He needs a little while to swallow so don't take it too fast.'

What could I say?

'Of course, not a problem.'

I took over the spoon and the yoghurt from her as she bustled out. Something about the sweetish, acrid smell of the substance repelled me. Now I was sitting in her chair McGee's eyes were fixed on me, without any gleam of recognition. His face was pale and cross-hatched with wrinkles, but there was still a trace of stubbornness in the set of his chin.

I brought the spoon towards his mouth and it duly opened and received the gloop. I noticed that my hand was trembling a little. Some of the yoghurt slipped out of the side of his mouth and I quickly rounded it all up with the spoon and scraped it back in.

Then I leaned towards him just as he swallowed and said, in a low voice but very clearly, 'What happened to your wife?'

His gaze stayed on me, a hard, uncomprehending grey-blue stare surrounded by rheumy, reddened lids. I locked eyes with him and said it again: 'What did you do with your wife?'

Not a flicker. Nobody home.

I delved for another spoonful, a deep, full one this time, and brought it back towards his opening mouth. The spoon landed and dropped off a significant deposit.

'I know your game,' I said, close up and deliberately. The belligerent assertion felt pointless and crass, hanging unacknowledged in the air.

I tried for one last time: 'Your wife. Where did she go?'

A brief pause. Then he shot the accumulated yoghurt back out of his mouth with sudden force, spraying it all over my face and jacket. The splattering took me by surprise. I recoiled sharply and was glaring at him when the carer suddenly walked back in.

'Och dear!' she said, 'I should have warned you. He does that every now and then. You can never predict.'

She extracted a wet wipe from a nearby tub and began fussing, dabbing at my jacket. I took it off her, gently: 'Don't worry, I'll do it.' I was still shaken. The clean-up gave me something to do.

'Sorry,' she said. 'Helping becomes a bit of a habit in here.' She looked regretfully at the half-finished yoghurt. 'Do you want to give it another go?'

'Ah no,' I said, 'I think I'll leave it to the professionals.'

I looked around the room. A large framed colour photograph of old McGee and his sons was on the windowsill. He was there in the centre, his heavy arms placed paternally around the shoulders of his two grown boys. They were all smiling, dressed in grey suits as if for a wedding, and Rocky's collar was open with his wee dagger necklace on show. Someone from the family had brought this picture up to the home and stationed it there as permanent evidence of familial affection, indelible testimony to normality. At some point far in the future, perhaps, this image might harden into undisputed fact.

She saw me looking.

'Him with his two boys,' she said. 'So sad.

Don't they all look handsome there. The younger one was killed a good few years ago. Terrible. Did you know him at all?'

'Just to see around,' I said, 'I remember seeing him around.'

'Such a pity.'

The silence between us on the matter widened. After a while she realised I wasn't going to try and close it. Neither of us could think of anything more to say.

'I think I'll head on out now. It was good just to drop in and see him.'

'Are you sure you wouldn't like a wee cup of tea and a biscuit?'

'Och no, I'll let you get on with it. Thanks.'

He turned his head towards me suddenly as I left, and for a second I could have kidded myself that something in his eyes knew me. Trick of the light. The spoon was already back hovering dutifully at his mouth. I walked downstairs and into the reception area. There was a special code you had to press into a keypad to get out and it took me a wee while to get the hang of it. The weather had turned and when the door finally opened the cool drizzle on my face felt like a blessing.

★   ★   ★

Before I flew back to London I took the bus up to visit Titch's grave in Roselawn cemetery in Belfast. Once I got off I had to walk for a while around the tidy boulevards of the dead before I found it, but in the end there it was. The black lettering on the mottled granite still looked sharp and fresh. It spelled out his too-short years and his full name, Rodney James Bell. No Titch — that was his joke name, and his ma wouldn't let him die a joke. The grave was well tended, with a pot plant flowering in front of it. She still fusses after him, keeping him right even now.

That's the legacy of it all, I thought, the long wound that cuts across the given and the stolen days: the noted but uncelebrated birthdays, the full past and the empty future. For those like Titch's mum, who are left behind, the skin never knits together in quite the same way again.

I took along some yellow flowers and a tall jar and a packet of Jammie Dodgers and I sat next to the grave and tore into the biscuits just like we used to. One biscuit for me, one for him, with his set down just next to the plant.

I ate mine slowly, crumbling it dry and sweet in my mouth and listening to the scraps of birdsong that laced the air. And I thought about the years that had passed and how everything had changed.

After a while, I got up and arranged the flowers in the jar and left them there for him like a patch of tethered sunlight. I left them there for him, and all the others.

Acknowledgements

With thanks to my agent Peter Straus for his wisdom and invaluable encouragement; my editor Nicholas Pearson, a beacon of reassurance; and all those who helped to bring this book into being, in particular Lottie Fyfe, Fran Fabriczki, Beth Humphries, Jordan Mulligan, Matt Clacher, Naomi Mantin, Matthew Turner and Jack Smyth. Thanks, too, to Rosemary Davidson, Nigel Farndale, Mark Law, Tristan Kendrick, Mark Jagasia, John Thornley, Andrea Tumelty, Karen McCartney and Sara McCartney for their generosity with time and advice; the memory of Ed Victor, whose belief in my writing first got this book started; and my beloved husband and patient listener Rajeev Syal.

My enduring gratitude also goes to those individuals from all communities in Northern Ireland who — during the bleakest days of the Troubles and beyond — refused to accept cruelty as our normality.

We do hope that you have enjoyed reading
this large print book.

Did you know that all of our titles
are available for purchase?

We publish a wide range of high quality
large print books including:
**Romances, Mysteries, Classics
General Fiction
Non Fiction and Westerns**

Special interest titles available in
large print are:
**The Little Oxford Dictionary
Music Book
Song Book
Hymn Book
Service Book**

Also available from us courtesy of
Oxford University Press:
**Young Readers' Dictionary
(large print edition)
Young Readers' Thesaurus
(large print edition)**

For further information or a free
brochure, please contact us at:
**Ulverscroft Large Print Books Ltd.,
The Green, Bradgate Road, Anstey,
Leicester, LE7 7FU, England.
Tel:** (00 44) **0116 236 4325
Fax:** (00 44) **0116 234 0205**

Other titles published by Ulverscroft:

HOW TO SAY GOODBYE

Katy Colins

No-one is ever happy to see Grace Salmon. As a funeral arranger, she's responsible for steering strangers through the hardest day of their lives. It's not a job many people would want — but for Grace, giving people the chance to say a proper goodbye to the ones they love is the most important job in the world. From the flowers in the church to the drinks served at the wake, it's the personal touches that count; and it's amazing what you can find out about someone from their grieving relatives. Or their Facebook page. But when Grace oversteps the boundaries of her job, she accidentally finds out too much about someone who's died — and those they left behind. Faced with a huge dilemma, Grace is forced to step out of the shadows . . . and start living.

MR DOUBLER BEGINS AGAIN

Seni Glaister

Baked, mashed, boiled or fried, Mr Doubler knows his potatoes. But the same can't be said for people. Because, since Doubler lost his wife, he's been all on his own at Mirth Farm, perched high above a small town. And that suits Doubler just fine. Crowds are for other people. The only friends he needs are his potato plants and his housekeeper, Mrs Millwood, who visits every day. So when Mrs Millwood is taken ill, it ruins everything — and Mr Doubler begins to worry that he might have lost his way. But could the kindness of strangers be enough to bring him down from the hill? Thus begins a celebration of food and friendship, and a reminder that it's never too late for a new start.

THE FORGOTTEN SECRET

Kathleen McGurl

It's the summer of 1919, and Ellen O'Brien has her whole life ahead of her. Young, in love, and leaving home for her first job, the future seems full of shining possibility. But war is brewing, and before long, Ellen and everyone around her are swept up by it. As Ireland is torn apart by the turmoil, Ellen finds herself facing the ultimate test of love and loyalty . . . A hundred years later, Clare Farrell has inherited a dilapidated old farmhouse in County Meath. Seizing the chance to escape her unhappy marriage, she strikes out on her own, hoping the old building might also tell her something about her family's shadowy history. And when she stumbles across a long-forgotten hiding place, she discovers a clue to a secret that has lain buried for decades . . .